ALSO BY ADAM SYDNEY

Yolanda Polanski and the Bus to Sheboygan

My Heart Is a Drummer

Adam Sydney

Newcraft Press ╬ *Tucson, Arizona*

MY HEART IS A DRUMMER

Published by Newcraft Press, Tucson, Arizona.

Copyright © 2012 Adam Sydney

The moral right of the author has been asserted.

ISBN: 978-0-9851636-0-0

newcraftpress.com
facebook.com/NewcraftPress
adamsydney.wordpress.com
twitter.com/adamsydney1

Acknowledgements

I would like to extend a very heartfelt thank you to everyone who was kind enough to share their time and energy with me in offering to read My Heart is a Drummer. Their input has been invaluable and their generosity very, very much appreciated.

My editorial team: Michael Baum, Denise Bjornson, Tre Cox, Ginia Desmond, Joséphine Dubois, Allen Gibson, Eric Kaldahl, Tim Keene, Bode O'Toole, Guy Rose, Ellen Shriner, Gail Sydney, Simon Woodham, and Rob Zonfrelli.

LOURDES

The first glimpse was always the sweetest.

Her car's transmission died and would never be fixed. Her daughter had a hypodermic needle in her sweater drawer. Her meatloaf was horrible—even though she'd made it exactly the same as every other meatloaf in her life—and Joselito yelled at her. Maybe things were a little tough, and Lourdes had wanted to cry on the bus with her forehead pressed against the sweaty, cold window.

But instead, she'd wondered about the first glimpse she'd have of him that day, and she smiled. Some mornings, it would be a little more difficult than usual, and she'd have trouble believing that he'd really visit her that afternoon, too. So she'd pull out the other first glimpses, which felt framed to her, like little paintings, icons, and review them for their actuality and their joy. Today, she had faith.

Always, always, Lourdes was baffled by what she'd done in her small life to deserve his presence within it, yet she denied herself the questions that could spoil, those signs of faithlessness that destroyed miracles because they offended the divine. Thinking of him was a prayer whispered, catching sight of him a prayer answered.

When it finally arrived, it was over Rodney's shoulder, right between Niqua at the register and Alfonso at the fry station. Donald was looking down at his phone, as usual, but she knew he'd seen her because he was smiling. His hair fell across his forehead toward the floor.

"Lourdes?" Rodney was breathing down at her.

"Sorry."

"No, I'm not looking for apologies."

She returned her attention to the monitor and worked a little faster than usual.

"I'm starting to wonder about that extra forty-five cents I'm paying you."

Lourdes focused on the smooth surface of the cheese slice on her fingers and replayed the first glimpse, between Niqua and Alfonso, over Rodney's shoulder. This time, his hair was a curtain.

The restaurant was a bit busier than usual, and it took an extra ten minutes before she could head out the door, certain Donald's eyes were trained on her. The sharp smell of winter would always and only ever mean New Jersey to her, and it smelled the most like New Jersey just after the layered stinks of the December Burger King. Today, the parking lot was humid with salted snow and laden with exhaust.

Situated at the back of the lot, his car was as far away from the camera as possible. Lourdes had taught Donald to park there. Of course, she knew they watched her; she'd watched them, too, smoking or making out. Everyone made fun of her out there, just as they did with each other, and she just smiled. If they really knew, they'd be silenced by the purity of it, only able to giggle as they cut their eyes at one another.

Now she stood by his car, and when he joined her, she was glad that she'd learned just kind things to say in English. Of course, she knew the other words because they had been directed at her so many times in the past thirty years. But seeing his face, knowing that his grin was all for her, she understood the uselessness of learning the bad things because they could never help in determining Donald.

"Lourdes." A gift.

She only blushed. Donald didn't speak Spanish, and when she thought about their time together while she was at home or at work, she cursed her handicap in English, an inability to say things exactly the way they should be said to him, about him, for him. There was so much to say. But now, when he was near and his gaze melted the space between them, she remembered that there were no languages, no barriers. There was only this one thing.

They entered the car, which was still a bit warm. As he moved his hand into her big coat, Lourdes stared effortlessly into Donald's eyes, a way to consume him and offer herself back. Helping him undo her pants, she allowed herself to moan as he encouraged her. In fact, it was the only time and place that she had ever allowed herself to moan—even with Jose, it had been too private. This was what she gave back to him, and she knew that it meant so much more to Donald than anything she could ever accept from him. But was it enough?

Right from the beginning, Donald had understood that Lourdes's whole life had been conducted in service to others, so she and Donald had immediately fallen into this particular way of appreciating one another, a way in which she was welcome to receive and never expected to give. It had never varied since, at first because Lourdes mistrusted her English, and then because neither of them seemed to want it to. But now, although fully clothed, she laid herself bare, and it was this act, so profound for Lourdes, that also worried her. Did he sense the loop that formed in her mind during their communion, the round of doubt that she regretted and was fighting against? Did he want more? Was he hoping desperately that she snake her way under his puffy jacket? She so wanted to return his kindness, and in fact it was this act that she thought about—if she thought about anything—as he drove her on, down in her lap. But as always, Lourdes's hands lay firmly on Donald's arm. She'd never betray her desire because she feared that any change could end her miracle, and she climaxed, and Donald smiled into her, deeply, and her worry was pushed out of their union for another day.

After seeping in his rapt attention for a few minutes, Lourdes touched his cheek. "You look so sad today."

"I have to leave you now."

"No! I have to leave *you*." Had any of them watched this time, and had they seen the faces she must have made? But she didn't care; let them see something pure.

Zaïda wanted them to see something when she was fourteen. The Pacific's breeze was colder than usual that day, and she'd spent the whole afternoon constructing her sand sculpture for her Aunt and Uncle in Punta Sal. Having spent all of her attention on the flourishes and details, she only realized how astounding the whole thing was when she waded out into the sea, the sun now at her back, throwing her work into sharp relief. It wasn't a few grains of sand shifted around—the thing was Zaïda. Her father had died having never seen a single thing from her, and her mother had never looked before, but now, finally, Zaïda had something for her loved ones to recognize.

Running up to the house, she quickly determined that no matter what she said or did, no one would ever come down to the beach to see the only thing that would ever come close to expressing everything in her soul. So she ate her shrimp that night silently, knowing that only their brothers and sisters had seen what she'd done, as the tide dragged her revelation out to sea. After that, she didn't bother to be seen, and she wasn't.

Donald turned his attention to the steering wheel, naked conflict at his eyes and his mouth. Lourdes never knew, she never asked, worried that her untrustworthy comprehension would only make things worse. But to witness his pain was unbearable, and to do nothing a crime she grappled with during quiet times, washing dishes, waiting for sleep to come.

He never asked for anything.

"I'm going to learn Spanish."

"No." She said it as gently as possible.

But how could she truly explain that she suspected these waves of sadness that periodically overtook him were due to the endless selflessness he showed her? That somehow, doing only one thing more for her would make his life even more miserable? That she didn't understand, but she wanted desperately to, and she'd be honored to do whatever she could to make Donald's life easier for him to bear?

"No, Donald." She said only this and prayed that he read the rest in her eyes.

WEDNESDAY

The sun was out, and it steamed patches of brown grass near Donald's car. Lourdes felt more uncomfortable being there with the sun so strong at the windows, but the innocence of the whole thing was so fundamental that anyone who came upon them would have to feel the same way. People weren't always nice, anymore, and they needed to be reminded, sometimes. Donald and her orgasm were both gifts from God. She wished the kids in the restaurant would someday be able to appreciate all the gifts that are already there, right inside of them.

She watched Donald eat the mistake chicken sandwich she'd saved for him, glad he'd finally told her that some of the other workers were doing things to his food. She'd been at Burger King for two months, now, and she just couldn't understand how people could care so little about others, about life. Nothing was important; nothing was serious; everything was *gay* or *cool.* Lourdes had been brought up to believe that most things were important and serious and floated on the waves somewhere in between. Your little opinion depended mostly on which coast you stood and how the waves moved that day, but all was tiny against the ocean.

Still, she laughed. "You have—on your—mayo." She pointed to the corner of his mouth, enjoying the lack of tension in her shoulder that his

4

tenderness had brought but that would return soon enough because of all the tomatoes and lettuce and Rodney, always over her.

Donald laughed, too, as he wiped it off. But he looked so much more tired than even Monday. "This is just what I needed, Lourdes. Thank you so much for thinking of me."

She stroked his face; his eyes were bruised from stress. "I think of you always. You know, I call you my angel in my head." She didn't know much, but she knew she could do this, at least.

Donald stopped chewing to tear up.

"Oh, no! I make you cry every time. I'm sorry."

"Please. Don't apologize to me, Lourdes. There isn't anything... You're the angel."

"No. Sometimes everything seems so bad, but then I think of you. Everybody should have an angel."

"I know."

His crying changed a little; with four grown children, Lourdes knew crying. "Oh, what is it?"

A strong intake of air steadied his breathing. "Would you come to my New Year's party?" Donald gazed into her, laying wide an exposed panorama of hope and pain and need. His intensity was a constant shock to her, but this was more so. "Please."

Lourdes averted her face and inspected the back of the restaurant. She thought of the bus to Newark that late at night, then the vomit and drunks. Then she thought of the other guests and how different she was bound to be. Then she thought of the private relationship that she and Donald had created, how she cherished it as it was and how it would have to change when put into words for others. Then she thought of the truth about Donald, which she knew he held close for her until he felt she was ready, experience obviously informing his actions and also at the core of the truth itself. This was in the car, too, somewhere.

She thought of her mortifying limitations and of losing her one and only angel.

Then she thought of herself, aged five, back in San Juan, when a neighbor boy the same age attempted to rape her, based on the relationship his father had established with him. Lourdes understood this, and also understood why the boy sold cheap wallets to tourists for ten years so he could finish college and become the executive director of a food bank in Schenectady. All the apologies, all the sacrifices—she knew it was easier than the other way, the hardening and dismissing and forgetting.

"Okay, Donald."

To see his joy was to see a raw, beating heart, and Lourdes knew that she'd never regret her decision. But a New Year's Party?!

Then the tears returned. "You're so wonderful to me, Lourdes, and I'm—" Donald trailed off into a slow shake of the head. "I *am* going to learn Spanish for you. I'm not going to let things continue like this. I promise."

Lourdes cursed her limited English and railed against her fear, but still she wouldn't ask what he meant by 'letting things continue like this.' They were honest with each other in so many other, gratifying ways. That alone was more than she'd ever asked for from her life, and she was determined to avoid anything that might alter her special gift for as long as she could. Things always change, she knew that, but in a way, she was barricading against old age now, collecting as many memories as possible that might save her when things got worse.

THURSDAY

It was so strange: her favorite car in the world, something with which she was so achingly intimate, parked in a street that was intimate for her in all the other ways. It was the first thing she saw, down at the curb, and Lourdes felt her heart spasm, not sure if she was thrilled or terrified by the situation. Or both.

Then she noticed the expressionless Asian man, a little older than she was, in her seat, staring through the windshield out into the heavy snowfall, into the night. Things were changing.

The man looked like he'd had a comfortable life, and Lourdes couldn't help but feel a little silly in her Wal-Mart sweat pants and old jacket with the stain on the back. She understood Donald wouldn't care, and right now she didn't really have time to care, herself, but she knew she would be reworking this moment over and over again over the next days and weeks, wondering how they discussed her poverty afterwards. Probably gently and charitably, if at all, but there would also be the mental echo of the shameful jacket, the boarded window on the second floor, the tennis shoes hanging from the wire above the car. These men couldn't help but retain those things, coming from Montclair, and a flush of embarrassment quickly crossed her forehead.

And just like the Burger King, there were youngsters behind her, watching her. Here, they peered down from the windows, wondering who on earth would ever want to associate with their mother. She felt their exhausting presence sixty feet above her, and prayed that the snow was thick enough to obscure the street below.

As if stung, Lourdes sucked air through her teeth: Donald was standing a few feet away from her in the shadow of the porch. Her heart misfired. Meeting him at night, finding him almost lurking, being asked to contend with a third person—so much was suddenly changing. It was the panic of slipping to the cliff's edge, so she took a deep breath and resolved to change as little as possible, herself.

But her eyes were adjusting to the light, and she saw that Donald was different. He looked drained and frail and his expression, in her experience an epic battleground where love quickly and easily triumphed, now just looked haunted and vacant, a dispassionate evaluation of her, somehow.

It was the one look her angel was never supposed to give her, and Newark the one place in the world he was never supposed to be.

"Donald, you look so... What's wrong?"

Relief at this flooded past the grayness around his eyes, and she felt a little better.

"I really want to hug you, Lourdes."

"Joselito's watching. Nobody comes to visit me. I said you were from work."

"I guess I am."

"You don't have to come here to say you're sorry about today." She glanced at the man in the car. "I know how busy you are."

"I'm so sorry."

Lourdes knew that look; she'd been giving it to herself in the mirror for the past twenty years. Back then, she'd let out the cat by mistake, a misshapen, confused tom, and hadn't bothered to look for him right away. She'd been nursing Carina, so she only moved the blinds and looked down around the dumpster, but the cat had run out into the street and been immediately hit by a car. He'd dragged himself to the gutter, twisted, and panted for an hour before she'd found him, only to die, staring up into the sky as she lifted him. It was the worst anger, the kind that could only be directed at herself, and it still felt the same, all these years later. Some things she had no right to forgive.

But she didn't want to be responsible for anyone else ever feeling that way. Especially poor Donald, who looked to be wearing right through his life. She wasn't a mute animal with only heaven ahead of her. She understood.

A weak wind blew snow into the alcove, wetting the outside of Lourdes's hands. The two of them couldn't even find shelter there.

"This is not right!" Taking one final look at the car, Lourdes turned back to the light and steam heat of her building. "I'll be right back."

*   *   *

The snow had muffled Lourdes's return, and she stood, a few feet behind Donald, clutching her two plastic bags and worrying that the men would notice that she'd changed her clothing. He was on his knees, leaned up against the passenger door of his car. The window was down and his head rested awkwardly on the seat before him as he stared down her street into the flurries. The other man was right next to Donald, in her seat.

"Donald?"

His hesitation was too long. "Oh, Lourdes! I'm just—"

The man removed his seatbelt carefully, so as not to hit Donald with it, and said, "Why don't we get you into my seat, and then I'll just drive you home." He smiled apologetically at Lourdes, and she came up to the car, instinctively aware of her role, rubbing Donald's shoulder before helping him stand up as steadily as possible. The man quickly vacated his seat, and the two of them got Donald strapped in.

As they backed away, the stranger quietly thanked Lourdes, who made no attempt to hide her distress.

"What happened?"

"He's tired. Maybe he has a cold. He's been so busy today."

Lourdes finally looked the man in the eye. "He has?"

But when she returned her attention to Donald, she found him staring at her, studying her and begging her all at once. She didn't understand what he wanted and was too disturbed to ask, so she turned to the man and tried to smile.

"Oh. Lourdes, this is Joseph. Joseph, Lourdes."

She shook the man's gloved hand, aware that snowflakes were catching on her eyelashes and glad at least that was still the same. But she felt Donald's gaze burning into her and understood only that it had something to do with this introduction.

"How are you?"

"Pleasure to meet you, Lourdes." The man pitied, apologized with his eyes: she must've been failing at hiding her distress.

Signs of Donald's illness were even more pronounced once he was in the car, and his head lolled against the seat. He turned away from her, defeated, disappointed, and massaged the gear shift. Lourdes had always been so thankful that his face was a window, a slave; this was the first time she had wished it wasn't so.

Deciding to focus on the one thing that still made sense to her, Lourdes peered down at him, poring over his appearance as mothers do for clues, and therefore, for possible remedies. All this craziness was probably just due to his sickness. "You should go home, Donald. We can talk later. Oh—" She looked down at the bags in her hands and then back to Donald, and in attempting to reconcile the two things, finally became overwhelmed. Her eyes welled up. "I don't know—I made brownies and thought—"

The man smiled politely when she handed her bags to him. "That's very kind of you."

Neither Donald nor Joseph acknowledged her tears, so she was certain, then, that her reaction must have been appropriate for the situation. Fear gripped her more tightly.

Without looking up: "Lourdes, my party on Sunday. Rascal's, you know the place?"

"Okay. You should go and get some rest now. Please."

"You're going to be there?"

"Yes."

Donald reached his hand out the window, and Lourdes took it deliberately, no longer concerned with what her children might think.

"Joseph will be there."

"Okay."

"At the party."

Lourdes looked up at the apartment buildings that loomed all around them, their lights and sounds so far away now, almost gone in the heavy snowing.

"Angels have hearts for everyone, Donald."

A note of harshness crept into Donald's voice that Lourdes had never heard before, but there was also the familiar self-effacement and contrition: "I'm not an angel."

"Then there are no angels." Lourdes shook her head at Joseph and backed away from the car, unable to experience any more. "I'm sorry. Go, go!"

She moved out of their decreasing sphere quickly, feeling already the frustration burning at her throat. He was leaving her now, and she'd failed in so many ways. She'd somehow even managed to make his life more painful. Lourdes didn't know what was wrong; she didn't know how to help him; she didn't know what she'd done to hurt him; she didn't have the capacity to understand.

Donald was still there, though, right in front of her! She still had time to make things right. She'd try until they understood each other. But she moved toward the car just as it pulled away. Lourdes could only vow to herself, then, as she watched the taillights dissolve into the silent, rapid snow flakes, that she would make things right when she saw him next. At his party.

ERIC

"Come in."

The morning was warmer, the dripping water reducing snow to clear, hard lacework. Its sudden humidity made Donald's hair limp, made him look like a bashful little kid. At this, Eric's mind stretched out electrically in several directions: naughty schoolboy; fevered recess; innocence stripped away. But he tucked these back and refocused on the goal at hand, the anticipation radiating from his solar plexus and warming his extremities.

Eric stepped aside, and Donald entered the apartment. One of the canvases was in the corner, covered by a cloth, and Donald turned away from it as quickly as possible. The many other images, displayed around the old, echoey loft, he avoided, too. Instead, he stood squarely in the center of the space, motionless, and faced the floor as he should.

Eric put Mindy down and inspected. Besides the hair, Donald looked thinner, sapped. This might work for the session, or it might work against it. His face was as plastic as ever. Even when it was supposedly controlled to the point of impassivity, Donald's expression was like the surface of a lake, rippled by any and every stone that broke the surface. It was still as round, as dimpled, but the cheeks were closer now, the brown, bottomless eyes correspondingly farther apart. Eric felt his breath catch: the legs, short in proportion, and the thickness of the body in general gave the impression of a giant baby, which never failed to delight Eric. He still couldn't believe his luck.

Donald literally gave no thought to what he wore, another facet of his gormless persona that invigorated Eric's creativity. Today, he had thrown on a Shetland sweater and old, brown corduroys that stretched across his backside.

Eric loved the middle-class ass, and he came up alongside it to scrutinize its form, which really did inspire memories of white bread, doughy and soft. Since Eric had known him, Donald's butt had grown and shrunk regularly over his naturally generous dimensions. Now, it was looking smaller, forgotten.

"You're losing weight again. Pull down your pants."

Donald immediately did so, the sweater drooping, the shirttails parting. Eric felt the thrill as forcefully as always: the unreality of a self-gratifying dream experienced over and over. It was the kind of perfection that had to include the phrase "once in a lifetime." It was the kind of perfection that could only come from gross, dismal imperfection. It was the kind of perfection that Eric was bound and determined to continue to exploit to its absolute extent.

But then he noticed new shoes peeking out from under the crumpled corduroy, a definite element of hip style about the red leather. They were clearly not a purchase Donald had made.

"I hate those shoes. Lift your leg." Eric pulled them off and walked to his sink. There, he opened a drawer that wailed into the cobwebbed, remote rafters of the space and removed his sharpest knife. For a moment, Eric considered keeping them for himself, as they would compliment his clubbing wardrobe quite nicely, but that felt as if it belonged to a different drama, so he simply hacked them up and threw them away.

"Next time, wear those old boat shoes. Take off your sweater and shirt."

Once again, Donald did as he was told, keeping his eyes down but unable to control his quickened breathing. The pale nakedness seemed to melt into the flesh-colored walls and soft, round shapes of the furniture, a coordinated element of the tableau. Eric liked that.

"Now I want you to answer me. Would you like to be thrown into a bath full of ice water right now?"

Donald always struggled with the questions; Eric feasted on this.

"I would like an answer to my question: would you like to be thrust into freezing water?"

"No."

Although he almost tripped on Mindy, Eric quickly recovered. He rushed up to Donald and pushed him into his bathroom, where a bath full of ice awaited them both. Eric forcefully handed him into the tub, squeezing harder on the tightening muscles, and Donald's eyes widened in what must have been profound shock. He was unable to stifle an eloquent groan, and Eric suddenly wished he'd had his audio recorder. He could've worked that in. But then, as he held Donald under the water, Eric saw black, spreading mildew at the corner of his bath tub, and it annoyed him. This wasn't about seediness, but then again, it did feel more authentic that way. Nonetheless, he'd have to re-caulk.

"I want to see how low I can bring your body temperature."

Almost immediately, Donald began shivering.

"Relax into it." Eric watched the skin turn pink, then white, then a light gray with purple undertones. "That's it." He watched all the involuntary movements in the toes, the skin across the neck tightening. Eric added all of this to the many wonderful things he'd seen the human body do over the past six months.

Bringing to mind steeping tea, Eric realized after a few minutes that he had reached perfection, and he pulled his camera off of the nearby basin. He'd already loaded it, the batteries were new. Wondering if black-and-white wouldn't better communicate the subtle, clinical changes in skin tone, Eric considered changing film as Donald held his arms stiffly at his sides, the thumbs gouging his hips.

"Put your head under the water."

Drawing a deep breath with much difficulty, Donald did the best he could and submerged fully. Eric then went to work, captured several images that promised to be arresting, the eyes searching to recall meaning under the bobbing ice cubes and the face seeming to bloat in protest.

Reasonably satisfied, Eric plunged his hand into the water and grabbed Donald's arm. He pulled him up, and then over spittle and gasping: "Okay, that's enough."

Donald struggled to stand, the shivering making voluntary movement difficult. Finally, Eric had him wrapped in a huge, nutmeg towel that he'd preheated. Mindy licked at the drops of water on the floor, purring unevenly, which made Eric wonder about her as an ironic element in the scene and if this were a popular motivation for pet ownership. When he'd first gotten her, he'd dressed her as a clown, with red-and-white striped satin and a jingle-bell in her hat, but it was too deliberate, too art-school, and he'd ceremoniously burned the whole sketch pad.

She might be in a couple of shots; he'd decide then.

"Come on."

Making sure to wrap the towel around Donald's shoulders, Eric gently led his subject into the adjoining bedroom. The room was dominated by a huge image over the bed: Donald's face barely recognizable under dried mud. Eric helped him lie on the unmade bed, then pulled the sheets over his ashen feet and calves. A space heater whirred nearby, and Eric adjusted it for optimal efficiency.

"How was that?" Eric lay next to Donald, carefully rubbing and patting, noting that the body hair was standing straight up, and that the scrotum had completely disappeared.

"Intense. You've outdone yourself. And this is great, Eric." Donald looked up into Eric's face, awed. "Thank you."

The shivering had become worse, interestingly, but the session was over. "Here. Get closer."

Donald pressed as much of his flesh against Eric as he could, and gradually, the spasms became sporadic. Considering a bright red ear, Eric wondered to himself if he'd managed to slow the heart rate, if he'd had the power to have such a profound effect on another human. Controlling a heart. "It's all over now."

Donald's body slowly flushed pink as Mindy observed the action from the dresser opposite.

"God." Eric pushed Donald away and got up, keeping his back to what had just formed between them both.

"Just another natural reaction, Eric."

Eric relived a certain hesitation, a delicacy during a diaper change at his sister's house the year before. Throwing a pillow on Donald's crotch, he swallowed his curiosity at the bald urgency he'd caught a glimpse of, a little annoyed that at that moment, the hard-on might have more power in the room than he did. At first, he wondered how he could control that, too, with contraptions or perhaps psychological tactics of some kind that might prove to be pleasantly confrontative, in a triptych or video loop, maybe. Then he thought about other ways to conquer the renegade organ. He'd wanted to avoid any salaciousness, but there might be a need to take hundreds of close-ups of Donald's physical, blunt craving, to reduce it to the helpless flesh it really was.

Eric frowned at Donald's chest. "But it's not entirely involuntary."

Holding the pillow against his crotch, Donald moved off the bed. "More of a surrender. I'm sorry, Eric." There, at the foot of the bed, he looked down. "Hey, you better throw this thing in the washing machine the second I'm out of here!"

Donald smiled at the dry chuckle he'd extracted from Eric, but it faded too fast. He threw the pillow over Eric's feet; he was flaccid. "Crisis over! Listen, if I'm late again to work, I'm really going to get fired, so. But I wanted to know if you have any plans for New Year's Eve." Donald had been unable to keep his tone natural, and the last sentence hung in the air, a pathetic act.

Eric was instantly disturbed by the breach. This hadn't been designed to be domestic, social. No matter how his art appeared to others, it was Eric who had truly embraced his own vulnerability in this situation. And he'd come to trust Donald with it completely, as he'd learned that there was no greater trustworthiness than one based on the kind of desperate inequality that fueled their partnership. Just like dressing cats as clowns, pure manipulation was at the heart of this work; and a contamination of insipid familiarity would destroy everything. If Donald's feelings were as deep as he professed, surely he should appreciate that. But now, penises and parties made Eric almost regret for the first time an experiment that he felt had been clearly prescribed.

Donald spoke first, quicker with nervousness. "I'm sorry. Never mind. Just give me a call if you need me again. This was really inspired. Really."

He passed into the next room, and Eric realized for the first time that his clothes were slightly damp.

"Eric? Do you have any shoes I can borrow?" No causticity, not even impatience.

Eric remained at the foot of his bed, arms limp at his side. Despite the lurking, unnerving undertones of his own, jack-in-the-box psyche and the occasional, tender window into Donald's, this was too productive, too ideal to end yet. He hadn't explored it fully.

Eric picked up the pillow at his feet and pulled its case off. Why, after half a year of fruitful collaboration, would Donald suddenly decide to risk everything on some Doritos-and-canned-salsa party? After all, he knew they were nearing the completion. If anything, Donald should've been thanking him for the opportunity to be documented in such an arresting, groundbreaking way, rather than potentially destroying the whole thing with his defect.

THURSDAY

Eric smoothed down the old, gray business suit, vaguely annoyed that it fit him so well. He'd even gone so far as to purchase cufflinks and throw on some trendy cologne he'd found at T.J. Maxx, which still couldn't drown out the Salvation Army smell of the worsted wool. How could people willingly constrict themselves like this? Why did they want to resemble each other to this extent? After catching a glimpse in his ancient mirror of the shiny tie constricting his neck, Eric decided that this had to be the subtlest form of torture: self-inflicted. He'd even gone so far as to carefully part his hair for the first time in fifteen years. It was all too bourgeois. His mother would have been proud.

Having just used her litter box, Mindy followed Eric to the door.

Donald looked more abject than usual on the doorstep. Eric's stomach tightened; it was going to be a good session.

"Come in. You look like complete shit, which is absolutely perfect. What the fuck have you done to yourself since yesterday? Actually, don't answer that. It's part of the mystery. I don't want to inform my work to that extent."

Mindy rubbed against Donald's ankles while Donald stood at the center of the room and looked at the floor. Eric was once again struck by what a perfect specimen he was for this series. The schlub. Eric's luck had really turned around in the last year, and some days, he could almost feel fame lapping at his door while he planned the installation at his desk, rearranging the experience for different spaces he had in mind.

And discovering the schlub was at the center of it all.

He handed Donald the costume. "Put this on." Then as Donald silently did as he was told: "How would you like to be trussed up and hung up-side-down today? And as a special treat, I'm going to be part of the session. I'll be playing the role of a worker bee from Stamford or New Rochelle or something. A commuter who's baffled by his existence, yet who continues on, following the rules, doing what's expected of him, until he dies at fifty-three of a heart attack. You should be flattered; I don't usually include myself in my own work."

Donald finished stretching the spangly women's shorts and tank top with "porn star" on it tautly over his body.

"Oh, and here."

Donald pulled on the Uggs Eric handed him and became still again.

Eric giggled. "My god, this is absolutely perfect! Totally what I'm looking for. You look horrendous. So, you feel like hanging up-side-down and squirming until your face turns bright red? Answer—"

"No."

Eric froze. Donald's response was different than usual, plaintive. Every other time, he'd sounded eager to please; now, he sounded eager for mercy. Eric considered the change and was delighted to predict that Donald would be doing even more desperate squirming than he'd dared hope for.

But then Donald did something else he'd never done before. He lifted his eyes and looked at the images of himself crowded into the apartment: the huge painting of his torso covered in crickets; the pictures of his forehead before and after Eric had shaved off his left eyebrow; the mannequin carefully papier-mâchéd over with the giant photo of his nude body.

Now Eric was annoyed. "Well, my dear sir, that's your—as they say—tough shit. Get in here."

Donald followed him into his study, which had been cleared of the furniture and the tipping stacks of Donald artwork. In their place was a rusting children's swing set, although heavy chains hung where the swings used to. Opposite, Eric's best camera and lights were trained on the scene.

Donald gave the set-up only a cursory glance. Where was the usual awe, the keenness?

Eric refused to acknowledge the shift: "I'm going to be a pedophile at the park, feeling my young victim up while I push her on the swing set. You're going to be up-side-down for a while. You may pass out, I don't know. Does that frighten you?"

Donald lifted his face to Eric, beseeching, and Eric's ogle passed away. He crossed his arms, willing himself to breathe. The room was suddenly stuffy and smelled of cat piss.

"Get over there." But Eric sounded squeaky.

Donald moved in front of the chains. The shorts were so tight that a testicle was now visible, but instead of delighting in this detail, Eric found himself wanting to look away. Things were quickly unraveling.

He'd carefully designed the swing set contraption and even tried it on himself, but Donald was much bigger and heavier, so that when Eric trussed him up and pulled the chains that would invert him, they bound at the top of the now creaking frame, leaving Donald only horizontal.

"God damn it! Don't move." As Donald swayed randomly with his breathing, Eric did his best to free the chains. He'd spent too much of his time on this project to let it beat him, even if it suddenly felt as if its artistic validity had been completely drained.

"If I don't get this fucking thing working, I might just shoot you with your balls hanging out like that. You look idiotic!" The harder he pulled on the chain now, the more Eric tittered, the muscles in his chest and throat contracting, the air being rhythmically pushed up and choked down.

"Fuck this! You're too fucking fat!"

The swing set's top beam collapsed, and Donald landed heavily on top of the pile of chains beneath him. His legs immediately started scrambling like an injured animal's, but the Uggs wouldn't cooperate, so it took him a moment to shift his position. His grunting finally caused Eric to tear himself away from the camera and approach him, but not before he'd gotten a couple of potential keepers of Donald struggling and grimacing. After all, Eric had been an artist long enough to know that sometimes, one has to surrender one's plans to the will of art and just roll with the bitch. The whole thing might still be salvageable.

He pulled Donald up, who had clearly injured his chest, and although he wanted to punish him, Eric mildly remarked, "That wasn't supposed to happen."

Donald's face was now animated with pain, his teeth bared above the "porn star" t-shirt in such a way that Eric was tempted to take a few more shots. But something about Donald's flashing manner warned him not to.

"Why don't we get you onto the bed, and I'll take a look."

Donald held himself farther away from Eric than seemed Donald-like as they shuffled out, and Eric told himself that it was the pain. As he helped Donald gently pull off the t-shirt, a series of bright pink welts presented themselves—something that he would never have gone for, exactly, but something he couldn't pass up now that it was right in front of him.

"Wow. Do you think you broke any ribs?"

"I don't know."

Eric could feel Donald's eyes on him and was suddenly enraged when he felt his face flush. "Listen, if you're going to start breaking the rules with this whole deal, then we're ending it! We're both getting something out of this, capiche?"

Donald looked away and lay quietly down.

"Now, hold still. I'm sorry, but this is too good not to get on film. Okay?"

Donald's breathing slowed down as he rearranged the shorts.

"Okay?!"

"Yes."

Eric found that after he left to retrieve his camera, there was a dread that now clung to their situation, their "partnership," and he didn't want to return to his own bedroom. Something fundamental had changed between this session and the one just a day earlier, and his mind rushed through ways to make sense of the situation, hopefully to salvage it. Donald had never wanted anything before, never expected anything. But this was a betrayal, and the one thing that Eric never excused was a betrayal.

When he was eleven years old and just before his mother moved out, it was the same thing with the dining room. The three of them always had dinner together, and even though it was clear that his parents were trying so hard for him, the time he spent in that room was like a lie he told to himself. He could still feel the strain on his facial muscles, forcing pleasant expressions that originated in shame, his eyes manically trained on some of the world's most boring foods: gray pork chops, burnt chili, stringy chicken. Nothing was ever prepared with enough salt, and their crystals coating everything was usually the only thing he could remember about those meals after leaving the table and retreating to his video games upstairs. The salt, catching the light at crystalline edges one moment and dissolving into coagulated gravy the next. His parents had done that to him.

Twenty years later, Eric had a lot of unusual items in his apartment: dozens of internet-sex-catalog oddities; exquisite, handmade, ethnic plunder; friends' shocking, brilliant artwork. He had a six-foot, foam-core pickle that recited a Hitler speech when you plugged it in.

But he didn't have a salt shaker.

As Eric stared at the door to his bedroom, refusing to allow Donald the upper hand, he began to wonder if maybe the whole project wasn't a bit too derivative, predictable in its desire to shock by figuratively raping the middle class. The whole thing suddenly seemed pretentious, over-reaching, and it was only the building, clenching rage at his subject that drove him back in.

Donald's chest was worse, but the bruising now looked to Eric like something private, something suffered alone and modestly. Even his bedroom felt like it didn't belong to him, anymore.

He put the camera down on his dresser and closed his eyes on the scene. The violated schoolgirl concept was at the center of his installation.

"All right. What the fuck happened? You know, I can sense that you're not participating. And none of this shit works for me if you're not participating."

"Why me, Eric?"

Now Eric found himself avoiding Donald's pleading gaze, and his anger at this new subversion screamed up from his guts, joining all the other causes of his fury that re-emerged and multiplied whenever he was thrust into this kind of shit. He could feel his face contorting uncontrollably, the same ugliness of a grown man about to cry, but without the possibility of inspiring pity. Nonetheless, he wanted Donald to see this; he could be naked, too.

"Because you're free and you're utterly nothing! And because you've always begged for it, at least up to now. So maybe the real question is: why *me*, Donald? Really, do you even have a clue how to answer that? Do you have a clue how important this is to me? Have you ever really given a shit about it? Because I'm not the one who approached you. I'm not the one that worked out this whole deal. That was all you, buddy. So now, to find you all of a sudden looking at me like I'm some kind of freak is not only unfair, it's also proof that you don't know the first fucking thing about what you call love! And I can't fucking stand hypocrites—you should have at least worked that one out by now."

Donald almost sounded surprised by it himself: "I still love you."

"And I don't love you. So I don't have to put up with any of this shit. I just don't! I don't even know you, and I don't want to. I already know too much. And you don't know me, so don't presume that just because you say I'm so important to you and that my success with this project is, too, that it has any impact on me, whatsoever."

The detached evaluation Donald performed on Eric was the worst affront yet, but Eric declined to rise to the bait.

Once again, the aching supplication: "So what do you think I feel for you? Eric, please, I—"

"I want you to leave now."

Donald got slowly up, the comforter gathering in his clenched hands. Eric had never dared attempt to inflict this particular kind of pain on his subject because he'd been worried he'd walk, but now that it was here, he had to capture it, Uggs and all. It was also a suitably brutal response to

Donald's questions, his shift in attitude, and Eric reveled in the rawness of his power. The camera flicked away, documenting Donald's winces, his eyes slightly crossed from the effort to move. He held his torso so stiffly that the tortured sculptures on and around Eric's bureau were an eloquent echo of Donald's suffering. As he photographed, Eric realized that this suffering could never have reached the level it had without Donald's sudden emotional turmoil, and he found himself relaxing into a gladness of it. Even if he never saw Donald again, he had this, and this was new, a nice addition. In fact, the submissive, desperate nature present in all of Donald's other images, Eric was now beginning to realize, limited their impact. Willing victim was suddenly too one-note. He began to wonder if the project wasn't worth the effort after all.

"How would you feel about me coming to your party and humiliating you there? Bringing all our work—a trial run of the show? For all your people to see? I wonder what they'd think about you, then. Capturing their reactions would finish off my project nicely. Do you love me enough to let me do that to you?"

Donald continued toward his pile of clothing silently. He removed the shorts with his back to Eric, but Eric grabbed his shoulder and turned him around, the graphic injuries a nice contrast to the paleness of the thighs and bound to look fantastic in black-and-white.

Finally, after getting most of his clothing on, Donald posed his own question, the tone of his voice better suited to the subject of chess or microbiology. "What *do* you feel about me?"

"I don't answer questions, buddy, I ask them. I'm going to humiliate you at your party. Look at the camera lens and tell me how that will make you feel."

A sentiment Eric never thought he'd see flower on Donald's face: the smooth brow and pressed lips of an academic detachment.

"I'll see you then."

Austin remembered the very second he stopped caring. He'd seen his cellmate beaten up for what had to be the twentieth time that month, and he actually felt a physical shift inside of himself, two monolithic stones scraping by one another, one coming and one going. The one going was the one that cared, and the one inside him now was blissfully hollow, free of needless, and therefore dangerous, things. It struck him now that they were both just stones, and one worked just as well as the other to mill things into dust.

His next concern was just dinner, and after that, just rec time and then just lights out. Just a single line of duties to manage, one at a time; just one, single life to live.

BRAD

MONDAY

Brad waited the full twenty minutes before going next door to their stuffy office: 9:22 to 9:42. He wasn't planning on going the exact moment the clock hit 9:42, but he finished reformatting the spreadsheet he was working on at the same time and didn't see a point in starting on the next step. It didn't have to be twenty minutes, either, because that might be a pattern people would start to notice if they became suspicious at all.

In the corridor, Brad considered alternatives: first fifteen minutes, then the next day maybe twenty minutes, then fourteen and nineteen, then thirteen and eighteen. But he'd lose track too quickly of the waiting period that way, even though he didn't really even need a waiting period, as such. Maybe he could tie it to a random event, like the first phone call after Donald arrived, or the first bird he saw in the tree near his window. Or maybe not the first, but the fifth. But there were a lot of birds, so maybe the first time he saw two birds together. Actually in the tree.

Stacy had her back turned when Brad entered, so he could smile at the top of Donald's head. The bright sunlight that was reflected off the snow outside passed under Donald's thin patch and glowed on his shiny scalp.

"You really have to start showing up on time, Donald."

Stacy turned back and took a pencil out of her mouth. "An old guy slipped and fell."

"Of course, he did. Can I—? For a second—?" Brad motioned to the door.

Donald rose and smiled broadly. "Okay, Brad."

Brad led, his mind focused exclusively on his ears, on noises that might determine what he'd do next. There was nothing else to think about. Everyone remained in their workspaces behind closed doors, so he continued down the short hall to the men's room, and Donald followed. They'd just remodeled the bathroom, and it was all black tile now, with strange, indirect fluorescent lighting that always reminded Brad of

23

somewhere. Maybe the morgue, only with more vertical shadows. Designed to draw attention away from unsightly stains.

The room was empty, so Brad backed into a corner behind the door near the paper towel dispenser. They had time to separate and recover back there if someone came in.

Closing his eyes, Brad soon had his face buried in Donald's shoulder, his hands grasping at Donald's shoulder blades. Perfectly silent, they hugged until footsteps echoed in the hall, and Brad quickly disengaged. He didn't look at Donald; rather, he kept his left arm pressed against Donald's right until the footsteps moved into an office.

He didn't want to say it. Donald didn't want to hear it. But there was only so much weirdness a guy could take: "So I guess maybe we should head, you know, back to the slog, as it were."

Donald shrugged, nodding, but then faltered, the shadows of the room taking over more of his face. "You know, Brad, if you ever want to ask me about anything at all, I'll be totally honest—"

"Shh, shh, shh! No, no, no! Go. Go! It's echoey in here. People don't have conversations in the bathroom."

"So you *do* want to have a conversation?"

"Just go, go, go!"

Donald frowned and left the bathroom first, as was the custom. Brad could only concentrate on counting to thirty-five because everything else in his brain was melted, and then he passed into the hall, flushed and loose. Back in the white space of everyone else, he could manage only to promise himself that he would reconsider the usefulness of the thirty-five-second rule later, once the real world seemed important again.

*   *   *

Brad hadn't thought about Donald's question when he returned to his desk, and he hadn't thought about it when he took a break and had a granola bar. He hadn't thought about it when he really did go to the bathroom—even though he'd been in the very room where the question was asked—and he hadn't thought about it when he went to lunch and had a burger with a huge red onion that lingered on his breath and hands and made him wonder why anyone would care enough about somebody like him to ever ask a question like that in the first place. He had fat, stubby fingers that almost wanted to reek of onion.

In fact, he hadn't thought about anything except the new contracts for the hourly workers until Elizabeth dropped the kids off at the office that afternoon. She was going to spend the night with her sister in Secaucus, who had just had a miscarriage, and the last thing she'd want around, Elizabeth had said, was the kids.

Only then had Brad had his first thought since Donald's question that wasn't work-related: the last thing *he* wanted around was the kids at work. And he only realized why when the kids had run into Donald and Stacy's office. Brad had raced in after them, his lips pressed against each other by the force of his furrowed forehead.

"Hey, guys. Come on now. Come back to my office, okay?"

"It's no biggie, Brad!" Stacy shook her perm in dismissal.

But Donald had frozen, his eyes glazed over and glowing from the light of his monitor. He looked terrified of Cooper and Emma's presence.

If Brad had instinctively felt that it wasn't a good idea to mix his work life and his home life together, Donald's disturbing reaction cemented the conviction.

Brad moved aggressively toward his children, who responded by staring, confused, up into his eyes. "Come on. Let's let them work. Sorry, guys."

He grabbed their hands and swiftly left Stacy and Donald's office, disturbed by what he'd witnessed there, yet relieved to have the kids' hyperactive antics to occupy his mind for the rest of the day.

TUESDAY

Of course, Brad knew the gentle knock. He swallowed down a little stomach acid that had suddenly sprung up as he reviewed all the tumultuous consideration he'd given the question, mostly the night before, staring at the digital clock on his bed stand. Every time a number changed, and especially when two—or even three—numbers changed, he felt his resolve click, stronger and stronger: too much knowledge about Donald would destroy what they had. On no account would he ask questions of any kind.

"Who is it?" Brad tried to relax his forehead as Donald entered. "Oh, hi, Donald. Close the door, would you?"

Donald did as he was told and sat down. "I'm so sorry I'm late, Brad."

Brad was suddenly up. "'I'm sorry I'm late *again*,' maybe?"

"You're really upset. And that's the last thing I ever want to do."

Brad paced behind his desk, rubbing his chair, touching the window blinds. "Donald! Look, I know that you always have legitimate reasons, somehow—"

"And that's what I wanted to talk with you about—"

"I'm not asking!" Brad sputtered out a humorless laugh. "All that, or whatever, is all your business. This is a work environment. So I'm sure you can see where I'm coming from."

"Of course, I do. Would it make it easier for you if I quit? We could still—"

"Easier?! Of course, it would! I don't think you've ever even worked a forty-hour week the whole time you've been here!" Brad stroked the back of his chair, almost tenderly, as he finally noticed that Donald's eyes were red, as if he'd been crying and might soon again. Brad never thought that in his life, he'd want to embrace someone and punch them so much at the same time. It was insane. Then he noticed that he more or less wanted to do the same thing to himself. And when Brad added these two reactions up, the result was his relationship with this situation, which he'd been concurrently needing and hating for almost a year.

He used to think of himself as a great manager. That was gone. But he also had begun to think of himself as ultimately alone, and that was gone, too. Because the last few years with Elizabeth had been like gradually losing sight of land.

If anything, the big news for Brad was that nothing worth anything is ever easy.

"Of course, it wouldn't be easier." Brad sat back down and studied Donald's broad, sweater-clad chest. "Elizabeth wants to go back to school for her MBA because 'I'm not really moving ahead here.' Not like she was expecting, anyway. And I was, too, I guess." The wool was gray-green and reminded Brad of his grandfather. "I know I'll feel even more of a failure if the kids are stuck with some babysitter. Someone who only wants to be around them because they're getting paid. Kids sense those kinds of things. And I know they only have one childhood. It's such a weight on my mind."

"Of course, it is."

Brad shrugged. "And I know that if I told Elizabeth my feelings, she'd just tell me to pick a nanny who could teach the kids piano."

Donald squirmed in his chair now, his face contorting with one of his shades of pain. "I'll just stay late every night. Maybe I can stay on top of things that way. Will that make things easier for you?"

Brad imagined the sweater vibrating along with Donald's deep voice. The wool would be scratchy and cool against his cheek.

"I appreciate that, Donald, I really do. But your job really requires you to be around when the rest of us are. You know that."

"What can I do?" Donald leaned forward, his right hand strangling his left wrist.

Brad wanted to strangle that wrist, too. Where had it come from? Why wasn't it like every other wrist on the planet? And why had it landed here, in the middle of this particular office in Montclair, New Jersey?

"What am I supposed to do if you're not here? Come in every day and what? What?!" Brad pulled a sheet of paper out of his top drawer. He'd filled it out a month ago, and it was a replacement for one he'd filled out four months earlier. "I need you to sign this written warning. Too many people know that this should have been done a long time ago. The next time, you'll be let go."

Donald sat back, nodded and shrugged. "You're doing the right thing. You always do the right thing."

Brad looked down at his desk. The useless paperwork that dominated his existence only exacerbated the sudden frustration. "I never do the right thing."

"You do, and someday you'll appreciate it. I just wish you did, now."

"Donald! Don't. Please!"

Donald quickly signed the document without looking at it. "And we could still—"

"No, we can't! What, meet up once every couple of weeks when Elizabeth lets me out of the house?!"

Now Donald did start to cry. It seemed like such a common process to him that he didn't even notice it, and this caused Brad to take a deep breath in an effort to regroup, which merely caught on a sob of his own. He attempted to control it by holding his breath.

This was a workplace, not a talk show.

"Brad. You deserve more than this. I know that. You deserve someone who's there for you twenty-four hours a day and can appreciate everything about you. Because it is *everything*. All of you. But I can't—"

"Please! Donald, please."

Donald ducked his head then looked expectantly at Brad, his face glistening and ravaged.

But there was a seam that ran along the shoulder of his sweater. Brad quickly walked around his desk and embraced his friend, lining the seam up with his jawbone and gently rubbing back and forth over it. Its hardness was just as comforting as Brad predicted.

The worry that was to come—the replay of the meeting, with two grown men hugging and crying about something that wasn't even clear to Brad, at least not in his brain—all of that dropped and became still for the insignificant future as he stood so, so close to Donald.

"You don't deserve this."

WEDNESDAY

Brad was sketching a unicorn on the corner of his desk blotter, which he had long and silently considered his signature creature. When he was ten, he had seen a horse outside of Lexington who appeared to have some sort of light brown horn, and he looked away before the mirage was torn apart. The horse was far away, at the edge of a stand of trees and had a bandage on its right rear knee. His father had driven by on the way to the Sears Tire Center. The bandage made Brad wonder how people could know about a unicorn and not share it with the world. It was the kind of question that he was now sad to realize was exterminated by adulthood.

Brad had been sketching unicorns ever since. His wife had noticed early on and made a wry comment, never verbalizing again but only turning her face away each time she saw another one. He wasn't ashamed exactly, but over the years, his desire to doodle at home retreated. This had been replaced by coping mechanisms, conciliatory gestures and unspoken resentments that never exactly went away, but instead stacked up in neat categories, providing each other with structure and support so that when a new one was laid atop, it was nearer the surface, closer to popping. Sometimes Brad imagined lancing them all at once and forcing his wife to swallow their contents, but then he thought of how she looked when she was sleeping, demanding nothing, relaxed and defenseless, and he became ashamed of himself.

Today, he was sketching a white unicorn with a black mane and tail when there was the knock on his door.

"Come in."

Donald entered, closed the door behind him and stood expectantly next to the desk. Brad immediately noticed he was wearing a pair of hi-tech sneakers and swallowed a snicker.

"Who gave you those?"

"My other shoes were damaged. These are actually really comfortable."

"And two sizes too small, I bet."

"You don't miss anything, do you." As he said this, Donald lifted his arm in Brad's direction, but let it fall back. Brad moved his hands to his lap away from his unicorn, and Donald's eyes welled up as he stared at the blotter.

In a way, Brad was glad for whatever was about to happen because he just couldn't do this, anymore.

"How's your family?"

"Good. Fine." Brad felt his own eyes stinging.

"So I have two things I wanted to talk with you about, if you have time."

"Okay."

"First, I'd like to invite you to a New Year's party I'm having on Sunday night." Donald froze in expectance.

"Oh."

"Stacy is even helping me set it up at Rascal's."

"Rascal's?" Brad was glad that the conversation was so unexpected because his dread subsided immediately.

"It would mean so much to me if you could meet my other friends, Brad."

A different kind of dread sunk into Brad's chest. Other. With no thoughts to speak of, Brad picked up his ruler and used it to surgically remove the unicorn from its corner of the blotter. "We're actually going to our friends' house, the Kriegs. We already, you know, set it up." He threw the unicorn into the trash next to an empty bag of Bugles. They almost looked like fat unicorn horns, and he wondered if that's why he liked them so much.

"Oh, that's sounds great." Donald's voice was cracking, and Brad continued to consider snack shapes in his wastepaper basket.

"God, I'm so stupid about things! I'm sorry. Of course you've got plans. It's just that I really need—"

"So. So, *others*. Is it the same?"

"No."

"Do you talk about me?"

"No."

"Am I... well. That's all right."

"Brad—"

"That's okay. That's all right. That's really okay."

Donald sighed unevenly. His hand was vacantly stroking the edge of the desk.

"Donald, what was the other thing."

"I was wondering." Donald paused in an attempt to even his voice out. "I was wondering if I could get out of here a little early today."

It was like breaking a dowel in his hand, the exact same painful shock of vibration. And with it, Brad could no longer ignore that he wasn't built for this. If there were tools or rules that he'd grown up with, but there was nothing. Twenty-first Century America offered a lot of maps, but not for whatever it was they shared. At least this wasn't his fault, and it was actually a relief that he would no longer feel that it would have to be, somehow.

Still, Brad couldn't keep the frustration from being the first emotion he expressed. "You can't do that."

Donald remained still, sniffling back his tears.

"Donald, please. Not for me, but for the job. I mean, what on earth is so important?"

"I—"

"No, don't tell me. You don't have to tell me."

"You know, I'm thinking that maybe working from home might be a better way for all of this."

Perhaps it wasn't that strange that Brad had only recently started wondering about Donald's life outside of work—after all, they'd both avoided discussing anything remotely personal about him. Of course, Brad had told Donald all about Elizabeth, all about the snowball of refusals, so light and inconsequential at the beginning, that had become so grievous and momentous lately. Only the day before, he'd realized that she consistently seated the kids between them at the movie theater.

Brad's chest ached: he'd never be able to tell this to someone who would understand now, someone who'd shared in the gradual accretion of his marriage—and who was so remarkably concerned with it.

"Brad, we can still—"

"Still what? We work together. It's not on purpose. It's just the way we are, here. Outside of here, I mean, maybe you want more—"

"No! You know I only want what we have."

Brad found himself smiling, nodding. "I know. Me, too! It's just a little weird, you know? And I'm not a weird guy. I'm sorry, but I guess it couldn't just stay the same."

This was going to be the last time. It had to be. Brad was surprised at how good the hug felt, considering the circumstances. It must be electric; it felt just like they were swapping electrons. Brad knew that when he'd pull away, much, much later, he'd smell Donald on his clothing, that this must be atoms from Donald's warm body, and perhaps some of these atoms would slip into his pores and might be with him when he lost their originator for good.

But Brad was the one who was going to be lost. He had no *others*. He hadn't swapped electrons with anyone besides Donald for a long while, and he may never again. The shock of this made him start to fiercely rework things in his mind to try and concoct a formula that might work, even while Donald rubbed a small circle on the back side of his heart. Brad knew he should just be focused on experiencing, but he couldn't help himself. And now, his desperation was going to ruin the last time.

His heart. The back side of his heart. And then Brad became aware of Donald's heart beating. Donald was a broad, thick man, and beside the considerable mass of his chest, there were several layers of clothing, too, between them. But there it was, and this was the first time that Brad had ever felt it. It was fast and strong, almost explosive between them, and probably only noticeable because of all the weight Donald had been losing lately. He was definitely bonier. As Brad wondered if his heart felt the same to Donald, he completely understood for the first time that this man was just as invested in the situation as he was, maybe even more so.

Their shoulders were damp now, but Brad didn't care. "How can you feel more than I do?" This was it; this was the end.

Donald hugged more tightly, tremor-ridden. "I don't know."

THURSDAY

Brad imagined what it must look like: the split-level at the end of the street. Small but surrounded by an expanse of what would soon again be a lush lawn, Christmas decorations rustling in the morning wind, a terribly elegant wreath that Elizabeth had picked out six months earlier on the bright red front door.

When he opened it, Brad could feel the artificially developed pine odor rushing out into the sun. He hadn't even been able to make it for a full twenty-four hours: "Donald."

Now that Donald was finally here, Brad felt his house bearing down on him, the sky pressing the air out of his lungs. He looked over Donald's shoulder at a car pulling away, Shara Delvecchio driving her mother to adult day care. "Why don't you come on in."

As soon as the door was closed, the room was plunged into stifling murkiness, the only really clear items being the white felt beneath the Christmas tree in the corner and the white spray snow that had been over-applied at its base. Glass hutch doors shuddered in response to the men's movement, the delicate sound echoing off shiny laminate floors. Now that the door was closed on Brad's neighborhood, the whole thing seemed a little more hopeful.

"Thanks for coming." No one was in the house. "I mean, is this all right?"

"Of course, it's all right! It's great. It's great to see you again, Brad."

The men stood in the small foyer, Brad aware of the new mahogany table behind Donald and the proximity of his coat zipper to its reflective surface. Then Brad sunk into the thought of what was underneath the jacket, the quiet, enduring humanity.

"Can I take your coat?"

Donald smiled as he removed his muffler and rustled his Gortex off. He seemed smaller here, somehow. Underneath everything was another one of his expansive sweaters, beige with rust flecks. Brad became aware of his own heartbeat at his neck and wrists as he hung the coat up in the closet, his mind beginning to swim and to drain.

When he turned back to his guest, Donald had moved a little closer. Brad plunged himself into the man's chest and buried his nose in his neck, searching for Donald's smell of pumpkin and motor oil and quickly detecting it. He savored the heartbeat, felt their undulations of breath, which moved closer, became one, moved apart. He became aware of their feet, their shoes, which were pressed up against each other, too. He resented the fact that this was taking place in the center of his home, but he had to do this. Over the course of his life, he'd learned how to compromise, and he'd come to accept that compromise was just one of the consequences for the uncreative. He was fine with that, now. He was fine with everything.

Uncharacteristically, Donald was the first to loosen his hold. Brad dropped his arms in surprise.

"I'm a little… Can I sit down for a second? Sorry."

"Oh, god. Sure." Brad walked into the kitchen and indicated the nearest, backless stool at the counter. The things were uncomfortable after a few minutes, and Brad wanted Donald upright again soon.

"Would you like something to eat or drink?" Donald's eyelids were gray, the lines around his nose and mouth deeper, unless it was the passionless northern light from the nearby window.

"That would be wonderful, thanks! Whatever you've got is fine with me. I've just been feeling, you know—"

"You look tired." The refrigerator was empty of most everything but condiments. And thank god of it, because shopping would keep Elizabeth and the kids away for a long time. "I don't have a lot, right now."

"Oh. Well, I'll grab something later."

"Maybe there's some soup." Brad knew there wasn't, but he needed some time to think about the next few minutes. It was just them, now. No immediate reason to part, no work issues to fill in the cracks of awkwardness that constantly shot through this thing, whatever it was.

Brad shut the pantry door and swung around at Donald, who was in his private space, now, who was from this moment a much bigger part of his life. "So what is this? I mean, what do we do?" He laughed in spite of himself. "You know? I feel like I'm cheating on my wife, for Christ's sake! I *am* cheating, in a way! I'm supposed to be doing this with her. I guess. Or maybe not this, exactly, but you know. It was one thing at work. I could tell myself that it was like some kind of weird work relationship or something. But the thing is, she can't do it! We never—it's always been something different. She's a regular person; she only cares about me so much. I mean, why are you *here*?"

"I know how difficult things have been for you, Brad, and I want to make things better however I can."

"But why?" Brad felt behind him on the counter, eventually grabbing the little air purifier. "What's so *bad* in my life? You know?" He had the pack in his pocket, and he lit a cigarette on the stove, bending over so that all the smoke was immediately processed by the tiny, whirring fan. "It's not *that* bad."

33

"I guess I don't know."

"And why are you even bothering? I mean, do you actually know what the reason is? Because I don't."

"There are lots of reasons." Donald seemed to hold his breath.

"But you hardly know me! I mean, work and everything. But not really. They can't be, you know, particularly realistic, these reasons. Accurate."

"Well, you might not want to hear all of them."

Brad inhaled a great wave of nicotine. "Try me."

"You're funny, but the kind of funny that most people aren't. You don't even know you're being funny, or if you do, I can't tell."

"I'm not funny." Brad put his face right up to the purifier and felt the smoke being pulled out of his nose. It was more pleasurable than he would have thought. He may have purred a little.

Donald chuckled behind him. "You see? That's funny. And you're so helpless, sometimes. How else would someone feel about a person who's so thoughtful and caring, but who just needs a little break, once in a while? And I know you don't want to hear this, but your wavy hair—"

"You're right; I don't want to hear this." Brad turned on the faucet and carefully dumped a load of ash into the sewer system.

Then he looked frankly into Donald's eyes. He wasn't lying, and there was more there, too. It was precisely why the situation was so uncomfortable: Donald couldn't or didn't hide things.

If it hadn't have been for that, the two men wouldn't be facing one another in Brad's kitchen. But Brad still had no idea if that was a good thing or a bad one.

"So, these others. What's that all about?"

Donald looked out the kitchen window. For the first time ever, he didn't seem as if he wanted to give Brad what he needed, and Brad was immediately glad that he wasn't going to get an answer. He didn't really want to know, it was just that he couldn't go on without asking the question that had always been there, waiting. Not if they were going to move it outside the office, this whole strange thing.

But then, Donald stretched out his arm toward Brad on the counter. He looked terrified, and Brad's stomach plunged from the possibilities.

"Brad. I'm different from most people."

Brad had to turn away, so he filled the purifier with another lungful.

"I fall in love with everyone I see."

There. It was only a surprise in that he'd finally said it, the words settling in the kitchen like ash. Brad wasn't special at all.

"And once I have, it never goes away."

Brad was an accident; their whole thing was just one of hundreds of things. Hundreds of strangers got the same treatment, or maybe better.

"No wonder you can't hold down a job!" Brad fumbled with his cigarette, his face hot. He was determined not to let Donald know how hurt he was. Probably everyone else made a scene; he didn't want to be more like them than he was, already. Just one of the crowd of pathetic, desperate losers, that they would let this happen to themselves, let Donald add them to his list.

"I haven't been telling people because all it does is make them feel bad. Or maybe they think that I don't really love them. But I do."

"Well, don't worry about me! I'm relieved, to be honest. Takes a lot of the pressure off! And now, you know, we can end this thing, which has gotten way too weird for me now, and I'll know that, you know, you've got a bunch of other people, so it won't be such a big deal for you."

Donald looked at his lap, clearly working up one of his crying fits again. But it was all his own fault! Brad didn't go around hugging his employees; he hadn't started it! And he didn't *love* Donald! He'd never said that he *loved* him!

"It would be a big deal for me, Brad."

"And the New Year's party…"

"I wanted everyone to meet you."

"But really… Really you wanted *everyone* to meet everyone. You wanted *me* to meet everyone. Wow. You're a little crazy, aren't you."

Donald lifted his face to Brad, to the window behind him, and revealed a massive wound. Brad needed him out of the house, needed time to process all of this, but he mostly needed a hug more than he'd ever needed one before.

Sergei promised himself it would be the last time, the night literally falling on the city, the kind of winter night that blows hell right into your bones. This would be the last time he would look for her. His mother had probably wandered down into the park, but there was always the slight possibility that she'd shuffled over to the much more dangerous Chaykovskogo, and he struggled with the same problem he always did: which first? Greater chance and less danger? Greater danger but less chance? No matter; this would be the last time he would ask himself this question because it forced him to admit that luck had such a stranglehold on his life. He hated this admission as much as he did his heart beat, which only ever reminded him how simply it could cease.

So next time, it would be his mother's luck that would matter, not his. Next time, he'd stay by the stove and drink tea while he did his crossword, and fate could take the blame.

Then Brad heard the extremely distinct, raspy sound of Elizabeth's brakes.

"Holy shit." Brad threw the cigarette down the sink and turned on the garbage disposal, pouring a large amount of dishwashing liquid in after it. He then looked at the expensive bottle in his hand, which had been mostly emptied. "Shit!"

Grabbing Donald's soft sweater, he pulled him to the French doors behind Elizabeth's grandmother's dining room set. "Wait out here for a second. And, you know, hide. Move away from the door a little. Just for a minute."

Brad raced back to the kitchen and turned the faucet on. Remarkably quickly, the sink filled up with bubbles, and the more he tried to wash them down the drain, the more were produced. Through the window, he couldn't see Donald at all, but Roberta Sachow and her ten-year-old son, Eli, were waltzing in their family room across the back yards, their mouths counting out the steps. They actually weren't that bad.

"What are you doing?" Elizabeth was right behind him.

"Oh, hey. I just, I guess I used too much and it went wild on me!"

She looked at the nearly empty bottle but said nothing. "The kids forgot to bring their recycling."

"Oh."

"I smell cigarette smoke."

"You can?"

"Is it a stupid rule? Do you think it's a stupid rule?"

"No! It's just that I had a friend over, and I forgot to mention it to him."

"You had a friend over. We've been gone ten minutes. What friend."

"Not a friend. A guy from work."

"He came and left in ten minutes."

"It was a work thing."

"And he had time to smoke."

"I had to fire him."

"What, like a firing squad? Did you blindfold him, too?"

Now, Elizabeth laughed, and it was a hard laugh, but it still seemed like maybe there was a bit of affection underneath. Brad wasn't sure.

As soon as he joined her, she stopped. She was staring over his shoulder.

Brad turned. Donald was waltzing by himself across the deck, smiling at the mother and boy in the other house. He was counting, too, like some kind of dashing clown. As soon as Roberta saw him, she stopped, waved awkwardly and slowly closed her curtains. He looked drunk and was even stumbling a bit, his horizontal plane tilting.

Elizabeth approached the French doors, determined, while Brad trailed her, wondering how it could have happened so fast for Donald. Roberta was awkward and a bore. But did that even matter?

When Elizabeth stepped out on the deck, Donald turned, his face drained of most of its color, and lurched forward, sitting hard on the deck and smiling apologetically.

"Sorry."

*   *   *

Brad stood over the kitchen sink, watching water run down the drain. Nothing was ever going to be the same, but if he told Elizabeth about it, maybe she'd understand. Maybe she hadn't understood for years because he hadn't told her anything for years. Basically because he hadn't had anything to tell her for years. And after all, it wasn't an affair because he never loved Donald—or anything else like that. Brad hugged his own mother, for Christ's sake. There wasn't anything wrong with that.

"What are you doing?"

He turned off the faucet and faced his wife. She only looked resentful. "Oh. How is he doing?"

"How could you leave him out there? Without a coat? Am I really that much of a bitch?"

"I don't know. I panicked."

"So I *am* that much of a bitch. Nice to know." She came up closer to him. "Well, I guess since I'm such a bitch, I should ask why, if he was the one who was smoking, why he doesn't smell like smoke, and you do."

"Well. We both were."

"But you felt like you had to blame him?" She dropped her voice. "I *know* I'm not *that* bad." She searched his face for a better explanation, and in response, he picked up the air purifier.

"It's like I'm in prison in my own house, Elizabeth."

She never altered her glare for an instant. "I don't want to get into it. The kids are going to be coming down in a minute."

*   *   *

The china tinkled with Brad's entrance into the living room, and Elizabeth rose placidly from her chair. She pulled some hand cream from the table behind her, and expertly worked it into her skin and over her subtle manicure. "So Donald seems like he's doing a bit better, Brad."

Donald was lying on the couch, smiling vaguely at the ceiling. He didn't look better.

Brad nodded awkwardly and stood as far as the room would allow from Elizabeth and Donald. He was never going to see Donald again—certainly never with his other people at some *party*—and he was never, ever going to explain any of this to Elizabeth. Let her go crazy wondering.

"Oh, that's great. Yeah, you know, I'm really sorry about all this, Donald." He pulled a cigarette packet out of the front pocket of his pants and fished for his next one. "Sometimes I get a little crazy with this one!" He pointed the cigarette at Elizabeth. "It's not her, though, it's—"

"What are you doing?" Elizabeth put the hand lotion away, now that the entire room smelled overwhelmingly of rose petals.

Brad looked down at the cigarette in his hand and laughed. "You see what I'm saying? You see?!"

"Kids?!" Elizabeth's raised voice caused Brad's smile to falter. "We have to go. It was nice meeting you, Donald." She looked down an instant at the cigarette in Brad's hand. "Maybe next time we'll talk more about yoga." She turned her head toward the stairs to her left, and Brad understood just how much she wished she was out of this situation. "You know, I'm at my class every weekday at ten at The New Day Studios. They've got some great instructors over there."

Brad carefully replaced his cigarette as Elizabeth passed from the room, her quick, purposeful stride an open contrast to the prone guest and slouching husband. "Kids!"

Brad dropped into the chair next to Donald and rubbed his face. Now, he was even whispering: "What the hell were you doing, dancing out there? I told you to hide! She can tell that something weird was going on."

Donald inspected the empty space where Elizabeth had been standing. "She's really something."

Brad's chest bounced up and down, but his humorless laugh was silent. "Yeah."

"I'll be able to stand up again in a second. I feel a lot better."

Brad watched as Elizabeth, Cooper and Emma passed through the hall and out of the house, fighting the squeaky storm door. Neither of his kids had bothered to look his way, let alone come to him.

"That's good." Brad coughed, noticing for the first time that his throat was scratchy. "I think I'm coming down with something."

As soon as Donald was feeling up to it, Brad was going to get him the hell out of the house. And no hugging. The whole morning had been a nightmare, and he was going to be utterly destroyed by Elizabeth when she got home—or worse, she'd never mention any of it again. His father had always said that you had to harden yourself to make it in the world, and today was the day that Brad would finally take that advice seriously. He found his mind drifting for the thousandth time back over the general unease he felt about all the moments he'd been weak, and all the times people found out about it. The time when he refused to dissect the pig fetus in biology, the black one who had a white spot over his left eye, and everyone tried to treat him the same at school but never did again. Then the time he refused to fire Dominic Carter at K-Mart, even though his speech impediment made it impossible to understand him, and then Dominic had a heart attack and no one understood what was going on until he passed out from the pain. Then the time Brad got mugged behind the CVS, and he didn't chase after the guy—even though he was so slow that Brad could have easily tackled him and bashed his head repeatedly on the side walk—just because the guy had on a t-shirt advertising an Aerosmith concert from 1976.

It never ended well, and it wasn't ending well now, so this was it. At the exact minute that Donald crossed the doorstep on his way to all his other people, Brad was going to be a changed man. At that exact minute.

"You know, you have to harden yourself to make it in the world, Donald."

Donald didn't seem at all surprised by the comment: "I know."

Brad watched Elizabeth's car move down the street. Somehow, she managed to keep it clean, even in the winter. Its chrome flashed in the sun.

Maybe one more hug, but it would definitely be the last

.

MARJORIE

"What is it, honey?" Marjorie looked up from her paperback after she asked the question. She moved her frizzy, grey-streaked hair out of her face, peered out at Donald, and then got up from the kitchen table and rubbed his arm patiently. The humid scent of cinnamon and garlic was even stronger here.

He stood in the center of the kitchen in his puffy jacket and his winter-reddened face, and she was reminded of her nephews when they came home from sledding, upset about a crash or an unfairness. But the analogies to young boys had to stop; the parallels were weak and they didn't help anything. Besides, Donald could sense them, somehow, and wasn't bothered, exactly, but certainly not flattered. Marjorie ran her eyes across his face: the look of surprised injury was there, too, the kind of look that usually only shows up on the faces of young children who don't see it coming, whatever it is.

"Uh-oh." Helmut quickly slid his wok onto a cold burner and approached Donald. He brushed the hair along Donald's forehead before determining that a long hug was in order. Outside, Marjorie noticed that crystals were beginning to form on the edges of the black window.

Donald had been fine that morning.

"Stacy? Or Brad?" Marjorie squeezed the closest, hairy knuckle of Helmut's left hand, which was buried in Donald's winter jacket.

"Maybe I should work by myself. Some kind of job here, at home?"

Helmut stood back from Donald, but only to search his eyes.

"Donald, that would kill you." Marjorie was glad that this time, there was a recognizable issue that could be addressed and solved. It was the depressions that were nebulous, sourceless that frustrated her the most.

"But *only* me."

Helmut and Marjorie stood back and watched Donald's tear-edged eyes for a moment. Her instinct was to sit Donald down at the table and

41

draw out the poison of the day, ounce by ounce, grievance by grievance. This was exactly how she saw him, and he would probably agree with her on this one: a vessel of purity that was continuously tainted by the ordinary excretions of the world's individuals. She wanted to help fish out this darkness that periodically settled in him, but amazingly, he had some process for this himself—at least as far as she could tell—because every morning, he would appear in every sense to be a fresh, open version of himself again. Mornings were always the best, and tomorrow morning, he would doubtlessly be fine. It was tomorrow night that she was concerned about. Amazing coping skills, but finite.

"Nobody's killing anybody. Now, Donald, do you want to tell us why you're so upset?"

Gently disengaging from Marjorie and Helmut, he peeled off his muffler and jacket. "Smells great." But the frown returned when he saw Marjorie's book on the table: *Tell Me Anything.*

"You mean, why I'm upset this time? Same old thing. The lies. I'm so sorry, guys."

Marjorie and Helmut exchanged a glance: were you allowed to change the things that people tortured themselves with, or did you have to grin and accept them exactly for who they were?

What if the things tortured you, too?

Marjorie resumed her rubbing. "I'm so sorry to hear that, Donald."

"I should have told Lourdes this morning, but I didn't."

The conversation would go nowhere, and Marjorie knew it. If he told people, their jealousy flared, sometimes to the point that Marjorie worried about Donald's safety. If he didn't, he was so troubled by what he considered "the lies" that people backed away from his recurring torment, spooked. Marjorie couldn't understand it: the more people he met, the greater capacity he developed for loving them. But for Marjorie, the behavior of each and every person that Donald connected with made her doubt the human race a little bit more. Even herself.

So what could she say or do? She knew that for Donald, his family was welcome anywhere, but there was only so far she and Helmut would go. Of course, the two of them had the normal goals of effect, change, improvement. But in Donald's case, these phenomena were achieved only in spite of themselves.

After a car horn outside: "Chickpea tagine?"

Marjorie was relieved when Donald nodded at Helmut. "You always know just what to say."

The three laughed and moved apart.

*　　　*　　　*

Later, the graceful arcs of headlights swept across their bedroom ceiling, as they did every night. Although they never actually discussed it, Marjorie's instinct was to find a pattern; if there were two cars driving down the street with headlights of exactly the same wattage, aim and height moving at the same exact speed, surely they would produce the same display. But they never did. Not exactly.

Donald was in the middle of the king-size bed. Helmut was on the left of him and Marjorie on the right. Useless imprinting from elementary school though it was, Marjorie could never completely banish boy/girl/boy from her mind, so a vague discomfort buzzed just below her consciousness. This only exacerbated the feeling that she was the inadequate one in the relationship, the outlier. Of course, she accused herself of being inadequate in a different way than Donald and Helmut accused themselves, something they could never wholly appreciate. To make matters worse, whenever she tried to explain her fears, she only felt more inadequate, occasionally even hysterical.

And then she didn't like herself much when she considered the inadequacies that Donald confessed to because she often agreed with him, if only silently. Of course, someone in his position could never be wholly adequate; the job was bigger than any man. But she still resented it, her irrational, self-centered response of a person held her whole life to a biamorous paradigm.

Helmut's feelings of inadequacy, on the other hand, were amorphous, personal, and he held them close to himself, managing them and mitigating their effects on his family as best he could. He was only seven years older than Marjorie was, but she tried and failed to block the term *father figure*.

Donald and Helmut already understood so much about each other out of the gate, and that was something Marjorie truly loved about her men. They both deserved to be well understood, and another guy could more easily do that. But that same connection needed to be moderated, too, and her cooling presence was less effective on the outside. As she willed her mental scribblings to end, she pushed herself closer to Donald and the center of their mass.

And it was always a warm bed. Helmut lightly rubbed the outside of her breast, exhibiting his comforting skills of affection, and was undoubtedly lightly rubbing a spot on Donald, as well. She wasn't in the mood, and he knew that by now, but he still rubbed. Between them, Donald had his face buried under his pillow, but the tension in his body told his bedmates that he wasn't sleeping.

Marjorie wondered when completely open communication was supposed to stop, when it did more harm than good, when it just became a list of impotent facts; then she slipped into another dream about Andie. For some reason sitting on a stool in the middle of the local organic market, Andie was making fresh peanut butter on the machine there. She'd always refused food she didn't see processed before her eyes—it was as if that one, dark brown, foul peanut that made it into consumer brands would somehow harm her or, in fact, be noticeable at all. After dumping some carefully chosen peanuts in the machine, Andie emptied her purse into it, and Marjorie watched used tissues, hemp lip balm, a canvas wallet, and red-hots swirl around with the organic nuts. The peanut butter that was produced looked perfectly normal, and Marjorie was surprised to find herself wanting to try it. This thought awoke Marjorie, and she wondered, the breathing of the men near her whistling into the dark, what it was that consistently brought her mind back to Andie. Gradually, she realized that Donald's breathing was conscious; he was still awake.

He'd always said that he couldn't remember his dreams.

TUESDAY

Donald had already been up an hour before Marjorie was, very odd for him, and he couldn't have gotten much sleep—an especially bad situation when he was in one of his depressive moods—so she was immediately concerned. Sure enough, she could hear him crying in the bathroom, drying up for five minutes or so, and then suddenly stifling an anguished sob in the shower. When she caught a glimpse of him in the kitchen as he was leaving into the darkness, she saw the dish towel in his hands, a forty-year-old rag covered in orange-gold paisley and tomato stains that he used for minimizing the noise.

Marjorie would have to get to the bottom of it that evening.

*   *   *

"Andie called." Donald turned away as he threw an old sandwich in the trash and inspected the sparse contents of their refrigerator.

Nothing really surprised Marjorie, but she felt the shockwave through the room, and she could tell that Helmut did, too.

"Oh?" The first image for Marjorie was of Andie at the vanity, combing her brown hair while humming something, probably a Whitney Houston song that she considered vintage. Marjorie had already forgotten her dream of the night before, but there still lingered a taste of the kaleidoscopic peanut butter, spiraling.

"I'm going to look at a boat tomorrow evening with Joseph, and I invited her to join us. In Connecticut."

A boat?! Joseph?! Connecticut?! It was always a crazy ride, and that was one of the reasons she loved being in Donald's life. But Marjorie was only getting older. For instance, she no longer found the thought of her grandmother spending weeks of old age knitting a single sweater all that hilarious.

"You look tired, Donald." Helmut stood squarely behind the other man and began massaging his neck. "And you must be starving."

Donald put a hand over Helmut's and quickly closed the refrigerator. "How are you guys doing? How was work?" Donald turned to face his partners, his eyes bouncing from one to the other with a rhythm that Marjorie was sure marked exactly the same time spent looking at each. "I'm getting the parent vibe again."

"We love Andie, just as much as you do." Marjorie sat down at the table, the scene widening, deepening.

"What should I do?"

Helmut hadn't let go of Donald and now tousled his hair. "Ahhh! We know! We know. But remember, buddy, this one kind of involves us, too. Directly. How do we not get a little parental, or maybe the word would be 'interested?'"

"Well, you understand *why*, with her, at least. And Joseph's such a wonderful man. I think that when she gets to know him, you know, focused on the trip, and he doesn't—I'm not sure if he even likes me." He traced the flowery vine on the tablecloth with a middle finger poised for a telegraph machine. "It's harder for some people when they don't know, and they start imagining the rest of my life. So this might be the perfect time for Andie to meet someone else. It would be very non-threatening, I think. Kind of a first step, maybe. And I think Joseph would actually prefer it."

Marjorie shook her head. "How can anyone *not* like you."

"I wonder how anyone *can*. But with him, it's not about me, it's about the effect I'm having, I think. You know."

She knew. She'd seen and heard about years of effects.

Donald sank into a chair. In the particularly vertical light there, he did look fatigued. "In fact, I've been thinking a lot about this. Because I'm coming into another hard patch, and I apologize in advance." Donald's face constricted; he pushed it down. "I know it's short notice, but I've started inviting people over for a New Year's thing. My people." Donald turned to Marjorie. "So, on a scale of one to ten?"

Marjorie looked up at Helmut, who was leaning against the refrigerator door. It was clear that the answer would be hers, so she swept back her hair, futilely, because it immediately sprung back with its mass like a sponge. "Okay. But you have tried this before."

Donald flicked a worried glance at Helmut, then sat up. "I was thinking that maybe this time, I'd tell them all."

Marjorie pulled her lips into her mouth and blinked rapidly a few times, processing. She was not going to appear to be dictating to him. "I mean, we don't have any plans. Helmut?"

"No."

"So? On a scale of one to ten."

"For us or for you?"

"For you. I already know what you're thinking about me."

"You'd tell them all at the same time?"

"Some of them already know. Eric. Hattie."

"Well, speaking for myself, I'm kind of curious, to be honest." Marjorie looked up at Helmut. Her response did not calm him. Then she dredged up the horrible mail carrier from about six months earlier: ugly, stupid, rude. That had been the first one that made no sense whatsoever to her and the point at which she'd started worrying about Donald's sanity. But it hadn't been long before she'd realized this really wasn't about that. Donald had reported back that the mail carrier was a wonderful storyteller and had a devoted husband—who wasn't insane, either. It was after that that his profound subjectivity really began to fascinate as well as concern Marjorie—after all, she was only receiving reports back, and those were pretty much all she ever got.

46

So she'd learned to trust Donald, to think of him almost like a psychic who peered into different dimensions, or at least farther back into the corners of this dimension than most. He seemed to catch things about people that everyone else missed. Since Marjorie had no uncanny perceptions of her own, she certainly didn't expect to agree with him, necessarily. But she still was curious as to what kinds of people would turn up on New Year's Eve.

Helmut shifted uncomfortably, so Marjorie adjusted. "You know that we want whatever you want, Donald. Honestly."

Donald smoothed out the tablecloth as if finished with it. "I have to do something. I've got to at least give something a shot, to try and fix this."

Marjorie stilled Donald's hand, grabbing it in both of hers. "Honey, I'm so sorry you're going through this, but I kind of wonder if it's going to work. I'm sure they're all wonderful and deserving of your love, but look at the rest of the world. The rest of us schmucks. We just don't get it. And that's okay."

Helmut knelt down in front of Donald, who had focused on the space a few feet before his chest. "Okay, so, what would be the outcome?"

"No more lies—"

"You're not really lying, if there isn't a two-way relationship there—"

"*No more lies*, and I really do think that if they get to know each other that they'll really like each other. It's harder to resent someone you've actually met."

"No, it's not!" Marjorie squeezed Donald's hand, wishing she didn't feel the welling frustration that always managed to reemerge out of sewn-together scraps of his notions. "Honey, for most of us, it's not. Okay, how about this. See how Connecticut goes. I mean, Andie can be a good trial run. See how it goes. Does the man—"

"Joseph."

"Does Joseph know?"

"About Andie, not about me yet." Donald really did look bad when he hung his head. "It's just that I'm not giving *anyone* what they need."

There was no arguing with that. Marjorie knew that people always needed more than what they got; it was one of the human traits that was wearing Donald down.

Marjorie remembered an incident from the scattering of her memories. A blazing day in Tunis, uncomfortable with her bare legs in a market full of fabric billowing right down around ankles. There were so many tourists just like her, but that made it much worse: her nakedness transformed into something more than just her own liability. She was a representative of immodesty.

Attempting to alleviate this unease, she threw herself into appreciating the goods on display. Her high-school French was just enough to position her as the perfect prey for the sellers, and the guilt that prevented her from avoiding this only soured into indignation over the afternoon. She'd collected an assortment of strange seeds, woven knick-knacks and embroidered slippers, wondering the whole time what she would do with them, as they'd never fit into her suitcase. For a moment, she'd even had a desire to plant the seeds in some back alley, the sudden miracle of greenery a delayed eulogy to her visit. Perhaps the old women would pick the desiccated seeds off of her mature bushes and crush them in their foreign kitchens.

Just then, she stopped at a stall selling souvenirs and looked back into the dim recesses of the building behind it. A teenaged boy was moving his hands ritually over something at a low table. Boxes of sunglasses were piled behind him, the Sahara dust filling in the cracks between cardboard and plastic. He waved his hands slowly over the item, then began to move his long, worked fingers in some kind of frenetic sign language. His self-contained focus was absolute; everything around and outside turned its back on him.

Marjorie was only an American tourist, but the boy's actions didn't seem Tunisian to her. Not Arabic. There were whispers of ancient profanity. She suddenly became terrified of his gaze and turned before their eyes could meet. As she hurriedly negotiated her bags around others, she felt the pinpricks of fear at her forehead and armpits. There were still unknowable things; the world wasn't yet New Jersey.

Marjorie imagined Donald's hands swirling and swooping like that over something hidden.

She said only: "Okay."

THURSDAY

Donald got up early with Helmut and Marjorie this time, his eyes unfocused by exhaustion. It was his turn to make breakfast, and despite the pleadings of his lovers, he brewed the most coffee the machine could handle and started on some eggs. They watched him from the table, unable to take their eyes off of him.

"Helmut's right. I'm not going to miss this time with you." There was a slight slur to his words, and Helmut grasped Marjorie's arm, as if to steady her.

"Donald, I don't think Helmut meant that you had to get up after only a couple hours of sleep. He's a selfish bastard, but even he's not that evil."

Helmut grimaced at Marjorie as his finger swirled around some sugar granules at the edge of the table. "I said that I wanted him all to myself last night." Marjorie stared at Donald's thick, white legs under his bathrobe. Their life together wasn't three times as much work as an ordinary marriage, it was exponential.

She arose and, kissing Donald on his neck, gently pried the spatula from his hand. She remained there, and they both stood over the burning eggs. Finally, she moved the pan off of the flame.

"I'm serious. Go back to bed."

Donald forced his eyes open long enough to look deeply into Marjorie. "I love you."

His pupils were dilated.

"We love you, too. Now, scoot."

After Donald left the kitchen, Marjorie dumped the eggs and sat down across from Helmut. She reached out and played with the hair on his arm. "Why am I the most aroused when he's at his weakest? I hate that. Are you like that?"

"No. I'm other, equally disturbing things." He looked back at the closed bedroom door. "He's worse than I've ever seen him. And I haven't helped things."

"I don't know how he continues to function at all."

"All those endorphins." Helmut moved so that his arm was no longer in Marjorie's reach.

"We all want him to ourselves, on some level."

"Yeah. But I got a little radical last night."

What was Helmut talking about? "Sometimes radical challenges demand radical solutions."

"I've seen it all before. I know that. But this guy last night never had a clue what was going on. When Donald suggested they get together again, you should have seen the look on the guy's face. It was like Donald asked him to fly to the moon with him or something. It was painful for me; I can't begin to imagine what Donald went through, what he's going through now. I mean, the man had stuffed dead animals in his—"

"Don't! Thinking about all that only makes me feel farther away from Donald, and I really don't want to feel that way, right now."

Marjorie knew that Helmut or Donald would tell her all about the previous night if she asked, but she didn't want that. Knowing wouldn't erase the fact that she was the outsider with this one, anyway. And somewhere, she resented the thought that she had to ask, because neither one of them was being particularly forthcoming. Something big must have happened. Something bad.

Still, she knew that she didn't have to be at the center of everything that took place in their family; that was self-centered and unfair. She jumped back and forth in her mind between Donald's sturdy, shorter frame, and Helmut's thin, aged body, realizing for the first time that she fell almost completely in the middle, with her regular body and slightly-taller-than-average height, her age. That this thought only now occurred to her didn't surprise her at all because she didn't like to think of the three of them in a line; they were always a triangle, there was always that extra dimension. Donald was most often at the apex, then she. Helmut rarely took that position in her imagination, and she wondered briefly why.

"Let's take a shower." Helmut turned back from staring at the bedroom door. "Come on." He grabbed her hand and pulled her into the nearby bathroom, which was always the coldest room in the apartment. This morning, it was especially cold, and Marjorie surprised herself by imagining and then dismissing her family living in a place with a warm bathroom. Rich, dark wood on the floor, a towel warmer, an invitingly tepid toilet seat.

"Christ, how does the tile get so cold?" Helmut had already shorn his clothes and was hopping back and forth, his long, graceful feet flexing and contracting, as he turned the shower on. "They've got the heat on downstairs."

"Shh!" Marjorie found herself a bit more matronly living with two men; she carefully placed her pajama tops on the hamper and slowly removed the pants, aware of the goose bumps coating her cellulite. She'd painted her toenails a dark blue but noticed that all it did was bring out her spider veins and the lurking indigo just under the cream of her skin.

Helmut drew her to him, rubbing her pliant skin, warming himself in the process. "So listen. I've got an idea, and it's a crazier one than usual. But I'm completely serious."

"Do I want to know?"

He reached one hand behind the shower curtain. "You first. I want to watch you."

"Get into the tub? I've stopped trying to figure you people out."

"What people?"

"Men. I never even bothered trying to figure women out."

The water was perfect; she and Helmut had the same temperature scale, too. The two of them had certain things Donald didn't share.

Helmut followed her in, clearly not worried about cleaning yet.

"So he can't hear us in here."

Marjorie stopped squeezing Helmut's hand, which was covering her belly. "What?"

"I've never kept anything from him. Or you. You know that, and it's completely true. Never."

She turned to face him. "You're scaring me now."

"This life is destroying him. Look at him. And it isn't something he's doing to himself. Not really. He doesn't control his life. It just doesn't work that way."

"Okay."

Marjorie frowned. She had to go to the bathroom now.

"Jesus Christ! You know what it's been like, Marjorie! On the sidelines. Don't tell me you're not just as frustrated as I am."

"We agreed we'd never, ever do anything like this, Helmut. Gang up. We're having a secret conversation, for Christ's sake."

"Did you see him this morning? He couldn't even walk straight."

"We're always there for him if he needs us. He knows that."

"Passively!" Helmut lowered his voice, massaged Marjorie's soft shoulders. "Look, the guy last night scared me. How many people is he involved with now who could be on the edge like that guy? I don't know if he was really on the edge or not, but wouldn't someone who was disturbed be more likely to get involved with Donald? I mean, it is kind of a crazy situation. And Donald is losing his strength to deal with things."

"Nobody who's ever gotten involved with Donald has really hurt him. Really hurt him."

"We don't know that. And anyway, that's not what I'm most worried about. I'm most worried about what's happening to him now."

"I don't want to do this, anymore—discuss him as if he isn't here." She pushed past Helmut and parted the curtain. The icy floor would be a relief.

"Marjorie, he wouldn't mind. When has he ever minded anything that we've done for him? Being passive means giving everyone else permission to call the shots. Who *should* be controlling his life? Because *he's* not."

"Giving up control *is* control."

"That's nonsense."

"But we're supposed to be supporting him, not manipulating him."

"But we do! Everyone does! What, do you think you're not on some level controlling his life? What about Hattie? You were the one encouraging him to drop her—"

"He was going to, anyway! I was supporting his decision, not making it for him!"

"You're getting the floor wet."

She closed the curtain and stepped back under the spray. Donald's New Year's party was three days away. Then, she'd see who was controlling whose life. Then she'd know if what Helmut was suggesting was necessary. He did have a tendency to take immediate steps. Decisive action always sounded good, but it could be regretted, too.

Rivulets of water ran down Helmut's elongated torso. Behind him, Marjorie followed the rows of pink tiles higher and higher toward the ceiling. When she was eleven, wintergreen was her favorite flavor, and back then anything wintergreen was exactly the same shade. One of her earliest Christmas mornings, her little sister suggested that she liked wintergreen more than Marjorie, so Marjorie slapped her across the face, just like the grown-up ladies did all the time on their mother's soap operas. She'd never slapped anyone like that ever again, but there were quite a few times when she'd wanted to.

She simply said, "He's entitled to his own life, Helmut."

"There's no more room inside of him for all of this, Marjorie."

"I know!" Marjorie grabbed the organic oat soap and started cleaning herself. "I know that."

Helmut ran his slender fingers over her back, ostensibly to wash her, just as he did so many things that were ostensible. She didn't often mind, but today, she did.

"All right. But just think about what I'm saying. Maybe it'll make a little more sense when he ends up in the hospital or something. Sick."

"He's not that bad, for god's sake."

Helmut just took the soap.

*   *   *

Passing quietly into the bedroom, Helmut turned on the light.

"Oh, no."

"What?" Marjorie came up behind him. The bed was empty, and there was a note on the bed stand that said, "I love you! I'll be back," in blocky, light print.

Marjorie pulled the covers over the pillows, which still hadn't cooled completely, and turned toward the kitchen. The top of Donald's head dipped out of view of the window in the kitchen door. The coffee pot was completely full and the sink empty.

"What did you tell him last night?"

Helmut joined her at the doorway and massaged her shoulders. "When was the last time you saw him eat something?"

*   *   *

Marjorie was in the kitchen when they came in, Helmut caught in the bathroom. She was repairing her caftan at the kitchen table, the rush of cold air attacking her ankles.

At first sight, he was clearly one of those older gentlemen who quietly kept up his trim appearance, who consistently managed his personal grooming habits and minded his clothing. For her, this was evidence that he continued to validate the earthly plane of existence and respected the condition of those who were still deeply mired in it all. He was clearly still here, rather than one of those old folks whose unblinking eyes reflected the hereafter, who slowly forgot one-by-one the reasons why they needed to present themselves as human. He still looked pretty damn good.

Donald looked awful, but more than that.

Marjorie stood and faced the old man, finally noticing that he was holding a plastic bag full of brownies. This clinched it for her; she liked him immediately and wanted to show him that she could be as appreciative and respectful as her younger lover, who she'd deal with later.

"Hi, Marjorie."

"What happened?"

"Oh, I'm fine. How are you doing?"

He kissed her, holding her cheek in his dry, cold hand. Something was lacking.

"Marjorie, this is Joseph. He was thoughtful enough to drive me home through all of this. It wasn't easy."

Joseph carefully removed his right glove, and Marjorie took his hand in both of hers. Of course, it was hot and moist, but there was a tremor there, too.

With him fully facing her, she could see that Joseph was older, that there were, in fact, a few signs that he'd taken a step or two in preparation for the next world. A certain distance, but nothing that couldn't be bridged. "Thank you so much. We were worried about Donald. It looks so terrible out there now!"

"It's gotten quite a bit worse, hasn't it."

"And you have, what are those, brownies?"

Joseph handed them to her, and she took them to the counter, ready to plate them up. "How sweet of you."

Donald watched her hands on the brownies, his eyes flashing.

Marjorie continued as if nothing had happened. "Please, sit down. Would either of you like some coffee or tea? Maybe something stronger?"

"Thanks, but I really should be getting home."

"Oh, good. So then *your* car's here."

"Actually, I drove Donald's." He glanced at Donald, who had slumped at the table, his eyes half closed. Marjorie looked away.

"But I just live up the street a few blocks. I'll walk."

"Oh no, we couldn't let you just walk out into that! It's officially a blizzard. I mean, that's how you and Donald met, isn't it? Didn't you slip on the side of the road?"

Joseph paused. He looked at his feet. "I appreciate your concern, but I'll be fine."

Marjorie sensed that she was making Joseph uncomfortable, and she knew of many potential reasons for this. But she didn't care. Donald usually kept his other people apart from her and Helmut, and she'd always known better than to ask him to bring any of them home. But now she had one here in her kitchen, shoes dripping on the coconut-fiber mat. One that had accepted. One that presumably knew everything, now: about her, about Helmut, about Andie. He looked unfazed, but then the word *inscrutable* passed through her mind, and Marjorie pushed it down, a racist description if ever there was one.

At Donald's party, it would probably be too surface, too hectic to really get much from the others, unless they became really drunk. But here was her chance to gain a little insight, to see if Helmut was right about Donald's state of mind.

To determine why one of the men she loved so dearly suddenly seemed alien, there at the table.

Pushing the fear out of her voice, the fear of whatever had happened to Donald since that morning, Marjorie focused on Joseph. "How long have you lived in the neighborhood?"

"Oh. Forty years. Something like that." Joseph put his glove back on.

"Forty years! You must have seen so many changes."

Joseph nodded politely. "I have. Well, it was a pleasure meeting you, Marjorie." He approached the door, and Marjorie's chest constricted.

"I'm coming with you, then. Please, it's the least that we can do."

"That's very kind of you, but I won't drag you out in this weather, too."

"No, hold on, I'll just get my coat." And Marjorie disappeared into the dark hallway.

She'd need her boots, too. It would be hard to have a conversation with the snow coming down like that between them, but she'd get something out of him, anyway. Joseph did seem a little resistant, but she liked that, his reserve, his old-fashioned pride. If she got nowhere, then she'd just ask the question point-blank. That was sure to disarm him, and maybe he'd warm to her. Then they might have a productive conversation about his friendship with Donald, about his impressions. And if not, she might at least get an answer to her question. Because a quiet voice told her she would never get the complete truth out of Donald about why he seemed so changed.

Helmut was in the kitchen now when she returned. "Hey, Marjorie, haven't you been coughing an awful lot today? Are you sure you want to go out in this?"

"It's just a couple of blocks." Marjorie pulled on her gloves.

"Oh, okay. Well, it was nice to meet you, Joseph. I hope to see you again. Maybe at Donald's party?"

Joseph threw on a dry smile. "I think so."

"Fantastic. Oh, you know what, Marjorie?" Helmut quickly passed out of the room, leaving Marjorie's gloved hands hanging at her side, interrupted.

"What?" She turned toward the indistinct rooms behind her. "Helmut? What's up?"

Marjorie shook her head at Joseph and moved toward him. "He's such a mystery, sometimes. Are you married, Joseph?"

"I was."

"Oh, is that right? Divorced or—"

Helmut thundered down the hall and straight to the back door, completely dressed to do battle with the elements.

"Colleen called earlier, Marjorie, and I couldn't speak with her. She really needs to talk to someone, and you're so much better at it than I am."

Helmut opened the door and waved Joseph through. "She really sounds bad, Marjorie."

She remained still, watching the men at the door. Something was going on, but she wasn't sure what it was.

"Pleasure meeting you, Marjorie." Joseph was outside now, and he stuck his head around the door frame. "I'll talk to you later, Donald?"

Donald coughed drily, got up and hugged Joseph, his sweater quickly scattered with beads of melted snow. Stiffened by Donald's physicality, Joseph walked into the storm, followed by Helmut.

"I'll be right back, guys."

Without looking at Marjorie, Donald passed her. "I've got to get some sleep."

A precious opportunity had just been lost. Marjorie pulled at her gloves instead of screaming. As she replaced her winter things in the closet, she grasped wildly for a sense of calm, for the most useful approach. Then she was confronted by Donald's naked chest in the bedroom mirror, his face mercifully cut off above it. Marjorie took a deep breath that came out like a gasp. "Gosh, Donald. Everything's hanging. And you seem hollow, too, somehow."

Donald's skin had slid down over his body and turned his nudity into a frown. It was something that happened to older women, not young men. But there were also horrible bruises that covered his chest, pitiful greens and yellows, and she couldn't ask about those. Not if he didn't volunteer.

He hadn't responded to her comment, and Donald always responded.

"God, it's cold in here." Marjorie just wanted to cover the void, which seemed to be gaping between them now. "Are you going to eat something before you go to bed, honey? You've got to eat something. I'm getting really concerned."

Donald turned to her so abruptly that Marjorie felt an actual rush of adrenaline, as if she'd been caught doing something wrong. "I appreciate that. But I'm beat."

He looked at her differently—critical, somehow, or doubting. It was different than the other times when he was depressed about not being able to give or be everything that everyone wanted. This was directed outward, not inward. At her.

What had she done wrong? "What about a bagel?"

"No."

"For god's sake, Donald, what's the matter?"

Donald instantly softened and hugged Marjorie, burrowing into her as if he really could. "I'm so sorry."

She pulled away. "What happened today? Did Helmut say something to you?"

He paused, studied the wall above their bed. "What did you think of Joseph?"

She had the urge to shake him, but he'd asked a question.

"He seems like a nice man. Why?"

"When you first saw him, before he even said anything, what did you think?" Now he was looking right into her eyes. It was impossible for him to hide how important her answer was to him, and she shivered, aware of the draught coming off the window behind her.

It was a test.

"Let's see. I thought he was very good-looking for a man of his age, that he kept up his appearance nicely. Very well put-together, very fastidious, maybe."

He nodded agreement, but she had utterly failed. Knowing that she would recognize this, he hugged her again, his voice in her ear an apology: "I love you so much, Marjorie."

She took a deep breath, willing herself into her counselor space.

"I love you, Donald. And if or when you're ready to tell me what's happening, I hope you know I'm ready to help in whatever way I can."

He merely nodded.

"Has Helmut said something to you? What's going on with you two?"

Donald patted her as if she was an acquaintance, and Marjorie could only imagine the rhythm being taken up by a knife sliding in and out of her skin.

FRIDAY

Hoping to sleep everything away, Marjorie awoke only after the back door closed.

The morning was gray, despondent, and she rose into consciousness with one thought very clear: Helmut and Donald were gone.

HATTIE

This time, Hattie had him tied up with pieces of rawhide. It was better, but still not quite right. And she had forced him to wear a black leather jockstrap with a zipper down the middle, but that was definitely not right. It contrasted with his pale, vulnerable inner thighs, just as she had envisioned. But somehow her erotic desires were like the things she bought for him. Nothing ever really fit Donald in person.

She caught him looking at her, eager for her enthusiasm. Before she whipped his legs lightly and he closed his eyes, she saw that he understood.

"You will not look at me!"

"Yes, mistress."

Hattie's generous breasts swung over her black satin corset as she looked down at Donald's open body, and she suddenly wanted to laugh or stroke his belly. But she wasn't going to give up that easily.

"Have you done things with other people since last week?"

"Yes, mistress."

She whipped him harder, and he tensed up.

"You are not to do things with anyone but me. Do you understand?"

He remained silent.

She whipped him across the chest with enough weight behind it to really sting.

"Do you understand?"

She could see Donald's eyes moving behind his lids, searching. She whipped him a little harder in a new spot and was glad to notice that all her humor was gone. His chest was turning pink because she wanted it to.

"Do you realize that you will be much more severely punished if you do not agree to obey me immediately?"

Still, he didn't respond. This time she aimed the lash at his soft thighs, and he jerked against the restraints.

"I'm sorry, mistress!" But it wasn't right, and they both knew it.

"You're sorry that you disobeyed me, or you're sorry that you didn't respond?"

He only breathed through his teeth, and she dropped down on the side of the bed, her breasts settling on her upper arms.

"'If you do not *agree* to obey me!' I should've just said, 'If you do not obey me.'" And Hattie chuckled.

"Yes, mistress."

"Donald." White men's skin always looked like it was apologizing, but his was especially so, the small tufts of hair on each nipple attempting to excuse the pink irregularities and failing.

"Sorry. Mistress."

"You have to want it."

"I do!"

"On your own!"

"I do now."

Hattie sighed and realized that she had been trying to time her breathing to his. "I know, but…"

She untied his arms and his legs, rubbing them tenderly. Hattie laid the side of her face on his cool, thin ankles. Today, she'd wanted to be the one who was tied-up, but there was absolutely no way that would work with Donald. Wanting to discipline her only for her own sake would make the scene even more of a parody than this was.

Fantasies.

In her fantasies, it was always so good, the absolute best with him. But when he was actually there, it was good in another way. She looked at each part of his body to try and memorize it. Then she noticed him looking at her, encouraging her to take from him what she needed.

In 1857, a woman named Marie brought her husband to a nearby insane asylum outside of Arles. His name was Jean-Jacques, and he was definitely insane. He repeated words over and over instead of going to work or sleeping.

It had actually been his suggestion, rather than something she wanted to think about, and as she stood next to him in the foyer of the building so new it still smelled mostly of plaster, she asked herself, "How can you respect the wishes of a mad man?" He was signing a document that attested to his desire to be incarcerated, but would he still feel the same way tomorrow? Did he really understand what he wanted today? Who was this man?

The signature looked utterly meaningless to her, blackness slowly soaking into an absorbent surface. When she went home alone, she renamed their spaniel Jean-Jacques so she could repeat her husband's name over and over.

"God, I love you."

"I love you, too. So much." Donald could go a long time without blinking, his body a slave to his feelings.

"I'd like to know what's bothering you."

Donald nodded slowly and sat up on the bed. "Thank you."

Hattie momentarily thought of covering herself with a bathrobe but quickly realized what an absurd waste of energy that would be. She could dress like Henry VIII, and Donald's feelings would remain constant, solid. It was such a wonderful thing to rely on.

Instead, she sharpened her focus on him.

"I started crying yesterday, and it hasn't really gone away."

"The crying, or the reason why you're crying?"

"Both. I think."

She'd met Donald when he'd come to her for counseling three months earlier. They hadn't managed more than two sessions before the relationship mutated, but this was still something she wanted to do for him, so she kept her responses minimal, distanced.

"Why do you feel that you're crying?"

"Oh, sometimes it's just a little tougher for me. I always get like this. Yesterday, it was all the lying, but now, it's the disappointment. The disappointment I am to my friends, the disappointment I am to myself." Donald smiled, but his eyes were turning red.

She wanted to hug him but recognized that it wasn't what he most needed. He doubtless got that from others. "Sometimes it's difficult to affect the feelings other people have about you, so their disappointment might not be something you can take responsibility for. Now, why do you feel that you're a disappointment to yourself?"

He looked around the room, distress working its way across his face. "Oh, because I still haven't been smart enough to figure out a way to live."

Now, she wanted to cry. "What do you mean?"

"I'm actually thinking about a party."

Hattie was so startled that the lump in her throat vanished. She'd come to believe that Donald was incapable of evasion, of denial. He'd always seemed remarkably self-aware, so completely at ease with the naked truths about himself and quite comfortable sharing them.

Of course, she knew it had really been one of his gifts to her, this effortless interaction. He instinctively recognized that so much of her work consisted of gingerly pulling simple truths out of people, months of gentle digging and stretching, truths that were plainly evident to *her* after only a few sessions. A lot of psychologists lived for the rewards of that dance, but she'd always preferred a more equal communication, issues quickly dropped on the table before her and her patient, so they could just get down to business together. She preferred putting the puzzle together, not hunting for pieces in dimly lit corners.

So she was surprised by his sudden change of subject. She hoped she wouldn't have to waltz around, not with him, but she remained a two-way mirror.

"A party."

"A gathering. Everyone in my life. I think maybe it's all the separations that might be the problem."

"No more lies?"

"I did try it, a few years ago. I wrote everyone notes and sent them out at the same time. Most people, I just never heard from again."

Hattie tried to imagine it: all her painful break-ups in one week. It was the vertigo of standing next to a gaping pit.

"And what about the people you did hear from?"

He lifted his forearm, exposing the parallel scars that cut into its outside edge. "People got upset, so now I usually keep it to myself."

She was upset. "Oh, Donald."

"So what do you think?"

"I think it's really great that you're considering solutions."

"Thank you." He sat up to stroke her hair, the proximity of his face a kind of radiation. *"So what do you think?"*

She relaxed against his legs. "I'm glad for one percent of a hundred percent of you. I don't know how I'll feel about meeting people with twenty percent of a hundred percent. But I wouldn't miss it for the world if it helps you."

"'One percent of a hundred percent.'" He focused on a gray dreadlock near her forehead, pain playing at the corner of his eyes. "That's it, exactly, Hattie. What an awful thing to do to you."

"Can anyone give a hundred percent of a hundred percent? What do you think that relationship would be like?"

Donald considered this, his eyes glazing. "I don't know. But at least the two of them would be getting what they deserve."

"You don't hear me complaining."

Donald snapped out of his trance and smiled. "How are things with Reggie?"

"A hundred percent of ten percent. Twenty on a good day."

"What if we'd never met?"

"Then I'd just be seeing him, a much poorer person."

He searched her eyes, then, and she felt him weighing whether she was right, whether she could even know if she were right. The pupils, widened by doubt, never closed around an answer.

Hattie found her mind returning to the night before. Reggie had asked to marry her, not five feet from where she and Donald were now, and it amazed her: the same room. But there wasn't—there never would be—the kind of genuine concern in Reggie's eyes that she was cradled with now, and her heart broke for Reggie and his desire for an arid, compromised future. Twenty percent.

THURSDAY

Hattie was playing the piano when he arrived. It was a languid, insistent version of "When the Saints Go Marching In," and he must've been patiently waiting, because the bell only rang once she'd finished.

"Donald." She wore an oversized shirt that hung over her jeans and provided a dark, private space before her. It was there that she wanted to store Donald, to protect him and own him and feel his hot breath under her bosom. Because he looked terrible. "You look tired." She dismissed the word that sprung to mind: cancer. But something was eating him away.

"You look great, Hattie."

She moved aside to allow him in, then kissed him gently, his lips rougher than usual. An alarming, coppery taste almost made her pull back, and she told herself it was just his chapped skin separating in the sapping air.

"I've missed you so much."

"Reggie's asked me to marry him. I don't know what to do."

Hattie could never tire of watching the march of bare emotions across Donald's face. It was so unlike anyone else she'd ever known—no one else had so much to manage. This time, it was surprise, then a flash of fear, followed by empathy, and finished up with pain, the emotion that was increasingly becoming the caboose for him.

Without further distorting any of his features, tears formed in his eyes. "Wow."

"I didn't mean to upset you, sweetheart. Why are you crying?"

But she knew before he answered: "You might know what to do if you'd never met me."

"Donald. Sweetheart. He's water compared to your cognac. I've had the best; it would be tough settling."

This time: gratitude, profound happiness, pain. He wiped his eyes. "You're settling now."

"When we give everything we can, it's not settling."

"But not everything I want to give."

"Donald. Why don't you come in. I bet you haven't had lunch, have you?"

Hattie's condo was filled with souvenirs of her trips around the world: African pottery, Indonesian baskets, Chilean photographs. Each specially chosen item was carefully and modestly spotlit, placed in a way so that none had precedence over the others. She'd always loved the quiet introspection that art galleries inspired in her; she wanted her home to do more than just provide places to sit. It had always been Hattie's ultimate goal to arouse higher, finer thoughts in others.

"That would be fantastic." He paused to take in her living room, as always. "I love you so much it's impossible to say."

It *was* cognac. Just a little at the bottom of the glass, warming the senses. "I've got some fresh greens and a French chicken salad I threw together a little while ago. Come join me."

She'd been careful to clean and tidy the kitchen. Although he didn't tell her everything about the rest of his life, she knew that its effect on him reflected a cluttered and harassed flurry of places and appointments. She wanted her share to be an oasis of time and peace expanding out around him.

"Reggie knows about you, Donald. Everything that we have. I guess one of the benefits of being involved with someone like him, someone who only feels so much, is that there isn't much of a jealousy factor. If we got married, I would still see you."

Donald nodded and leaned against the counter, processing. "I want you to be happy."

"There would be some advantages with Reggie. Financial. I think things would be easier." She ran her hand over the cold marble work surface, remembered its expense and how much she'd wanted it. "How are you doing?"

"Oh. Things are tough right now."

This came out sounding unconcerned, a sign that he wasn't looking for her professional input, so Hattie remained silent.

"Yesterday, I experimented a little. I tried giving one person a hundred percent, just like you and I talked about. And I just couldn't do it. I'm not strong—or maybe smart—enough."

Donald's tears returned. "And I tried introducing a couple of my friends to each other, but I have a feeling that's not going to turn out too well, in the end."

His shrug was final; he didn't want to discuss this any further, but he didn't want to keep it from her, either. It was his permission to revisit it later, after some distance had been gained. But he was hurting too much, right now.

"Have you ever been hypnotized?" The question had come out of Hattie's mouth before she'd even really willed it, a very similar experience to being hypnotized herself.

"I never have. Have you?" He slumped on a bar stool, his arms collapsing on the counter before him.

Hattie pulled her lunch out of the refrigerator, warming to the plan that was forming in her mind. "You know, I used to smoke."

No one else on earth could have been half as interested: shock, concern, relief. "Gosh."

"What would you most like to change about yourself if you could?"

"Everything." His smile did little to dampen the harshness of the statement. "I guess I should have said 'nothing.'"

Hattie moved in front of him, holding his face up to hers. "Honey. Sweetheart. You don't ever, ever have to say anything to me, if you don't want to. Not me. And whatever you do say, you know I can take it, whatever it is. Besides, from you, it couldn't ever be anything but true. I know that. So why 'everything?' Do you think your friends feel that way?"

"They'd each like to change a part of me, and when you add up all the parts they'd like to change, it equals everything."

She searched his face, unable to formulate a response to this that could make it any less harmful. "What would I like to change about you?"

"Oh." His hands rose to hers, his grip tighter than usual. "You'd like to change the fact that I know all that."

She couldn't help but chuckle, although it really was the last thing she wanted to do. "Well, that's true. I guess we all want to change you, even if we think it's for your own good. That's a lot of pressure, huh."

He kissed her hand, and the shadows on his face deepened, revealing hollows that shouldn't have been there.

"I really want to feed you, Donald. You're getting so thin." Turning back to the food, she continued, trying to strike a casual chord in her voice. "So, what would you change about yourself if you completely forgot about the rest of us for a moment?"

"Oh, god, I don't know. I wouldn't be me without the rest of you."

"How are you sleeping?"

"I guess I could use a bit more."

"Okay, then. That sounds like a plan. What if we worked on that through hypnosis? That's something *you'd* like to change, isn't it?"

Hattie couldn't keep the gravity of her desire from the question, and she felt it betrayed by every movement she made, like a heavy, soaked blanket covering her. She didn't want him to do it just for her, but when she flashed a look toward him over the brimming plates, she could see a deep gratitude in his face that attested to the fact that there was really never any other motivation for anything he did. On one hand, it was profoundly satisfying to her, nourishment to the core of who she was as a human being, to be so completely and accurately appreciated by another. And yet, his complete self-effacement was a fact she had finally to accept at that moment as a force she could never really change. She hated surrendering to this defeat because it meant that she simply wasn't as smart as she thought she was. But she was nothing if not a pragmatist, and perhaps it wasn't quite defeat just yet.

"After lunch, then."

*　　　*　　　*

When he was under, Hattie tucked a story away into Donald's mind. It was about an old man in Cairo who could only sleep at the top of a minaret. Sleep had become something holy to him, after he'd dreamt of Mohammed resting in an oasis. Mohammed, too, had drifted off to sleep in the old man's dream, but the old man was too respectful to acknowledge what the Prophet dreamt of.

*   *   *

Later, it almost smelled like spring to Hattie when the wind blew in just the right direction. After the last two months, she was glad even of the scent of a false season.

"I have another reason." The mall's parking lot was a lot busier than she'd expected, people plodding toward the entrance, stone-faced.

"What do you mean?"

"Oh! It has to be the sales and people returning Christmas gifts. I couldn't imagine why anyone would want to come back here so soon after all that holiday shopping."

Donald looked down at the foot well of Hattie's car. "You said you have another reason."

"I do." She spotted an SUV backing out into an empty lane and turned toward it abruptly. "Sorry. Let's just get inside, and I'll explain everything to you. Does that sound all right?"

"Of course." He waited until she opened her door before deliberately getting out, himself.

To Hattie, when he was thrust into public, Donald resembled a cloistered nun. His eyes were always averted, yet an unfocused, beatific little smile played on his lips. It had the effect of him seeming both aloof and apologetic, but she understood why, at least, which made it heart-breaking, too.

She grabbed the shoebox off of the back seat. "My store is on the other side. Do you want to walk around the outside, or cut through the middle?"

"Outside." The odd grin was still there, but his eyes were comfortable on her.

Their path was fortuitous: most of the way, they were on the back side of the mall, where the trucks would back in to make deliveries. The area was mostly empty.

"So, I've always wondered, Donald. When did it start for you?"

He nodded; clearly, this was a question for which he'd been waiting and was prepared. "I always say that it's kind of hard to pin down. It's always sort of been the same for me."

"'You always say.' Is there any part of it you don't say?"

He frowned at the salt-encrusted sidewalk, the sun highlighting the many thin strands of his hair that lifted in the breeze. "Let's see. I don't usually say that I thought everyone was like me until I was about eight, and my cousin beat me up because I wanted to kiss him. He broke my collar bone. I also don't usually say that the first time I had sex with an adult was when I was six. And the reason why I don't say any of that is because it upsets most people and makes it look like I'm fishing for sympathy."

Three teen-aged girls rounded the corner toward the two of them, and Donald flung his face toward the holly bushes next to the building.

After they'd passed: "And I almost never say that I liked it. The sex."

Hattie was silent a moment, more concerned with her response than her internal reaction. "I've always thought that a life lived differently was better, somehow."

They walked in silence, the only sounds the hum of the far off highway, her clicking shoes and his breathing.

"Do you believe that, Donald? That your life has been better because of your difference?"

She was hoping for a particular response, and she got it: "It's hard to say. I don't know what it's like to be anything else."

Fewer cars were parked near the back entrance, and fewer shoppers passed in and out. A concrete bench was tucked into an alcove near the doors, and Hattie wordlessly tugged Donald to it. Its chill took a moment to work its way into her flesh, but she didn't mind.

"You're one of the most suggestible people I've ever hypnotized, Donald. Like everything else, you're a dream to work with." She took his hand in hers. "Wow, you're ice-cold, baby. Maybe we should get inside—"

"No." He looked warily at the entrance. "No, this is fine. So I'm suggestible."

"I don't know why I'd be surprised by that. It seems right for you, somehow. And I think you're really going to find that you'll be sleeping better from now on."

The luxuriant smile was such a contrast to his shadowed face that Hattie looked at his collar, her throat constricted by sudden doubt. "Well, do you remember another suggestion that we discussed when you were relaxed?"

His smile thinned. "No."

"Well, the other reason we came to the mall is because I wanted to test that suggestion out a little. I think it might make things a bit easier for you. How does that sound?"

Anyone else would've asked Hattie what she'd done. Donald squeezed her hand. "Thank you."

"Well, don't thank me yet. Come on, let's go."

Hattie led Donald gently into the mall, the humid heat saturated with the odors of wet wool, candied nuts, overheated wanderers. His eyes dipped below every face, and he seemed unnaturally interested in dried sausage and designer teddy bears and fluorescent handbags.

Hattie was beginning to seriously question the whole thing, but she reminded herself of his increasingly muddled behavior and his eye sockets, which seemed to be widening to the depths of an invalid's. Doing anything had to be better than doing nothing.

"Why don't you take a look at a few of these people, Donald. There's a lady over there, by that plant, on her cell phone. Why don't you take a look at her."

"Okay." Donald raised his eyes in the direction that Hattie indicated. He seemed to be having difficulty focusing. Then he stared openly, eventually attracting the attention of the woman, who stopped talking when she saw the profound disappointment on Donald's face and glared back at him, baffled.

Donald wrenched his eyes off of her and looked at clusters of other shoppers, and families, and lone, old men on the couches in the middle of the concourse.

"What did you do to me?"

Donald's voice rose in panic, and Hattie willed any trace of her own nerves out of her response. "I just put a suggestion in your mind that when you see someone, you don't automatically have feelings for them."

He glared around at more shoppers, his mouth open in confusion and disbelief. "But—it was that easy? You can change someone that easily?"

"I didn't know if it would, or to what extent, but—"

"And this is what it's like for other people? Everyone else is… You can change me back, right? Hattie?"

"Yes. I'm sorry, Donald, I didn't think you'd be so upset—"

"Can you change me back now?"

Hattie took a deep breath and looked around her. It had never occurred to her that she could so completely misjudge an action; professionally, she was almost always correct in her choices. She had to gather her thoughts but for some inane reason found herself revisiting that desperate love letter to Professor Shigura that had only resulted in shaming both of them. He'd kept calling her 'dear' as he let her down, and she'd never used the term since.

Hattie too took a deep breath. There was no place she could relax him in the mall, and as she formulated the quickest route back to her car, she found herself frustrated with the throngs of bodies wandering around, blocking easy access to an exit.

One of them approached Donald, the woman on the cell phone.

"Excuse me. Do I know you?"

He inspected her in such a distracted, almost disdainful way that the woman's hands clenched into fists.

"No, I don't know you. Sorry." He turned to Hattie, pleading. "Can we get out of here, please?"

"We can go back around outside—"

"Why? No, just the fastest way."

The woman was still there. "Excuse me, then why were you looking at me like that? Like you're pissed at me or something."

"I'm not mad at you." Donald shook his head and placed his hands on his hips, looking down as if he'd been winded. "I thought you were someone else, okay? I'm sorry."

The woman was glad for the apology in Hattie's eyes, but backed up a step at the fear there.

"We're sorry. It was just a misunderstanding." She pulled Donald off toward the center of the mall, leaving the woman in front of a cheap jewelry cart.

"You're fucking right you don't fucking know me!" It should have been yelled, but it just came out like an apology of its own.

Machtelt Pluijm and her family still talked about their disappointment in TV dinners, even though they'd tried them only once, so long ago in their old house outside of Springbok, and even though it was more than that. She'd even gone so far as to purchase the tables that you could set up on your lap so you could eat while you watched television, something she hadn't allowed in her house since they'd gotten the set a year before, 1977.

She still shared some of the South African government's lingering mistrust of the new TV service, and it seemed to her that it might be harder to guard against subversive messages if you weren't completely focused on the program. However, her children had begged and begged, so she bought the slabs of frozen food and cooked them just as it said on the package.

Pulling the foil off had caused the first stab of guilt and disappointment for Machtelt: the food looked gelatinous and small. However, Anselm and the kids didn't seem worried about it, so she passed them around the front room as the TV flickered in the semi-darkness.

It wasn't just the taste; the channel had just started broadcasting commercials, too, and they'd quickly gone from amusing to a bore. As she held up a piece of meat to her mouth that was simultaneously wet yet somehow like pressed sawdust, and she watched a commercial about a plane ride to Europe she could never afford, Machtelt looked over to her children and realized that the world would never stop lying to them. It made her want to kick in the television screen and dump her grainy potatoes into the wires there just to smell something really cooking. But then she noticed that her kids looked back at her with much the same thought on their minds, and it wasn't so bad.

Later, she stood at the sink, the sea-foam chiffon curtains moving in and out, and the taste of metallic green beans still under her tongue, and she watched her children playing in the back paddock, which would always look a little smaller now.

The mall was endless, cavernous, yet Hattie felt even more pressed in by the slow, bovine march of humanity. Ashamed that she didn't want to hear anything else about his altered perception, Hattie talked mostly about her plan to work with him in her car as soon as they made their way back to it. His seatback could be reclined, and the heater would make only a pleasant hum in the background.

When they finally made it back, she wasn't surprised to find that getting him into a relaxed state was much more difficult than the last time. His agitation had grown with every glance at another person, and Hattie realized that the woman's reaction in the mall had been an appropriate one: he did appear to be angry at everyone.

Finally, though, she believed that she got him to a state in which he'd be open to her, and a few minutes later, he raised his seatback, emerging back into the winter light.

"How do you feel?"

"I know what you said this time." Donald's eyes were averted again, but the smile was gone.

"Absolutely. Now, do you want to take a look at someone? There's a family walking by right over there."

"What if it didn't work?"

"It worked."

"How can you tell?"

"Donald, you'll be able to tell for yourself if you just look over there."

He picked at a pill on his sweater, then quickly looked to his right. Hattie ran her eyes over the back of his head, wishing she could undo what she'd done there. At that moment, his bald patch almost resembled a scar, a mark of misfortune.

He threw open the door and threw up the lunch she'd prepared for him. Hattie rubbed his back, wishing the layers of fabric weren't there, wishing that they were just in bed at her house, chatting about his latest love. Perversely, she also felt much closer to Donald because she was experiencing so intensely at least one of the factors that was at the core of so much of his own anguish: sometimes entering a person's life to make it better only makes it worse.

Rubbing his back felt almost like an insult, but she didn't stop.

"Sorry about that. I didn't get any in the car."

"I'm sorry, Donald. How are you feeling?"

"It worked."

"It did." She stroked his hair. "I'm so, so sorry about that. I don't know what else I can say. It was a very, very poorly thought-out idea. I honestly don't know what I was thinking."

He looked at her nose momentarily, apologetic but something else, too, and turned back to the wads of wool on his sweater.

"It's all right. I'm back to normal, whatever that is." He rolled down his window and spat.

This must have been his version of furious, this simmering. It made her feel better to see that his palette of emotions might be as wide as most, even if this also disappointed her a bit. Nonetheless, she'd deal with her own reactions later. Right now, she felt she stood on much more solid ground; she could deal with run-of-the-mill anger.

"You must be very upset with me right now."

He jerked his head her way, genuinely surprised by her comment. "I'm not upset with you!" Leaning his head on her shoulder, she could feel the vibrations of his voice run up her spine.

But this way, he also didn't have to look her in the eye. "It's just... Anyway, I don't want you to feel bad. I'll get over myself. And anyway, I've got to get going. I've got another..."

"Of course, Donald." She put the car in reverse as he pulled away from her.

"Please don't give it another thought, Hattie. Honestly."

It was the first time he wasn't completely available to her, and her heart fluttered. If this was his version of punishment, she deserved it, so she didn't press the matter. She had to respect his reaction, whatever it was.

Still, the space between them, where the heater released its warming contents, was thick in a way it had never been before. With what, exactly, she didn't know, but Hattie could feel it, and it slashed at her insides.

Compromise might've been distasteful, disappointing to her, but right at that moment, Hattie realized that she could never do this kind of damage to Reggie. The safety net she'd mentioned to Donald two days earlier—and bored herself with, if she was honest—was much more than financial.

JOSEPH

MONDAY

The car slowed to a dead crawl, and Joseph turned his face away. But this only caused him to slip, and he landed hard on his backside. Pain radiated down his legs, up his spine, and he remained immobilized in the snow bank with no thought of getting up or moving or resolving the situation. He honestly couldn't remember when it had been anything other than winter.

The driver pulled over as far as he could and jumped out of his car, leaving the door open to keep other motorists from running over Joseph. As he stared straight ahead, Joseph's coarse white hair bounced side to side in the cold breeze but never threatened his part. If nothing else, he had his faithful part.

"Sir?" The man stopped ten feet away, as if he were worried that he'd frighten the older gentleman, invade his space. Joseph slowly turned to face him and laughed mechanically.

"That was quite a trip I just took!"

But Joseph observed. The man was in his mid-twenties, white, with a young, round, open face and eyes that didn't fit, somehow. They never stopped changing.

"Are you sure you're all right?"

The man was broad, Joseph guessed doughy under all the winter gear, but not particularly tall. And even Joseph could tell that he wasn't dressed fashionably, his clothing clearly just a distracting necessity.

"I'm not sure of anything. Could you help me up, please?"

He gently reached down and grabbed Joseph's upturned, gloved hands. Now that the young man was within his clear vision, Joseph recoiled at the nakedness of his face, his look a plea that hadn't been leveled at Joseph for forty years. And as it mutated, it gained strength.

After he was upright, Joseph turned away. The soreness would reverberate in his bones for the rest of the day. "I'm fine."

Across the street, the dead branches jiggled in the wind, a rejection of some kind. The close sky glowed, a dismissal. The houses extended in every direction, strangers, strangers, strangers.

So Joseph returned his attention to the man and found the brown eyes still enveloped him.

"Good."

The man's voice was just as blatant in its exposure, and a faint echo rose up from Joseph's distant store of social conduct: he should be galled at all this. But he experienced this message merely as a weak imperative, rather than a natural reaction, and this intrigued him enormously. He'd forgotten the last time he'd been intrigued by anything.

Then the scene froze, and Joseph controlled it. It became increasingly clear that he'd gained a certain level of power. He felt the man's intense interest like the stinging wind on his cheeks and found himself almost enjoying the discomfort of the widening silence.

For the past two months, Joseph had felt neither enjoyment nor discomfort of any kind. He'd only been considering ways to end his life. But at least for the moment, he was *feeling*. He wouldn't be the first to talk.

Fifty-two years earlier, at the exact same corner of Princess Avenue and Lindy Street, a young woman had paused, wondering why she didn't feel more pain at watching her boyfriend, Mark, walk away. The subdivision was being built, and on nice days, there was always activity with large vehicles. She watched a bulldozer at the corner pushing a sapling over and realized she should have been horrified by what was happening. But she wasn't. Mark was gone. Mark was gone.

She stood there, her cigarette hanging limply between the fingers of her right hand, weighing inaction versus action in her mind. She thought the honesty inside her mind would be too much for her, that she would have to chase after him. But it turned out it wasn't. The damp, sunny spring day just reminded her that she'd have to hang her laundry out, so she turned back to her parents' pink house. Her romance novel was going in the rubbish when she got home, though; none of it was right, so why waste her time? There was laundry, then lunch, then her room to straighten up.

"Would you like me to drive you home?"

Joseph hardly heard him. His world had become so small that it was a pinprick.

"Yes."

"Good. I'm Donald."

The old man stared at Donald's large, soft right hand and removed his glove to shake it.

"Joseph Takemura."

The same hand gripped Joseph's shoulder as he stepped along the icy street. The car was clean, older. Nothing personal was in evidence, although Joseph had no idea why he would look for clues or what he expected to deduce if there had been any. He was more interested in his own motives at this point, anyway.

Donald got in and returned his overwhelming gaze to Joseph. "Where to?"

The man was the opposite of a threat, but Joseph noted that his own defenses remained in place. "Not far. Just over that hill, as a matter of fact. I can go shopping later."

Finally, Donald turned his attention to something else and began to drive.

Joseph hadn't been in someone else's car in years! It was a realization like a blow, and he felt his lips press tightly together, his usual response to blows. This was certainly the kind of information he should keep to himself: embarrassing, pathetic, raw. Revealing it would do no one any good.

So why did Joseph want to, with this man? He'd always been proud of his tact and discretion, but that very carefulness might well have closed doors as much as it had kept him above the petty fray of everything. Why was he only realizing all this now? Why had he never questioned his behavior before?

He hadn't been in someone else's car for years. It was a fact, just like the hard winter light, just like the plastic door pull in his hand. Just like the man's disconcerting concentration on him. Just a fact.

"I haven't been in someone else's car in years."

Donald shifted into third, his big hand covering the gearshift.

"Really."

"I'm an old man."

"I know."

"It's the white one right there. The second driveway."

Donald pulled up. He looked at his steering wheel, pained, as the car idled roughly. Joseph found himself feeling the way he did at the corner.

"How old are you?"

"Twenty-five."

Joseph looked up at his house. He used two of the eight rooms now. The others he closed up and let the winter have.

"Thanks for the ride. Was it Donald?"

"That's right."

The whole thing was ludicrous. It should have been perverse, too, but it was just ludicrous. Joseph looked at his house again. The gutter was peeling away. He stared down the dull street; it didn't even bother to stare back.

"Donald." Joseph's only plans were to get his hair cut in two weeks. This was like a date; the man was actually waiting to be asked in.

Maybe it was perverse. "Well, goodbye, then."

He turned to get out of the car and encountered more icy snow. Donald was by his side in an instant, firmly guiding him along through the danger. It had been so long since a hand had touched Joseph because it wanted to. After his wife had died, physical interaction was an obligation; this was always evident in the touch. Now, he could've lain back, and Donald would've been honored to carry him into the house. It certainly wasn't something Joseph wanted to think about, but its reality surrounded them both in a way that made him feel a little bit warmer, in spite of himself.

"Well, thanks again." And Joseph fiddled with his keys, the man's stare oppressive behind him now. When he finally got the door open and turned to close it, he started at the man's arm extended toward him.

But it was just his business card. *Donald Hanak.* "It was very nice to meet you, Joseph." A eulogy.

Joseph barely grinned and closed the door. There'd been a time when he'd confronted Viet Kong, shot at young boys in the black jungle. He'd had the fortitude to take lives once; now, he could barely take a business card, and he stood behind his door, trying and failing to determine which one of them had been ludicrous, which one perverse.

TUESDAY

Joseph couldn't clean like he used to. Although he couldn't see it himself exactly, he assumed that Donald would surely notice the dark crust where the linoleum met the wall, the oily dust that clung to the light bulb above them. But Donald simply stood behind Joseph, still and expectant.

"I haven't had anyone over for ages. It's terribly dirty." Again, the unguarded truth. But guarding implied that there was something that needed guarding! Joseph reminded himself to relax. "Would you like to come into the kitchen?"

Donald quietly followed and sat on a chair in the corner.

"Are you from Montclair?" Joseph chose a question he felt both of them would care about least. He retrieved a couple of very old tea bags. Even they were dusty.

"That's right."

"I'm from Indiana, originally. Fort Wayne. My wife was from these parts."

"I'm sorry."

"Thank you." There was nothing worth guarding. "But what I'd really like to know is—well—why?"

Donald only dropped his head and studied the clasped hands in his lap.

"Do I remind you of someone?"

"No."

"Then what is it?"

"Well. When you slipped and fell, you laughed. Your coat's frayed at the bottom, but you don't care. I can see by your hands how powerful you've always been. Even though you sense something different about me, you invited a complete stranger into your home—"

"But don't you see, ordinarily, I never would have!"

"Exactly—"

"But you know absolutely nothing about me! You know, I'm not, what is it, now, queer. Gay."

"I know."

Joseph stared at Donald. He knew.

"I should be—I don't know what I should be." Joseph filled his kettle. He used to be so many things when he was younger: a yielding husband, a competent audit manager, a fair racquetball player, an amateur acrylic painter. With so many of these titles gone, he found that he had less and less data upon which to base his behavior. His reactions felt more and more random as context fell away. Although lately, he'd been wondering if random might be underrated, as far as reactions go.

And then, as if on cue: "Did you spend time in the internment camps?"

His first disappointment in Donald, and oddly, only because he'd acted normally. Ordinary. Americans were always so secretly pleased with themselves when they demonstrated their knowledge in this way, and the question always came up. Joseph hated talking about it, but it seemed so important to Donald that he didn't mind as much. In fact, Joseph's reactions were becoming cracks in fathomless ice.

"Jerome, Arkansas. But I was so young. I just remember the wooden huts and lots of mud. My parents didn't dwell on it, either."

"Were they both Japanese?" Donald's eyes roamed over Joseph's face, appreciating his sagging jaw, worrying over his worry lines, open and eager and naked.

"No, I'm sorry."

Donald immediately understood and stood, while Joseph put down the dusty teabags and turned off the stove. Then a random memory: his parent's black maid, Aggie, when he was ten years old and she'd pinned her arm between the refrigerator and the wall. She'd been attempting to clean out behind it. Refrigerators were very heavy then, and when he'd returned from school, Joseph had to listen a few times to her patient, hopeless call before he came to her aid.

Help me. Help me.

"I'm sorry."

Donald moved to the front door and Joseph followed. He watched the alien young man walking before him and was absolutely unable to make any sense of the last twenty-four hours. He found that he liked that, but it wasn't enough. He needed the house to himself for a while.

"Right now, it's all a little too much."

"Of course it is." Donald's attention was diverted behind the couch, where a hundred years' worth of photographs stood. A different emotion played on his face for each face he inspected. It was much easier, a relief, when his eyes weren't trained on Joseph.

"After I'm gone, I guess they'll all be thrown out. I don't even know where my nephew lives, anymore. My last relative. It was Seattle twenty years ago, but people move around so much, nowadays."

Joseph looked at the picture of his mother, black-and-white smile still projecting, still a presence in the room after death and so many years. When was the point you died all the way, when there was finally nothing of you left? Joseph suspected that his death would be immediate, a snapping sound then silence.

"You know, it's funny how some stories stay with you as you get older, but so many of them just dry up. Little incidents in your life. Maybe they stay with you until you figure out the reason, and then they just," Joseph frosted the air with his hand, "fade away."

"Hmmm."

Joseph listened to the words as they came out of his own mouth: "When I was in drafting school in New York, more than fifty years ago, there was a man, a fellow student. One day, he told me that he was a socialist. I can't even remember his name. I hardly knew him, but for some reason, he told *me*. And only me, as far as I know. At the time, it was such a dangerous thing to do, but I didn't care. Why would I care if he was a socialist? Maybe that was why he told me. Maybe he assumed things about me, I don't know."

Joseph thought about that man a lot, especially lately. They were the same age, but how differently did the two men's lives turn out? Or had they turned out more or less the same? Because so often, the wild differences of youth all ran together over time, turning a uniform gray. Joseph felt more and more like a simple animal the older he got, and saw the world's humans in much the same way. He and Donald were just a couple of creatures, radiating heat, shifting around, sometimes attentive to stimuli. Things once of incredible importance, gray, gray, gray.

"Why do you suppose that one's still with you, Joseph?"

"I have to say that I don't know, but I'm glad it is. The old days…"

Donald remained silent, smiling.

This would be the last time. Joseph stamped down the fear and the discomfort and continued.

"And there's another. On a bus. I was about eighteen and heading to New York for the first time, and this young man sat next to me. It was an overnight trip, because back then, it took a lot longer to get across the country. We never talked. I don't think I ever even looked him in the face. At some point I fell asleep, and during the night, I would half wake up and realize that his head was on my shoulder or he was curled up around me. Funny thing was, nothing seemed to matter to me in that state between sleep and consciousness. Maybe it was the same for him, too. I don't know. And then the bus stopped in Erie, Pennsylvania, and he got off."

Donald nodded his head. He presumed to understand it as much as Joseph did, and Joseph felt a rush of anger bubbling up his throat.

But he'd had a studied life of betraying his emotions, and he recognized this might be an instance for feeling things later. So he calmly continued, intent on saying the last thing he planned to share: "It seems as if my resistance has been worn down at the same time that anything requiring resistance has disappeared from my life. I suppose that's convenient." Joseph laughed, but it was so humorless that even Donald's gaze weakened. He looked down at his shoes. "It's funny, but I thought that it would be the other way around when I got older. Old men always seemed so cantankerous to me. But I guess a lot of them still do."

Time was supposed to be the great leveler, but Joseph realized that there might be two sides of the line: the old men leveled down, and the old men leveled up. He still believed that he'd gotten smarter as he'd gotten older. He hadn't closed up like a rotting lily blossom.

"I can't help feeling that I might be taking advantage of this situation. But that's resistance, isn't it."

Donald shrugged again. He wasn't taking sides, and that made Joseph feel calmer.

"How about this: I'll worry about me, and you worry about you."

Donald relaxed along with Joseph. "That's a plan I can live with."

Joseph was only relieved for a moment before a chill of fear worked its way back into his gut. "Okay. Anyway, I know you have to go to work now—"

Donald sheepishly sidled toward the door, clearly anxious not to spook Joseph now that a détente had been reached. Then, just before the door closed on the winter glare: "You know, maybe some stories stick with you because you're supposed to tell them to someone else."

As Donald walked to his car, Joseph realized that he still knew absolutely nothing about him. Neither of them had been in the least interested in that topic. The imbalance made Joseph dizzy, but dizzy was an experience, and he found that it was pleasant, trying these human experiences on again, long after he thought he'd put them away for good.

But he'd kept a story back, too; if he decided that the situation should continue, it would still have to be a gradual process. Joseph hadn't let his nephew fade out of his life. If anything, their bond became greater as their family became smaller. Instead, it was simple. One day, the phone was just disconnected, and Daniel just vanished into thin air.

For Joseph and so much of his family, the urge to commit suicide often arose earlier than the alternate urges that develop in most people, and it was stronger and clung on. As he watched Donald carefully maneuver his car down the icy street, Joseph wondered why it had come so late to him and whether anything, even this strange man, could really ease it.

*   *   *

Donald was fumbling with the wrapper of a sandwich and talking on his cell phone. The light was gone now, another desperately cold night working its way into every corner of the suburb, and he was parked in front of Joseph's house again, his car idling. The sandwich, which had never really neared Donald's lips, slowly descended into his lap as he talked.

Joseph approached the passenger window. He'd been waiting for Donald at his front door in his coat and gloves. Earlier in the day, he had chipped at the undulating ice on his boat's deck and swept the grit off of its white vinyl seats and onto his driveway. It looked even smaller than the last time he'd been aboard.

The afternoon had been a series of bold moves for Joseph. His first act had been to finally take a look at eBay, and his second to telephone Donald at work. He was easing into it, or the order of his actions would have been reversed.

Still, chipping the ice off of his life had been easier than he'd imagined so far, although what he found underneath was worryingly liquid. His interaction with the world had always been vigilantly ruled, so not knowing where he stood or why was having odd effects on him, making him even more of a mystery to himself. For instance, here he was, waiting at Donald's car like a shameless basset hound, electrified by his utterly uncharacteristic act.

But who could be ashamed around Donald?

Donald waved warmly to Joseph and indicated that he would be with him shortly. Only at this point did Joseph notice the sub-zero weather and that he could hear what Donald was saying: "Of course I do, Andie. That will never change." Donald wrapped the uneaten sandwich back up and stuffed it into the bag on the seat beside him.

*   *   *

There were little waves in the toilet bowl. So much of Joseph's life had been spent staring down in this way, but he'd never noticed the waves.

83

Maybe they'd never been there before, or maybe he'd just been seeing a composite interpretation of a toilet bowl all these years, too tired of staring at the same thing to recognize when it was different.

And another thing: his pubic hair was still jet black. It was the last part of his body that hadn't gone silver, and he found himself reviewing the ways he'd dealt with discovering each of these little deaths on his body: amused at the chest, disgusted at the face, contemplative at the temple, dismissive at the legs. Joseph wondered how he'd deal with the last frontier of his body, in light of his brand new attitude. He hoped he'd be too busy to notice.

It became clear, then, that the disturbances on the surface of the water were due to Donald's footfall in the next room, and Joseph relaxed enough to open up a weak stream.

When he returned to the living room: "I've found a boat online that I'd like to look at, and I was wondering if you'd like to come with me."

Donald immediately began bobbing his head. "Wow! Absolutely! That would be great, Joseph!" He looked momentarily to the right of Joseph's knees, a flash of doubt interrupting his enthusiasm, but only for an instant. "When do we go?"

Joseph hardly noticed the momentary hesitation. "It's a '67 Erickson. Twenty-six feet. A sailboat. I found it on eBay, and I'm not particularly sure how the whole thing works, but it seems like a good deal to me."

"Let's see the pictures!"

"I didn't know you sailed."

Donald chuckled and laced his fingers over his knee. "I really haven't done much sailing before." As usual, his gaze was raw with emotion. "I'd just love to learn more."

Joseph fought to suppress a wave of distaste, but Donald noticed it, anyway. "Actually, my computer's not working too well—"

"Oh, okay. No problem." He pointed a false grin in the general direction of Joseph's coffee table.

The thought of any silence at this point was galling to Joseph. "I have an old motor boat. A nineteen-foot Bowrider, but it was never what I really wanted. I compromised, although I don't know why I felt the need, looking back on it. My wife didn't really care what I did after I retired. A sailboat just seemed more reckless, in a way. Less practical, more work. I don't know. It seems silly now. I've hardly ever taken it out. It's just rotting away in the driveway. You probably saw it; it's under the tarp."

Everything seemed silly to Joseph now. He rose. "My computer's upstairs, in my bedroom."

Each stair found a foot; his house was still solid, reassuring. Joseph had been followed up his stairs only one time since his wife had died. The woman, Phoebe, had been surprisingly strong for a woman her age, and much lonelier, he thought, than he'd ever been. It was so easy for memories like this to die with him.

"The last time someone else was in my bedroom was about three years ago. A friend of my wife's who couldn't stand being on her own. We only met like that once; it didn't really work for either of us. I guess *help* either of us." Joseph looked back at Donald for a reaction and got nothing but pure interest. "I don't know why I never asked before, but do you have another person? A, uhhh…"

They reached the upstairs landing, sloped walls and deep shadows cooperating to push the two men together. Joseph felt dizzy again, but he at least had a right to know.

Donald was silent for a while before finally swallowing. He stroked the railing next to him, studying it carefully. "I live with two people, Joseph."

Joseph peered into the dark recesses of his bedroom. He noticed the picture of his wife on the dresser for the first time in months.

"Huh." Joseph was surprised to find himself empathizing with Donald, the first step in what he suspected might be a certain freedom, a further relaxation of his assumptions. He'd welcome it.

Keeping his eyes on his wife: "I guess emotions don't really… If you think your emotions are supposed to make sense, then you're going to have a pretty rotten time of it. I guess I know that much."

Donald's voice cracked. "I guess so."

"But it sounds—complicated."

"I don't know what else to do."

Joseph realized that any more would be too much, right now. But he was starting to get the hang of it, this odd ebb and flow of revelation and emotion. For a split second, he was twenty again, an explorer. But only for a second.

"Let me show you that boat."

WEDNESDAY

A young woman stepped out of Donald's moving car, and as if choreographed, landed right in front of Joseph.

"Hello."

Donald was a young man; it made no sense to be shocked by a young friend. Still, Joseph's first reaction was to feel absurd, some old fool who should have known better than to get mixed up with people who were vital, who mattered, who were at the core of the modern world. But that might be a form of resistance, too, and Joseph had promised himself: no resistance, no reserve. He had decided to do this. He wasn't going to do it half-way.

"Hi. You're probably Joseph."

"That's right. And you must be Andie."

She turned back toward the car and sighed, a little dramatically, Joseph thought. Donald looked pale, panicked behind the wheel.

She said, "Jesus Christ."

*   *   *

Hundreds of houses passed by, each one harboring its own drama. And there was drama in the car, right now. Some altercation had taken place before Donald and Andie had picked Joseph up—why else would she have jumped out of a moving vehicle?

But Joseph settled into his coat and the warmth there: his goal was to exist with discomfort, rather than to ignore it or alleviate it. Donald's back seat was actually quite cozy.

"Joseph's wanted a sailboat his whole life. Wouldn't it be great if you fall in love with this one?"

"Well, let's take a look at it, first."

"Where would you sail it, Joseph?" Andie twisted herself into his direction, her leather jacket squeaking against the leather of the seat.

"Well, I thought I'd start with a lake. When I get the hang of it, the ocean, maybe. It might be too much for me." She was pretty, but the angst!

"So Donald told you that he and I used to live together, along with a couple of other people."

Was she attempting to provoke him or Donald? "He hasn't told me too much about you."

At first, Joseph hadn't known what to expect when Donald called to ask if he could bring a friend. Then he didn't care. Initially vaguely curious, he realized that each member of their little party would be moldering underground in a very short time, anyway. Along with anyone who knew them. Then no one would care or remember or take any kind of interest in any of this; there would simply be headstones that provided antiseptic dates and series of letters that were once names. In fact, Joseph was more or less in that grave now: there was no one left to be shocked at his new acquaintances and behavior. A freefall.

Of course, his new acquaintances could be shocked at his behavior, and he was surprised to find this a reassuring thought. But the girl, at least, was clearly on the defensive. She had never gotten completely right with Donald; that was clear.

Joseph imagined the level of desperation Andie must have felt to expose herself in such an uncomfortable way as this, then considered the desperation that seemed to tinge everything that Donald did or said. Finally he marveled at his own, sudden desperation to follow any path toward human contact, even one as unexpected and ludicrous as driving to Connecticut with a couple of strangers. He leaned back in the seat, pleased to be there, and uncrossed his legs: they did have something in common, after all.

There was a declaration buried in Joseph that rose like a bubble right out of his mouth: "I don't want to sleep with Donald, but why not get to know someone who believes that they've fallen in love with you?"

Donald looked back at Joseph in his mirror. Surprise, then gratitude and admiration were plain in the rectangle of his eyes. When they came to a traffic light, Donald turned around to face Joseph.

"Joseph. Actually, I'm like this with everyone I see, and it never goes away."

Joseph sunk back, drew into himself. He wouldn't act yet, but he was in the car with a lunatic, possibly two. He'd have to get away. The light was fading; they were entering a short, winter twilight. Then, darkness. Joseph wasn't even sure which state they were in.

But only a week before, he'd been considering cutting the rubber hose that pumped gas to his stove and taping up his doors! And anyway, Donald might've been a lunatic, but love was harmless, right? Joseph felt his chest rise up and down, up and down.

"Is that so? And you've never met someone that you didn't feel that way about? Ever?"

"If I don't look people in the eye, it doesn't happen. But I want to look everyone in the eye! That's the problem."

"Well, one of the problems." Andie's voice dripped with annoyance, and she stared at the side of Donald's face.

"That's incredible. Although this means I really shouldn't be all that flattered." But it was a relief. "How can you possibly manage to live like this? It must be hellish."

"It's everything."

Joseph replayed the odd looks, right from the start. "No wonder." He met again the intense pain and pleasure that would flash across Donald's face, his finesse at gently opening Joseph up, even this far. He'd had years of practice.

Joseph chuckled at himself: he'd never really been in control of any of it. "Hmm. Forgive me for asking, Donald, but have you ever seen a professional about this?"

Donald shot a look at Andie, but she faced her window, the lights of a gas station making the outer stragglers of her hair glow.

"My parents tried, when I was smaller. And recently, but it didn't work out."

Andie swung around at Donald. "Hattie?"

Donald shrugged.

"Oh, Donald. Fuck."

There was quite a bit going on in the front of the car, and Joseph reminded himself that he had absolutely nothing to lose. Why not get the answers he wanted?

"How did it happen for you, Andie?"

She kept her face on the passing strip malls. "It happened for both of us. We met each other in a parking garage and saw something in each other."

"But he sees something in everyone, doesn't he?"

Andie paused; Joseph was annoying her. "Everyone deserves love, on some level. It doesn't mean that it's worth less."

"But isn't that like saying that standards don't amount to anything?"

"We all have our own standards. Who's right?"

"Maybe the majority?"

"Is that why your wife married you? I mean, was she wrong about you?"

Donald had discussed Joseph's life with this girl. She continued: "So if your wife felt that way about you, why shouldn't Donald?"

"My wife loved *me*, not *everyone*."

"But was she wrong about you?"

"It's not right or wrong—"

"Exactly!"

"But wouldn't you rather have someone who loved only you because you were the only person they could love?"

Andie's voice rose, strained. "I'm not about ownership. I know it's hard for most people to understand."

"But you don't live with Donald, anymore. Why not?"

"Maybe part of ownership is living together."

"Then I suppose I want to own and be owned."

"Then what are you doing here?"

Joseph found himself chuckling, back in the dark recesses of the car, stretching muscles that hadn't been called upon in years. "Good question." How long had he avoided arguments, disagreeable situations, people, feelings? Truths? "I think I'm taking advantage of someone who wants to be owned."

"And it's you people who are destroying him."

Judging by what Donald had just revealed, refusing to see him ever again might be equally damaging to the man. Still, there was no denying a portion of responsibility, if there was any destroying going on.

"Donald, you've kept pretty quiet. Is it people like me who are destroying you?"

Donald choked on his first few words. "Nobody's destroying me. I'm not being destroyed, guys. I just wish you two would see how much you have in common."

"No offense, but I don't see much at all, except for you. And what's wrong with that? There's no right or wrong with any of it." Joseph found himself wanting to say quite a few things, things from his past and things from his present. He wished he knew these people better so that they would understand.

"You look like shit, Donald."

"No, I don't." His voice slipped under the hum of the wheels.

"Can you let me out here?"

Donald kneaded the steering wheel with both hands. "It would get better with you, Andie."

"Let me out. Please!"

Donald quickly pulled into the parking lot of a transmission shop and parked next to a Plymouth Valiant rusting and pining. "How about after we see the boat, I'll—"

Andie got out of the car and closed the door on his voice.

"I'm sorry about that, Donald."

Once again, Joseph marveled at Donald's hundred-and-eighty-degree swing from watching Andie walk away, devastated, to shrugging into the back seat, pained but completely devoid of resentment or blame.

"Why don't you come up here with me?"

It was a life that had to take its toll.

*   *   *

Joseph knew the moment that he saw the sailboat that he didn't want it, and he was just as sad as he was glad that he could still fool himself with schoolboy fantasies. The obsession, the exaggeration: pure, base materialism. Of the world.

"We really don't have to do this."

"Of course we do, Joseph."

"I think I wasn't being completely truthful, a while ago. I said that I was taking advantage of you. That's kind of like saying someone in a burning house is taking advantage of a fireman."

Joseph watched carefully. Donald turned to face him, concerned by this statement, not flattered. His eyes were still red from tearing up on the ride over, but he only stored this information.

"Okay. Let's take a look."

The house was a saltbox replica painted dark red in a neighborhood with recurring facades and Subarus. Before Donald and Joseph had reached the front door, a tall man had passed through it, pulling heavy gloves over his hands. His cheeks were pockmarked and his frizzy brown hair was almost at the point that someone would call him bald, but Joseph was most reminded of a cornered lynx. The man's eyes, lidded darts, restricted themselves to mouths.

"How's it going?" He approached Donald first, shaking his hand with the vehemence of a threat. "You Joseph?"

Donald looked instead at the boat in the driveway. "No, I'm Donald. A friend."

Joseph felt the man refocus on him. The pressure of his hand was almost ridiculous, and Joseph had to fight down a smirk, then a wince. "Nice to meet you, Stu."

"Yeah, you, too. So did you guys see my baby? You know, I really don't want to sell her, but things are looking pretty well fucked at my company now, so. Fucking idiot general manager screwed the pooch, and now we have to pay for his stupidity. Fucking pisses me off. I fixed her up just the way I wanted her, too. She is a real beaut, though, you got to admit that."

They had reached the sailboat at this point, which looked lost in such a landlocked, ice-covered place. Its lines urged anchoring in a remote cove for the short duration of a storm or skipping past whitecaps that gathered themselves at the distant, sun-dazzled mansions of Newport. Joseph felt something like relief when the floodlights on the garage suddenly extinguished themselves, and the craft's shame was secured again in darkness.

Stu waved his hands, and the glare returned. Donald was staring at the back of the man's head.

"What do they say? Yar or some shit? I'm telling you, this baby really handles. I used to take her out to the Sound every weekend, and man, would she turn some heads. If you want to make an impression, this is totally the way to do it."

Stu was directing all of his comments at Donald, who nodded more and more supportively, who ran his hand along the bow.

"One time, I took her all the way from down here at New London over to Montauk and back. You guys are from Jersey, right?"

Now Donald was looking at the man. "Yeah. It wasn't too bad of a drive. So what got you into sailing, Stu?"

"My granddad used to take me out when I was real young. I guess it made an impression on me, you know? Shit! I don't know if I can let her go, guys, I've got to be honest. Fuck! All right, so let's take a look at the cabin. It was just reupholstered like eight months ago or something."

Stu had reflective stripes on his futuristic sneakers, and they flashed aimlessly as he worked on dragging a metal staircase over to the boat. Joseph hadn't been particularly surprised when he'd met Andie. She was pretty, spirited. She had dimples, and if nothing else, she was emotionally invested in Donald. In fact, she'd vehemently defended Donald, although it could have been herself she was defending. Joseph wasn't sure which, and he wasn't sure if she knew, either. Of course, he couldn't believe that anyone who became involved with Donald to that level of intensity could be completely sane, but Joseph could understand Andie.

Stu, on the other hand, was wearing shoes that looked like snowmobiles and talking about how much pussy he'd conquered because of his baby.

Once again, Joseph felt pointless.

*   *   *

Later on, at the bar, after Stu and then Donald had gotten up, Joseph stared at the obscenities carved into the table's Formica and remembered his retirement party. It had been fraught with undercurrents, with little deaths, and they'd just kept continuing since. How much could he really change?

In fact, he was more than ready to leave. The stuffy, humid bar smelled of burned fries and mold, and he wasn't used to drinking, anymore, so he just felt dizzy, confused. The trip had been eventful, which was all he'd dared hope for, but now he simply longed for relief from the pressure in his bladder, a quick, easy ride back to Montclair, and his silent, cool bedroom. The morning would rearrange this evening into a more manageable entity.

Kathleen Dodge had just finished her last day at the local Hallmark store and was feeling decidedly unHallmark about the situation, so her coworkers offered to take her to the best bar of a bad lot in town.

Charisse, Kathleen's best friend and mastermind of the visit, was the most daring employee at the store, and this was frequently pointed out by the others. She would occasionally wear electric pink and bake extravagant pastries like croissants and Danish herself. Once, she even made a squeaked reference to a vibrator, which only added to her mousy yet outrageous persona.

The others were ready to leave after nine o'clock and one drink, but Charisse and Kathleen urged them to stay for one more margarita. Then Charisse admitted that she had cancer and would soon have her breast removed. The others weren't at all sure if another margarita was the right or the wrong thing to do, at this point. But then Kathleen looked down at the charm bracelet that dangled from Charisse's bony wrist, its Kewpie doll and racehorse the most weathered, and finally admitted to herself that she had noticed a lump in her own breast a few months back. Immediately afterward, she had taken to using a shower mitt exclusively.

So Kathleen ordered a pitcher made with gold-label tequila this time and leaned her head against the wooden railing that encircled the booth, its coolness outweighing its questionable cleanliness. They'd been friends for such a long time.

Joseph started unzipping as soon as he entered the restroom. Approaching the urinal, Joseph saw Donald's legs under the stall partition and was glad that his battered shoes didn't look like they were from outer space. Then he noticed an arm directly next to the crack in the stall door, and the bathroom immediately shifted five feet to the left.

Glad to be occupied with the task of keeping upright, Joseph carefully left the bathroom and passed through the dark bar to the street outside. A taxi was idling directly before him, and Joseph entered it. Managing the heat and stink of cigar was his next undertaking.

"Hey, there. Where can I take you?"

Joseph had to urinate furiously, and even after all his years of seeing bodies betray loved ones and himself, he was still surprised to find that his physiology wasn't in the least affected by the situation. He stared at the plastic Virgin Mary on the dashboard. She looked a lot younger and better fed than she usually did.

"A little too much to drink, eh?"

"I'm sorry."

Joseph got out of the car and returned to the other stench, approaching the bartender because he didn't want to go back to the booth. The man had a very large mole on his nose that Joseph wrenched his eyes from as quickly as he could, but not quickly enough.

"Are you kidding? In a place like this, filled with drunks? They call me 'The Mole.' I'm—"

"Hey, Mick." A younger man with teeth that looked like they were fighting each other sidled up to the bartender. "You know you got a couple of fucking faggots going at it in the john, don't you?"

"What are you talking about now, you fucking idiot?"

"They're doing something in there, dude! I ain't making it up. Go in there and see for yourself! In this bar! I don't know what the hell they're thinking, but it's fucking disgusting." He exhaled sour alcohol.

Mick removed a baseball bat from underneath the bar. "You better not be fucking around with me, Johnnie, or I'm going use this thing on you."

Joseph grabbed Mick's arm. "Hey, hey, hey. Listen, that's not what's going on in there."

Mick shook off Joseph's hand and looked at him in a very different way. "How do you know?"

"Because the two men in there are the guys I came in with. My friends."

"So what's going on, then?"

"It's not what you're thinking at all." Joseph looked around the room, his eyes suddenly blind to detail. He leaned in closer to the bartender, and Johnnie leaned in closer to him. There was nothing left to say in him.

"Fuck me, Johnnie! If you don't back your ass up and out of my face with that reeking breath, I don't know what I'm going to do to you, but it ain't going to be nice."

"Jesus, Mick! You're the one that served me."

"Yeah, and I wish I'd served you Listerine, you fucking moron."

The two men suddenly burst out in laughter, but it only lasted a few seconds. Mick's eyes were cold dots on Joseph.

"So, I'm waiting."

"It's kind of embarrassing. I don't know if I should even tell you."

"I can find out for myself. What, some kind of toilet thing? Is one of them retarded or something?"

"No." Joseph lowered his voice. "Nobody's retarded, but one of them has a catheter."

Mick frowned.

"What do you mean, a tube up his dick?" The younger man tittered. "That's, like, the worst thing ever."

Mick's eyes narrowed. "So, what, he needs help with it?"

"Yes! Now, don't let on that I told you. They're going to be coming out in a second. My friend would kill me if he knew I was telling people about it."

Johnnie squealed and grabbed his crotch. "That is fucking messed up!"

"I'm serious! Don't even look at them when they come out, or they're going to know that I said something."

"Are you fucking kidding me? I don't want to look at them! I don't even want to be in the same fucking room as some tube up some guy's dick." Johnnie swayed away from the bar. "I'm fucking out of here."

But Mick continued to stare right into Joseph. "Don't people do that for themselves?"

"They can't always."

"So why's the other guy doing it for him?"

"He used to work in a nursing home. You know, you could always go in there if you want to see it for yourself."

Stu emerged from the men's room as if distracted by an important task, his trajectory the booth at which they'd been seated earlier.

Joseph raced to the same spot. Stu stared at his neck as they stood near the dirty chrome at the edge of the table.

"So, what's the deal. Are we going to talk price or what?"

Joseph looked over at the bartender, wondering intently about the acoustics of the room.

"It's a very nice boat, Stu, but I'm going to have to think about it. It's kind of a big—"

"Fucking timewasters." Stu pushed past Joseph and out the door. Mick's mole was pointed at the booth as if seeking out its own ugliness, and it was soon rewarded by the appearance of Donald, whose eyes were encircled with red again and whose face was slashed with despair. He took Stu's place next to the booth. "So—"

Mick's eyes narrowed at Donald's inappropriately raw expression, recognizing that this was probably not the result of a catheter change. But the profound devastation was laid bare so completely that even he couldn't watch Donald for long, and he turned back to the game on the television above his shoulder. Joseph knew that you had to dismiss a lot at a bar.

Nonetheless, he was annoyed. "Can't you hide things better than that?!"

Donald was genuinely surprised, and Joseph was at least glad for this brief moment of relief from the sight of his pain.

"I thought I was."

*   *   *

Thankful for the silence on the way home, Joseph kept working the incident in the bar over and over again in his head. Each time, it came out differently, as if he were standing before a slot machine, amazed at the different combinations, a detail rising to prominence in one pull, forgotten the next in favor of another. But they were all facts, memories. What he couldn't determine was how to feel about it all. That skill was still rusty.

Finally: "That was exactly how I didn't want this evening to go, Joseph. I'm so sorry. But Stu was—"

"No, no, no! I don't want to know about him."

"But today was supposed to be different. I wanted to give you all of my attention instead of fitting you in for an hour once or twice a week. I do that with everyone else, but I wanted things to be better with you. Right from the start."

The man was constantly in tears. And with no clue how to respond to Donald's statement, Joseph waited.

"I also usually don't tell people about me for a while, but I thought that with you, I'd be honest right away, even if it meant that you wanted me to leave you alone. But you didn't." A smile invaded Donald's face, as arresting as ever. "You're okay with it."

"I hardly know you. Why would it bother me that much?"

"For a lot of people, it does."

"But if you wanted to spend the day with me, why did you invite your friend to come along?"

Donald nodded to himself. "I want to be completely honest with you, Joseph. Keeping things back just makes it worse. I want my friends to get to know each other. In fact, I'm having a party on New Year's so that everyone can get together because you're all so wonderful that I know that you'll become friends, too. And that way, everyone will know everything."

"So tonight was a trial run." Joseph hadn't given Donald a single thought when he'd provoked the girl. Andie. "I guess that ended up a disappointment for you, too. But I liked her well enough, I suppose."

Donald remained silent at this, waves of agony returning to his face. Joseph couldn't stand the thought of witnessing such pain again, and only then did it dawn on him exactly how he should feel.

"Gosh, I can't remember the last time I was in such a tight scrape! And it was looking kind of hairy for a second there. But we pretty much squeaked out of that place scot-free, so I have to say, they must not make them too bright in Connecticut."

Joseph waited for a chuckle, and he got it. Of course, he got more: "You see? I knew you were the right person to do this with." Donald attempted to wring out all the pathos from his next question. "So what are you doing tomorrow?"

Joseph leaned back in his seat; the front was a lot more comfortable than the back.

"Not a goddamned thing."

*   *   *

The night had plunged into a slicing hardness of cold and black, and things exposed to it for long became brittle or chafed. As Donald pulled up to the curb in front of his house, Joseph noticed Andie sitting in a car across the street, and she gestured for him to look away.

He did as he was told.

THURSDAY

The moment Joseph found Donald in the bar, a woman joined them, so he couldn't ask Donald what was wrong with him.

"Stacy, this is Joseph. Joseph, Stacy."

"Oh, pleasure to meet you, Stacy." She was another one Joseph couldn't understand. Hard eyes, thin lips ready to sneer.

"Hi. So, anyway, I'm going to have to get out of here—"

"You don't want another drink? Or lunch?" There was hardness in Donald's eyes, too. Did he change that much to accommodate people's personalities?

"You're buying?"

"Of course."

"Okay." It was a graceless acceptance, her tone flat and exasperated. Joseph began to work on ways to excuse himself.

But she led them to a table in a darker area of the bar, and Joseph watched Donald in front of him, almost shell-shocked as he shuffled along, his shoulders stooped under some new, unknown weight.

"You know, I haven't been in a bar in years, and now two in as many days." Joseph might not get the whole story, but he had to do something: "So, how are you doing, Donald?"

"Oh, you know. I think I may be coming down with something."

They sat at the table, Donald looking away from his friends. Joseph couldn't believe that someone in Donald's situation could possibly be this affected by jealousy—wouldn't that be the height of hypocrisy? But if he was, Joseph would have to take decisive action pretty quickly.

Consequently, he was less subtle than he liked to be: "Have you spoken with Andie since last night?"

Donald shook his head, distracted, and only then did Joseph recognize that over the last minute, sweat had been rapidly building up under his jacket. He wanted to take it off, to open his mouth, but decided to keep things as they were. Something had happened to Donald, and this had to be his first concern. If only the woman wasn't there.

"So how do you guys know each other?" She couldn't have sounded less interested if she'd tried.

Joseph answered: "We're neighbors."

"Oh. So, Donald, I'm thinking about dyeing my hair. I always liked red. I'm getting real sick of brown." She said it again, like a disappointment: "Brown."

Then Andie was standing over them all, and Joseph's sweat glands resumed their work: Donald was in no shape for this now.

"Hey, Donald."

Failing to catch Andie's eye, Joseph realized that it was up to her to recognize the change in Donald. He couldn't imagine how anyone wouldn't, but this Stacy woman certainly seemed unconcerned. Then again, Joseph really had no idea if Andie was capable of seeing the change in Donald either, and the thought scandalized him. He barely knew any of these people at all; how could he expect to deflect the impending drama?

Surprise, then delight momentarily covered Donald's pained distraction. "Andie! What are you doing here? Sit down!"

Andie hesitated for a moment; she knew something wasn't right.

"This is Stacy. Stacy, Andie."

"Hey."

"Nice to meet you. Listen, I can't stay long." Andie exchanged a laden look with Joseph, and Donald watched them both, clouding back up.

"I don't mean to be rude, but I was hoping I could speak with you alone for a couple of minutes. Just for a couple of minutes."

A week ago, Joseph was opening cans of soup and sleeping in the middle of the day. He'd almost stopped believing the local newscasts: the wins, the escapes, the rampages. Now, he was about to order a burger with Swiss cheese, and a pretty, odd girl with frankly great tits was shooting him meaningful glances.

He was still a man.

Donald ducked his head and spread his hands on the table. "Okay. Why don't we—"

"Just over there. Sorry."

When the two of them rose, Joseph felt the scene's axis go with them. And he was stuck with its polar opposite in the middle of some dark, depressing bar.

"So you guys are neighbors. What's it like living in the same neighborhood? Because working with him was insane."

"Oh, you two worked together?"

"Yeah, up until yesterday, when he just decided to get up and leave in the middle of the day. Our boss can put up with a lot of stuff, but Donald's just too much."

Donald had gotten fired because of Joseph.

Across the room, Donald was looking worse and worse, his conversation with Andie intense already.

"Tell me, is it that Donald's too much or that the rest of us are just not enough?"

She snorted at this. "What?! I don't know about you, but there's nothing wrong with me. And there's definitely something wrong with him."

Joseph was having a taste of the frenzy that Donald must have had to manage on a daily basis. All at the same time, he found: his respect for Donald decreasing because of this stupid Stacy woman; his guilt building because of Andie and Donald's firing; and his adrenaline levels rising, a surprisingly welcome thrill. Joseph was up to his neck.

He inspected Stacy for a response to the kaleidoscope of emotions that must have been playing across his face, but she just sucked on her straw.

"Anyway, I promised him that I'd set his little party up here. I owe him a few favors, I guess, and he's not that bad. Are you coming to that thing?"

"I think so."

Stacy looked back impatiently at Donald and Andie and then moved along the vinyl of her seat to escape.

"I'm not."

*   *   *

Joseph's adrenaline won out.

It was riveting just to trail someone else through a supermarket, to be empty of intent and a list of pressing, menial goals. As he watched the snow falling outside the window in Pathmark, Joseph simply experienced the heat and movement of the other shoppers. The colors and shapes of the dairy products they walked past repeated and altered, altered and repeated. For the first time in his life, he noticed their patterns formed waves of sensory information, if he didn't focus on any one container.

He wondered how many total hours of his life he'd spent, stationary in front of the dairy aisle, studying individual containers. Joseph wanted to arrange every dairy product he'd ever bought into a display that pleased the eye with its rhythms and contrasts, starving each one of its history and mundanity.

He hadn't asked for any of this nor done anything wrong himself, really, so guilt about his relationship with Donald was illogical. And as for respect, he'd just have to let that work itself out. But eventually, Joseph would have to get to the bottom of what had happened to Donald and was affecting him so profoundly.

A memory arose: the girl one block over, Nicolette, after she'd been attacked by some man. Raped. Afterwards, when he'd talk to her, she would giggle, a sound so close to crying that Joseph had avoided her ever since.

Donald was walking ahead of him, quickly, but not quickly enough to explain the sheen on the surface of his skin.

"I wonder why flowers come in so many different colors. Did you ever wonder?" Joseph had become used to his friend keeping his eyes on the ground in public, but now a bead of sweat had formed at the tip of his nose, three days before January and in the middle of the freezer section.

"Donald, do you want to take off your coat?"

Donald stopped and turned to Joseph. His gentle grin rose with his gaze, as he carefully followed the trail of Joseph's body up to his eyes.

But then his attention veered to a woman who passed quite close to Joseph, and he seemed momentarily troubled. "There are billions of dandelions, and they're all exactly the same color."

Joseph chuckled. "Dandelions. Only you would think of a weed first. I was thinking of roses and lilies."

"But every dandelion is beautiful, too, right?"

The woman was a short, stout older lady with earrings that dragged her earlobes toward the earth and a coat that still smelled of mothballs.

"If you say so." Then: "I suppose so. You're right."

"What's that?"

Joseph looked down at the red and white container in his hand.

"Greek yoghurt. I've never had it before."

"Greek yoghurt."

"Speaking of food, why don't we pick something up for you while we're here? We could get something that wouldn't be so tough on your stomach."

"Yeah, those wings were pretty…"

As Donald's thoughts trailed into oblivion, Joseph became aware that they were holding up the aisle, always a primary worry of his when shopping.

But this time, he had something else that came first. This time, he had a priority that made the ten seconds at the supermarket he'd always saved others, with his careful cart handling and rushed grabs, seem as trivial as most everything else a lonely person does.

Donald seemed to be struggling with what to say next, his mouth working wordlessly. The glares eventually became too much for Joseph, so he nodded pleasantly toward the back of the store, satisfied that he had expanded his own comfort zone, and Donald moved on.

For the rest of his life, Joseph would often replay moments he'd shared with Donald. In fact, just before the aneurism, he would be painting a cathedral and the many cars marching along its buttresses, each a different shape and hue. His mind would pass back to Pathmark and the particular combination of dairy products there and how he'd never let Donald finish what he'd wanted to say in the freezer aisle. Then Joseph would have an odd and final sensation of actually tasting and smelling his thoughts, which he would also feel between his eyes. Roaming, warm, colored pebbles.

Joseph remained seated while his friend picked up his prescription. He did wonder what the drugs were for, but wondering didn't mean that he really wanted to know. Then, only later in line to pay for his yoghurt, did Joseph test the waters.

"So that Andie's quite a gal."

"She is."

"You know that I'm just—I suppose I shouldn't say 'just playing along,' but there's an element of truth to that. I guess I don't need to tell *you* that, though."

Donald shrugged good-naturedly, but it looked more of a trial for him than usual.

"Still, you know, don't you, that she's like you are to me. I'm seventy, Donald. There are increasingly less and less opportunities. I can feel them shrinking and it's worse than death."

Donald's face cracked into empathetic horror, this time without any tug of self-consciousness. "Joseph, I wanted you two to meet."

"She said there wasn't much between you two, now. But I suppose that's just on her side."

Donald fondled a pack of Juicyfruit vaguely. "It's only ever on the other person's side."

"I don't know how you stand it. People like me."

"It's funny. I used to wonder how other people could stand *not* feeling what I'm feeling. *Not* feeling." He put the gum back on the shelf, but kept his eyes trained on it, and the rest of the impulse purchases strategically lined up and offered on either side of the two men fell away for Joseph, too.

"Donald, you seem, I don't know, is something bothering you? More than usual?"

Donald swung his body toward Joseph. "How do I seem?"

"Well, for a start, to be honest, you've been looking increasingly ill. And today, you seem almost, not angry, exactly, but as if there's something weighing on your mind."

Whatever hard-packed notion that had lodged itself behind Donald's pleasant and accommodating aura momentarily dissipated, and his eyes moistened. He reached for Joseph's arm before correcting himself. "I was right about you, Joseph. I knew you'd understand me, and I was right."

"Sir?" The cashier smiled without humor and stared at Donald's chest. If she'd looked up, she would have found him doing the same thing to her.

"Sorry."

Joseph handed the cashier his yoghurt and then the pack of Juicyfruit, which he imagined felt still warm from Donald's touch, although it couldn't be true.

Then Donald hissed between his teeth. "Oh, no! Oh, god!"

"What is it, Donald?"

"I forgot—I don't believe this! I forgot to—what time is it?" He consulted his cell phone. "Oh, god! I completely forgot someone!" Donald had raised his head in his distress and was now freely looking around at the other patrons, murmuring wildly.

"Can you call to reschedule?"

"No! No, she doesn't have a cell phone. Oh, this is bad. I never do this. I never forget." But Donald's voice had disconnected with his frustration and now floated off into the general din of the checkout lines.

"I'm sorry, Donald." This could be something else that Joseph might find himself feeling guilty about, later.

Donald fixed his eyes on the little old woman who had attracted his attention earlier in the freezer aisle. She fussed with her square, shiny vinyl purse a few lanes away. The people behind her looked upset; evidently, she had been digging for a while. The shopper nearest her, a middle-aged lady in a gray, leather jacket, rolled her eyes and delivered a piece of her mind as she leaned over the young child strapped to her shopping cart. The little girl looked up at her mother with the frown of concentration specific to toddlers. Joseph noted the exact same frown on Donald's face now.

"Donald? We can go."

Donald nodded absently, and a moment passed before he moved toward the exit with Joseph at his side.

"Or if you want to, uhh… Talk to that lady—"

"No." It was a declaration that seemed to surprise Donald, and he looked back at the old woman quizzically.

For some reason, it wasn't until they hit the moist, cold air and Joseph looked up at yet another, pink, darkening sky shedding its precipitation across Northern New Jersey that he realized that the only thing the two of them had picked up for Donald to eat was a thin pack of gum.

*   *   *

Joseph should have been glad, then, that they were entering the airlock of a restaurant, as the cold, heavy gust from the evening mixed with the fried, disinfected air blasting out from the kitchen. But a terrified woman awkwardly grasping a boy ran past them and out into the snow. The boy looked to be around eight, his face bright red and covered with tears, his screams momentarily slowing the routine bustle behind him in a wake of dismay. Joseph's immediate thought: malevolent omen.

After a delayed processing, Donald ran out after the woman, and Joseph watched as he approached their car and signaled to them through their windshield that he was ready, willing and able to be of service. The woman waved her dismissive thanks, nearly rammed into a car leaving the parking lot, and flew off into the gathering slush and headlights.

Donald dragged himself back toward the restaurant, his breath shorter and more visible.

"There probably wasn't much you could've done there."

"But what happened?!"

Joseph fought back a sting of annoyance by reminding himself that his friend's baffled concern was nothing like that of the people in the restaurant. But then he found himself annoyed with them, their attention so easily redirected back to their sloppy burgers and cell-phone whining. He hadn't been in one of these fluorescent places in years but found that they'd changed very little, which only made him all the more irritated by the customers' continued participation in such a rape of the senses.

But Donald was looking more lost by the moment, so Joseph put aside his encrusted disgust with the human race.

"Don't worry about them; I'm sure he'll be fine. Gosh, I haven't eaten in a Burger King in years."

Bernadette Bentley watched her bus glide off to school without her on a muddy, spring day. The driver was Negro, too, and she couldn't help but feel that he hadn't waited for her because of her dress, which wasn't really that short, although it had big, silver paisleys on it, and because he somehow could tell that she was humming a new tune that her mother didn't seem to like: Lalena, by Donovan. Even though he could never have told.

Bernadette knew that after she was done with school and on her own, the bus driver and her mother could never take the song away from her, so she told herself not to mind and that this was proof she would be powerful some day. A neighbor stopped his car and gave her a ride to school not five minutes later, and it was almost the cosmos agreeing with her.

Then in 1994, while frying bologna for her grandson in Highpoint, North Carolina, Bernadette found a strange phrase from the song, "that's your lot in life," float up into her consciousness. It was only then that she realized that spring morning with the kite wind was the last time she ever wholly believed in a story she made up for herself.

As they chose a table in the dining area, Joseph told himself he could ride out another attack of fatigue, brought on this time by the hard chairs that made him feel his bones and by Donald, who stared back into the kitchen, blinking like a beaten dog.

Joseph's adrenaline was wearing low. "Is she still here?"

"I don't see her. How could I do something like this to Lourdes? Now I can't tell her where the party is." Donald rubbed his eyes, which were welling up. "She doesn't deserve this."

"Donald, I have to ask you: who *does* deserve this?"

Taking a deep, uneven breath, he considered his response. "I just mean that she'd never do this to me."

"How do you know?"

Donald was pulled momentarily out of his misery, and he thought about the question carefully. "She's always been wonderful to me."

"Okay. So what happened today that made you forget about her?"

Donald nodded as his thumb ran along the edge of the table, an agreement to the question's validity. "Do you see other people as if they're just things? Organisms? Just creatures moving around?"

"Well, we are. Organisms."

"But what about all the differences?"

"Differences." Joseph looked around the dining room. There didn't appear to be anything even remotely special about any of the patrons there. Some sheep had spots, some didn't. "I don't know. Maybe they're not *organisms*. Just other people. But you know by now, surely, that it's the only way the rest of us can make it through life. We wouldn't get anything done if we were all like you."

"But why do you need to get anything done?"

"God, I don't know." The sensory overload of the last few days was making Joseph feel scattered. He had to stretch to reach thoughts. "But why now? This can't be a conversation you're having for the first time."

Sighing, Donald shrugged. "When you love someone, sometimes it's hard to really believe something about them, even if you thought you understood."

"But today you understand, for some reason. About the rest of us. That we see each other as organisms."

"And it's, you know." The tears reappeared, and Donald's voice rose. "It's tough. I still *feel* the same, but knowing that about people makes it harder to... I don't know."

"What a roller-coaster ride you're on."

Donald chuckled, which forced some liquid out his nose. He quickly grabbed a napkin. "I'm sorry."

"For god's sake, don't apologize to me. Don't ever apologize to me. Or any of us. We certainly don't deserve it."

The snow was coming down much heavier and quicker on the other side of the plate glass. It conspired with the violet night to provide a kind of psychological insulation to the space, and Joseph imagined it padding homes and businesses from each other all over New Jersey, each place more separate and autonomous until the air became transparent again.

But he had to concentrate on the problem at hand. They were among a group of people brought together by time and space to this particular spot. They had to share other things.

"Maybe we do it, Donald, because we don't know any better. We haven't learned. Not because we can't or don't want to. Does that help?"

This question staunched the flow. Donald wiped his eyes and stared down at his chicken salad. "It definitely helps that you said it."

Joseph wasn't satisfied. A few feet away, a man with thick, black eyebrows and skin as pale as if it had been drained of its blood was reading a comic book. He wore much gold jewelry at his neck, wrists and knuckles, and Joseph could imagine absolutely no reason to ever appreciate him as anything more than a fellow living thing.

Embracing the moment, Joseph lifted up his sore body and approached the man.

"Excuse me, sir?"

The man looked up, politely blinking at the disturbance. "Yes?"

"I'm sorry to bother you, but is that RoboWars you're reading?"

The man looked back at the cover, and Joseph fought down his customary irritation with anyone who'd actually have to revisit the title of the book he was reading to answer such a question. But then he wondered if this uncharitable reaction wasn't just what was troubling Donald about other people, so he suppressed it, taking a deep breath of the air they were all breathing.

"Yeah. Volume two." The man had a Middle-Eastern accent.

"I'm sorry to bother you like this, but I'm thinking of buying one of those for a friend, and I just don't know if it's worth it."

"Eeehhmm, yeah. I think so."

"Really?"

"Yeah."

Now it was Joseph's turn to look at the comic while his brain grappled with itself.

"Is there a comic that's better, maybe?" Once again, Joseph swallowed his disdain for the situation, for the man. It really was a law: strangers were guilty until proven innocent. Or perhaps not guilty, but valueless. He hadn't always been this way, but Joseph couldn't move far enough into the past to pinpoint the moment the scales shifted. At some point, he became convinced that the majority of his fellow earthlings were bores or unkind or cursed with flat personalities. For him, the numbers were now simply against the human race. Donald was right.

"I don't know. This is my daughter's. I just grabbed something to read when I came over here. You know, I don't like sitting alone in a restaurant with nothing, you know, to read or to do. And she likes to talk about her comics."

Joseph should have been encouraged, chastened: the man had glanced back at the comic because he wasn't familiar with it, not because he was an idiot. And it was a favor for his daughter. But all Joseph could do was look at the man's hairy fingers, which reminded him of an old sergeant of his who'd repeated himself, convinced that no one could ever, ever comprehend his simple commands the first time around. Joseph searched his memories for a fond association with hairy knuckles and came up wanting.

But Donald was within earshot.

"Your daughter likes to read comic books? That's unusual, isn't it?"

"I don't know. She likes the computer games, too. She's only thirteen."

The man closed the comic book without marking the page, and Joseph stared at it, a dull grin on his face.

"Oh. Thirteen. So she's what, in the eighth grade?"

"Ninth. She skipped a grade, actually. She's very smart. She takes after her mother." The man gestured toward the window. "I only drive a cab."

Joseph's burger was beginning to turn over in his gut. "But that must be very interesting."

"Sometimes. Some of the people. I had a lady who practiced, what do you call it, an aria for a performance a few weeks ago. She asked first, though. I don't know opera."

"Me, neither. Well, I'm sorry to bother you. I'll let you get back to your dinner."

The man looked down at the flattened bun and the morsel of processed fish left hanging inside it. "Okay. Bye."

"Bye."

After carefully inspecting Joseph's face when he returned, Donald looked quickly away and out onto the crawling, careful traffic illuminating the heavy wads of snow drifting down onto the street.

Joseph dropped his voice. "Donald. I don't know what to tell you. He's not an organism, anymore."

"A woman sung opera to him in his back seat, Joseph."

"And hundreds of people didn't. They just sat there."

"But they're beautiful in other ways. In ways that maybe only they know."

Joseph continued to find things coming out of his mouth that he knew were the wrong things. "Probably. But not all of them. Some of them don't do anything for anyone." He had to correct course. "Look, just because I don't like the guy doesn't mean that I dislike him."

Donald turned back to Joseph and leaned toward him. "It doesn't?"

"No." He lowered his voice to a hoarse whisper. "And I certainly don't want to do the man any harm. Look, we're like ants. We just do our jobs, cross paths once in a while."

"Is that really what you think?" Donald's expression flared up in the kind of horror borne of pity.

Joseph deflated; the day had been too much for him. "I don't know what I think, anymore."

"Ants." Donald stared at the man, who had returned to the comic. "Do you really feel like an ant?"

"I don't know. Go talk to him."

"I don't need to."

Joseph could see the clash of reactions in Donald's eyes as he inspected the man. Underneath it all, as always, was love, but there were other things there besides the caution. It was something new, almost disdain, and Joseph marveled how he could manage so many conflicting emotions, a marionette with a dozen enemy puppeteers.

"Donald, prove that I'm wrong."

"But, Joseph, I can only really prove it about myself. And that's exactly what I don't want to do."

Joseph was only dimly beginning to understand the issue at the center of Donald's anguish, but he knew that he had failed at something essential. He could sense it in the way Donald extracted himself from his squeaking, steel chair and held his salad out. He'd barely touched it. "Do you want to take this home?"

"That's all right." Had the green substance in the center of the black plastic really ever come into contact with the earth? Joseph had the urge to take the salad from his friend and fling it across a furrowed field. To get it back to where it belonged, its real home, and out of this place of rigid, clean, unappetizing surfaces.

"Hold on a minute."

Joseph approached the counter. An older, black lady with a kind, round face stood at the register, inspecting a receipt. He didn't stop to plan; planning would only make him awkward and his story, whatever it was going to be, stilted.

"Welcome to Burger King. May I take your order?"

"How are you?"

"Just fine. How are you?"

"Fine. Actually, I was wondering if you might be able to do me a great favor. It's an awful lot to ask."

"Well, I guess I can certainly try."

"You know Lourdes. She works here."

The woman lit up. "Of course, I do! She's just wonderful."

"My friend over there, the guy in the puffy jacket? He, well, he owes her a bit of money, you see, and he was supposed to get it to her today."

The woman distanced herself a bit from the conversation now, although she remained still, polite. "All right."

"He feels just awful, and I know you can't give out people's addresses or numbers, but if you're not too busy, maybe you could give her a call to let her know that Donald's here?"

The lady searched through her interpretation of the policies and procedures of Burger King. "Well, I don't know. I would need to speak with Ken, our manager."

"Well, you see, the thing is—" Joseph surreptitiously looked around the dining room. "I think that neither one of them wants too many people to know about this." She remained closed, unconvinced. "I just, I don't know—and maybe I'm wrong—but you just seem to me like the kind of person who would help us. He thinks I should have kept my mouth shut, but I don't know. You just seemed like you would help."

In truth, she did look the kind of person who would help, the kind of person who would bend rules and take the consequences in heaven. But she also needed this job.

"I'm sure Ken will say it's all right. Hold on just a minute."

Passing into the white bowels of the kitchen, she returned with a bald, middle-aged man with a moustache who looked like he'd been beaten down once too often to rise to any occasion.

This might be more difficult than Joseph originally thought. He hated to do it, but he bowed his head slightly, something that seemed to make non-Asians feel a little less threatened.

"Sir, I'm sorry, but we can't contact employees for customers."

"That makes perfect sense." Joseph glanced over at Donald, who had turned his back on the scene and was watching it in the reflection of the window, slouched over, his face blurred by the barrage of the snowflakes.

"It's just that my friend was in here a few days ago, and he forgot his wallet, and Lourdes was nice enough to pay for his lunch."

"He can leave the money with us. I've got envelopes in my office, and I'll be sure to give it to her when she's in next week."

"That's very thoughtful of you, but…" Joseph turned back to Donald to avoid Ken's eyes. Was Donald falling for Ken, too? That truly would bring Donald's sanity—and by association now, Joseph's too—into question. But he'd said *everyone*. Everyone. Which had to include Ken.

Joseph was on the verge of giving up the whole thing.

"Actually, my friend really wanted to give it to her himself because, well, I know he doesn't want me to say, but he's going into the hospital tomorrow, and it's… This is just really important to him, finishing up loose ends."

Now Joseph stared meaningfully at Ken, who looked over at Donald critically and then swiftly turned on his heels. "I shouldn't be calling her. I can get into a lot of trouble."

A moment later, he returned with an address, and Joseph was forced to once again question whether maybe Donald wasn't right about people, after all was said and done.

*　　*　　*

The snow was beginning to accumulate on the front steps of Lourdes's apartment building. It was the same snow that was falling on Montclair, but in Newark, it looked almost mistaken to Joseph. Sorry for the contrast it provided.

Joseph remembered when Lourdes's building would've been considered an okay place, but he'd been around long enough to see the tide wash 'okay' farther and farther out, and in fact, his own family had been dragged out with it, too, into the pines and lawns.

It was surprising to find that he was still somehow shocked by one of Donald's relationships, or at least his attraction. After all, this one looked like it made the most sense; from a distance, Lourdes appeared to smile kindly, beaming with a devotion that he'd yet to see in any of the other individuals Donald had introduced him to over the past three days. But he also recognized in himself what Donald had somehow only lately become aware of in others: Joseph's immediate impression of Lourdes was of a short, dumpy, unattractive, poorly dressed woman in her late fifties. What saints did he pass in the street?

Having torn his eyes off of Donald's most interesting relationship yet, Joseph watched the traffic on McCarter in an effort to provide the woman with a little privacy. The last thing Donald was concerned with was discretion, and in fact, Joseph had had to turn down his friend's invitation to come up and meet Lourdes. But it had been more than that. From everything Donald had said about her, it was clear he was hoping she would disprove his theory about organisms with Joseph. While her kindness surely included giving strangers the benefit of the doubt, Donald needed more than that from her now, and Joseph didn't want to provide him with another opportunity for wrenching disappointment. It was cold and late and the thought of Donald watching the poor woman for any sign of an immediate and profound appreciation of some old man she'd just met was just too much to deal with. No sane person behaved that way.

So Joseph wasn't moving from the car.

The snowfall made the neighborhood feel safer, somehow. Something more important, more distracting was happening than everyday human melodrama, thanks to the storm. Still, Joseph had locked the car's doors the second Donald slammed his shut, and he understandably gasped when a face appeared at his window.

"She isn't mad at me."

After regaining his breath, Joseph rolled down the window, and Donald dropped to kneel near him.

"You see? Anyone who's as nice as you described couldn't be."

Donald stared at the snow hitting the windshield, and Joseph joined him. There was an intermediate stage from flake to droplet, dots of wet slush threading a path downward, and Joseph pondered why a term for this particular state of precipitation had never been developed, why English chose to bless certain concepts with a single word, while others had to be awkwardly aimed for with a shotgun spray of unsatisfactory reachings.

So much of Donald's experience with life must have been just as frustrating: never being able to rely on communication, desperately attempting to convey thoughts and feelings that would never completely translate. The little gaps might as well have been canyons.

"Say, Donald, what exactly did someone say to you about the rest of us? Our failure to see the beauty in others."

Donald continued to watch the little transformations take place on the windshield, even as they proceeded on his face and neck. Joseph noticed his own neck was unusually relaxed, and he leaned back against the headrest. There must have been some reason that Donald wasn't getting into the car, but he had absolutely no energy to find out what it was.

"I've always thought that I was dumber than everybody else. Or more screwed-up."

"No one's ever said that to you, surely."

"Oh, some people have. And some people get mad at me for believing it, but it always kind of explained everything."

"And now, you're worried that you're smarter than everyone else."

Donald turned to Joseph, but his thoughts distracted him so completely that Joseph could've been looking at a hollow mannequin.

"No, not *that.*"

An especially large slushy wad slowed down before it came to rest on a windshield wiper. It was clearly going to take a lot longer than the others to melt and pass away into the bowels of the engine compartment.

"Then what is it that's bothering you?"

Donald laid his head against his arm, which was resting on the door.

"Gosh, I didn't realize that I was so tired."

Donald was shivering and rivulets were running down his neck.

"Donald, why don't you let me drive you home?"

"Donald?"

Lourdes had changed her clothes. She was standing only a few feet away from the car, a plastic bag in each hand. Her coat was now funereal, a twenty-year-old black, and her slacks a cheap rayon.

Joseph's heart sank.

"Oh, Lourdes! I'm just—" Donald looked like he was going to pass out.

"Why don't we get you into my seat, and then I'll just drive you home."

Lourdes deftly helped Joseph get Donald into the passenger seat. "What happened?"

"He's tired. Maybe he has a cold. He's been so busy today."

When she looked up at Joseph, he saw the fear in her eyes, the fear that should have been in everyone's eyes who knew Donald that day. "He has?"

How could he tell her that there was something else to fear, too?

And then: "Oh. Lourdes, this is Joseph. Joseph, Lourdes." Donald watched Lourdes as she politely shook Joseph's hand.

"How are you?"

Joseph sensed Donald's eyes slip off of her, troubled, and refocus on his reaction. The wrinkles bunched up on Joseph's cheeks as he pushed the edges of his mouth up. "What a pleasure to meet you, Lourdes." But his voice wavered falsely, and he hated himself for it.

All this was made especially absurd because tears were forming in her eyes; the tension of the introduction hadn't been lost on Lourdes, just its cause, and she looked from Donald to Joseph confused, pained.

Donald obscured his face from her in the dark interior of the car, and Lourdes moved in toward him. "You should go home, Donald. We can talk later. Oh—I don't know—I made brownies and thought—"

Then Joseph was holding the two bags, furious with himself for immediately noticing crusty, black edges. "That's very kind of you."

Her eyes begged Joseph, but he looked away, too.

"Lourdes, my party on Sunday. Rascal's, you know the place?"

"Yes. You should go and get some rest now. Please."

Lourdes took Donald's hand, sheltering it, at least, from the blizzard.

"Joseph will be there."

"Okay."

"At the party."

Looking up into the snowfall, she seemed to find something. "Angels have hearts for everyone, Donald."

"I'm not an angel."

"Then there are no angels." Lourdes shook her head at Joseph and backed into obscurity, her voice the last link. "I'm sorry. Go, go!"

It had been such a long night. Joseph joined Donald, moving the seat, adjusting the mirrors. He was completely overwhelmed now and refused to dip into the emotional maelstrom because the weather was getting worse and the day had been so much work and he'd run out of the energy necessary to offer even the simplest, considered response.

So he merely said: "Boy, it sure is coming down now. I'm going to take my time here. I'm really going to have to concentrate."

"It is getting worse. Do you mind if I turn up the heater?"

"Be my guest."

"I've dragged you all over the place today. I'm sorry about that." Donald's words were slurring together now.

"Oh, that's fine. But I am getting a little tired, myself."

"It's beautiful, though, isn't it?" Donald hugged himself as he watched a snow-plow truck make its way down a side street. "Do you think Lourdes's right? That there are no angels?"

Joseph sighed. He'd learned this lesson in childhood, the dark slope downward that always waited on the other side of excitement. Only now he had the old man's duty of selfless sagacity, even if his bones ached and the snow made his eyes water and refocus. But he had no idea what to say in Lourdes's defense and spent a good minute squinting at the road, making worried noises at intersections and other cars.

The light pressure on his crotch saved him. "Donald, the brownies. She handed me *two* bags. See?" Joseph tore his hand, which had clawed up, off the wheel just long enough to hold up both. "Two bags. She'd never even met me before."

Donald took the bags and placed them on his own lap, moving them around under the plastic. Finally, he opened one and took a square out, which was suitably crumby and gummy. There appeared to be M&Ms lurking around the surface.

Joseph didn't have to look at Donald to know that he was crying again. He felt the drive stretch out before them, longer and longer, the stress mounting from the road conditions, from Donald's needs, from the late hour. He was still so far from home.

Donald took a bite.

"How is it?"

"Okay."

"So how come you can forgive almost anything else—and I know because I've seen you do it—but you can't get past this?"

It was an effort for Donald to swallow.

"Well, I've been mad, and I've been hurt, and I've been stupid. So I can understand what that's like."

A red light suddenly came upon them, and the car fishtailed a bit before coming to a stop.

"Jesus!" Joseph was sweating again. "I'm just going to turn this down. I'm sorry." As he reached out to the heater, its scalding air blew up his sleeve. "So you can understand all that, but you honestly can't understand feeling nothing?"

Sirens were suddenly upon them, although from what direction, Joseph wasn't sure. He also wasn't completely sure where the curb was, so he waited until a parked car made itself known, and he pulled up behind it. The screaming, always disturbing to Joseph, was very different now because the vehicles were approaching so slowly. Something that ordinarily meant swift-moving danger was now the most frustrated sound Joseph had ever heard, and he couldn't help but imagine the emergency on the other end: young kids waiting and choking on smoke, or an older person convulsing in a corner somewhere while her husband split his impotent time between staring at her in horror and pleading out the window at the sweeping, silent weather.

It seemed as if the emergency vehicles were right on top of them, but there wasn't even so much as a pale tint of red or blue reflected in the denseness.

Then the screeching stopped.

"Oh, no. We should see if we can help."

Joseph found himself chuckling at this statement, and he took advantage of this relaxing, momentary surrender to lay his head on the steering wheel. "Donald, look at us: you can't even walk straight, and I'm sweating bullets, here, some frail old man trying to get us home through all this! They should be helping us."

Donald's chest jiggled, but Joseph was disappointed to notice that it was a cough. Still, he grinned as he wiped his eyes. "See, I knew it."

"Knew what?"

"That I should've brought you along." He lifted the brownies. "Two bags. Two bags!"

Even though he'd said this solely for Joseph's benefit, it was something. Joseph pulled back out onto the deserted street, the steering wheel making only broad suggestions to the tires.

*   *   *

Donald didn't bother to watch either one of them when he introduced them; he just sat at the table, defeated. By now Joseph recognized that everything was probably in their voices, anyway.

He was desperate to sit down—to lie down—but at home. The warm scent of alien spices and the orange glow of the room allowed him to feel just how tired he was. He wouldn't be able to carry on any kind of conversation, and this woman wasn't going to let him go easily. He could sense it as she gripped his hand, staring meaningfully into his eyes.

She wasn't all that much younger than he was, but just as Joseph had turned into his father thirty years before he'd needed to, this woman had turned into her daughter thirty years too late. It was a discrepancy that Joseph knew from experience would work in his favor in the relationship, but not hers. People like the both of them could spot each other, just as two beetles in the Amazon would pass each other with absolutely no move to mate or fight, immediately aware that the other was an entirely different species. Joseph experienced a similar kind of disconnect now, although where his response to her was wary blankness, Marjorie's assessment of him was generated entirely by a list of assumptions.

Of course, some people might seem as if they were appreciating a stranger if they took one look and believed they already knew all there was to know about him. Donald must have understood this, because he seemed to grow smaller, cave in on himself in his corner of the room.

And then she took Joseph's bag of brownies from him. Lourdes's brownies.

"How sweet of you."

He glanced at Donald. It was no more than irritating to Joseph, but he could see that Marjorie's complete misjudgment of him was the last thing Donald needed to witness.

"Please, sit down. Would either of you like some coffee or tea? Maybe something stronger?"

"Thanks, but I really should be getting home."

"Oh, good. So you drove your car here."

Who was this woman? "Actually, I drove Donald's." He glanced at Donald, relieved the change that had taken place in him that day was masked partially by his fatigue. Maybe Joseph would get out of their house without hearing Donald explain and apologize.

But this woman hadn't even so much as glanced at Donald since they'd arrived, so either he looked like hell an awful lot or her priorities were not in the right order.

"But I just live up the street a few blocks. I'll walk."

"Oh no, we couldn't let you go out into that! It's officially a blizzard. I mean, that's how you and Donald met, isn't it? Didn't you slip on the side of the road?"

The patronizing had begun earlier than Joseph expected. "I appreciate it, but I'll be fine."

"How long have you lived in the neighborhood?"

"Oh. Forty years. Something like that." He pulled his glove on, certainly a plain enough gesture of departure.

"Forty years! You must have seen so many changes."

"I have. Well, it was a pleasure meeting you, Marjorie. "

"I'm coming with you, then. Please, it's the least that we can do."

"That's very kind of you, but I won't drag you out in this weather, too."

"No, hold on, I'll just get my coat."

She raced out of the kitchen, and Joseph felt his manhood being dismissed, his potency for dealing with life discounted. He'd been around a long time, and over the years, he'd discovered that this was simply what happened to old people. It was also true that each time it happened, his value eroded a little more and his reaction became a little more resigned, to the point that he couldn't even remember the last time he'd even bothered to object. Calmness made more sense, and behavior didn't really indicate self-worth, anyway.

But the events of the past few days had brought him back, had dredged up an old vitality that now had him reacting in a decidedly immature way. It was a laughable response, he knew, and much of it had to do with his exhaustion, but damn it, he wasn't going to let this woman walk him home like a little school girl.

Joseph turned to escape.

"She'll follow you." His head was still resting on the kitchen table, but Donald's eyes shone keenly.

Joseph paused as he caressed the door handle. "I just want to go to bed."

"I should've seen this coming." Donald flared up at himself through his exhaustion. "Do you want the brownies?"

"Not especially. No."

"So is anybody really even *aware* of anybody else?"

Joseph wondered if Donald's particular condition included really understanding how other people felt, if the empathy extended that far, because his expression almost seemed to say that he did. He seemed sorry for Joseph and the answer he had to give. "Eventually, I think."

There was the sound of a toilet flushing nearby.

"Wait a second. Watch what happens."

It was so unexpected that Joseph's bile completely drained away, and he found himself grateful again for Donald's ability to surprise him.

A tall, thin man emerged from the shadows of the hallway, his smile being the first thing Joseph saw. It was so wide that his molars were dry.

"You must be Joseph." When the man looked at him, quite a lot was seen. Joseph prayed that he, at least, was truly aware of Donald.

"And you must be Helmut."

A second later, Marjorie's heavy boots crunched as she returned to the kitchen.

"Hey, Marjorie, haven't you been coughing an awful lot today? Are you sure you want to go out in this?" Helmut's concern permeated the kitchen.

"It's just a couple of blocks."

"Oh, okay. Well, it was nice to meet you, Joseph. I hope to see you again. Maybe at Donald's party?"

For some reason, Joseph was disappointed. "I think so."

The party. He'd just somehow make up for all his failures then. He'd redeem himself there, and maybe the human race, too, if he could just develop a plausible response to Donald's dilemma. He owed the man that much, although he'd have to stay clear of him for a few days. Joseph could only solve one problem at a time, and any more wild stimuli certainly wouldn't help him at this point.

"Fantastic. Oh, you know what, Marjorie?" Helmut rubbed her shoulder as he passed the woman and left the room.

"What? Helmut? What's up?" She refocused on Joseph. "He's such a mystery, sometimes. Are you married, Joseph?"

"I was."

"Oh, is that right? Divorced or—"

Helmut returned, dressed for the weather, and threw Joseph a reassuring glance as he opened the back door. "Colleen called earlier,

Marjorie, and I couldn't speak with her. She really needs to talk to someone, and you're so much better at it than I am."

Helmut opened the door and Joseph quickly moved outside. "She really sounds bad, Marjorie."

Joseph was glad she didn't detect his relief as he passed out of the hot kitchen. "Pleasure meeting you, Marjorie." But he'd been a little too hasty, and he peaked around the corner of the door frame: "I'll talk to you later, Donald?"

Even though, at just this moment, Joseph understood much more about Donald than either one of his roommates, and he might've even been closer to him, Joseph was still highly uncomfortable when Donald got up and hugged him. Looking up at the stained ceiling, he counted until it was over, the silly thought passing through his mind that the whole scene could melt down into an orgy if he so much as loosened his belt buckle.

"I'll be right back, guys." Helmut closed the door on Marjorie and Donald, and Joseph was alone with him on the back porch.

The dark cold was a relief, but not the indistinct stairs that quickly disappeared into the storm. The last thing Joseph wanted was to slip and have to be carried back up into the apartment, everyone standing over him, concerned about his well-being.

"It's awfully nice of you to walk me home, but it's really not necessary." Joseph was aware of how weak he sounded.

"To be honest, I was going to use this opportunity to grab a smoke. No one likes me smoking at home."

Joseph was surprised to find that there was already a cigarette hanging from Helmut's mouth. "Oh. I see."

Helmut peered at the brightness of his home through the thick, weightless snow. "They can't see me, right? I'm a real outlaw, eh!" He cupped a lighter to his mouth. "I'm staying right here. Or I could come with you. I mean, would you mind that?"

"Yes, I would." This man perhaps put Joseph too much at ease.

But Helmut paused for a second, then choked out a hearty laugh, and Joseph decided that he could understand this one. He liked Helmut and looked forward to telling Donald how much so when he saw him next. In fact, Helmut could be the key to his argument disproving the idiotic supposition he'd made earlier that evening—and a hundred years ago—that human beings were nothing more than heartless ants. He'd felt positively about Helmut from the moment he laid eyes on him. Was that a form of love? And then, of course, there was Andie, too, although Joseph wasn't sure if she was the key to much.

The cars parked ten feet below them were getting vaguer now, and Joseph could feel the snow building on his shoulders in the short time he'd been pondering the situation. "That being said, I would appreciate it if you did join me."

"Oh, good, because I'd freeze to death just standing here. Which way are we going?"

As the men carefully navigated the stairs, Joseph vowed to repay some of his debts and develop an answer for his friend's suffering—at least until the next revelation concerning his fellow man visited itself upon Donald, and he was crushed slowly again under its weight.

ELIZABETH

THURSDAY

She couldn't believe what she was seeing. Some man was dancing on the deck. Her first thought was that it was a crazy homeless person, and she immediately wondered who it was she should call. Probably the police, but she didn't want him arrested, for god's sake, just moved or returned or whatever they did with crazy people, because she could tell that he wasn't dangerous.

Brad turned to look, too. He was disturbed by the man's behavior, though, not his presence, so Elizabeth walked to the French doors and stood out in what was left of the snow to make herself known.

The man looked ill, but when he noticed her, his face took on such a pleasant expression that Elizabeth immediately began to recalculate. He was waltzing, of all things, and faltered, dropping on his butt, but there was no sign of intoxication when he opened his mouth: "Sorry."

She wanted to laugh, but she wasn't quite that person, anymore, especially when Brad was around. And even though it was funny, it was also embarrassing and pathetic, too, so she went with those reactions and merely smiled with her mouth but not her eyes.

The man's eyes, on the other hand, were magnets, and she felt things being pulled from her before she looked away.

*   *   *

Elizabeth had a mass of black hair that she pushed onto the top of her head, exposing her funny pink ears, and the long twists of her neck, which Donald was staring at when she sat near him on the edge of the couch. She had a cherry cough drop in her mouth that repeatedly cracked against her teeth and many bracelets at each wrist that were tinkling slowly into knots.

"I can't believe he did that to you. Last month, at a party we had—a fiftieth anniversary party for his parents, right?—he tells his sister that she has bad breath. And there were, like, ten people within earshot."

"Does she?"

"Have bad breath? It's like rotten garbage, but no one ever says anything. So his father had to do a toast, which didn't come out too well, unfortunately, because he'd already done all of his toasts earlier in the evening, so it was just another one about having his family and friends together, which he'd already done when he thanked us for the party. And the only reason Frank gave the toast in the first place was to cover the awkward silence after Brad's comment. Can you believe that?"

A small laugh quivered out of Donald as he refocused on the ceiling. "I can believe that."

She was glad that she was putting him at ease with her stories, although he seemed a little too at ease now, his brown eyes melting into something almost like intimacy.

"I can't imagine what it must have been like working with him." Elizabeth picked a glass of water up from the nearby table and handed it to Donald. Already, she could understand why Brad had fired him: the man made him nervous. He was clearly some kind of loose cannon, a person with unusual sensibilities, a feeler rather than a thinker. Brad, meanwhile, was a feeler trying to think, and that had been funny for a while—for a few years, in fact. But not anymore. Elizabeth, on the other hand, was a thinker who liked feelers, which was probably why she had been so attracted to Brad in the first place: she recognized his true self in ways he still didn't. And that was also probably why he had initially been attracted to her. She got him better than his parents, who saw him predominantly as an occupation, and his friends, who mostly saw him as an easy touch. But now he shied away from her recognition and forced himself to think pretty much all the time, rather than what he was built to do, which was to feel. And this tedious fact, coupled with the loss of her primary role in the relationship as the recognizer, the appreciator, had been disastrous to it.

Still, there had been times he'd redeemed himself. When they'd gone to Fran and Joe's cabin last summer, Brad had skinny-dipped in the lake in the middle of the day, his white legs and back visible ten feet underwater, his paunch for an instant somehow a trophy. He could have been arrested.

At the time, the thrill had lasted them both for weeks, but then he started closing down even worse than before, and now, she couldn't tell if he was really still in there somewhere, or if he'd jumped into the lake bare-assed just to shut her up for a while. But didn't he know that she *wanted* to shut up?

Donald offered a shrug that was more energetic than she would have expected from someone who looked as drained, as fragile as he did. "I loved working with him. He was a great boss."

Something made her rise at this. "I'll be right back."

Brad was standing over the kitchen sink, watching water run down the drain.

"What are you doing?"

He turned to her, and Elizabeth finally, really looked at him. He seemed relieved, of all things, and Elizabeth noticed a tickle of hope buried under her confusion. Maybe this strange morning was the first sign that Brad was opening up, befriending peculiar, spirited people.

But he only asked how Donald was doing, and Elizabeth quickly closed down. He was the one who had changed; he had to make the first move.

"How could you leave him out there? Without a coat? Am I really that much of a bitch?"

"I don't know. I panicked."

"So I *am* that much of a bitch. Nice to know." She didn't want Donald to hear the harshness of her voice, so she moved right up to her husband, his eyes crossing when he looked into her face.

But Brad didn't have the balls to be honest about any of it.

"Well, I guess since I'm such a bitch, I should ask why, if he was the one that was smoking, why he doesn't smell like smoke, and you do."

"Well. We both were."

"But you felt like you had to blame him?" Feeling Donald's presence, feeling it drawing her back, she lowered her voice even further. "I *know* I'm not *that* bad." What in the hell was going on with these two?

Brad picked up the little air purifier by the coffee maker. "It's like I'm in prison in my own house, Elizabeth."

He wanted to continue talking about cigarettes. "I don't want to get into it. The kids are going to be coming down in a minute." And she left Brad slouching at the sink.

Donald's eyes were closed, but he opened them as soon as he was aware that Elizabeth was standing above him. He smiled extravagantly up at her, and it was at that point that she began to understand her husband's turmoil: Donald was open, enthusiastic, simple. It was terrifying. It was gratifying. It was something to feel, not know.

"I'm sorry if my husband gave you the impression that I would've actually killed you if I caught you smoking in the house, because I'm really not like that—except with him, because lung cancer runs in his family, and the kids, and he had asthma when he was younger. I would've asked you to do it on the deck, but I would've at least let you wear your coat." She shook her head toward the kitchen. "You look a little better, maybe?"

"Sure."

The absolute smile made her move back, find a chair. "The kids will be down in a second. They're running around collecting the recycling. So you two are friends? Because he never mentioned."

Donald shifted his whole body to face her. "Work friends. You know."

"I'm glad to hear it. So, right now—I don't know. Are you hitting on me or something?"

Donald hesitated, his mouth gaping as it twisted through several complicated thoughts.

"All right. You know what? Don't even answer that. You're probably just a very friendly guy, or maybe the lightheadedness or something. And I really am a monster if I'm asking guests in my own home things like that, only you are, aren't you, or maybe not hitting on me, but something, right?"

Then Brad was there, and Elizabeth moved farther away from Donald so that she could catch her breath. "So Donald seems like he's doing a bit better, Brad."

Brad was even more nervous. "Oh, great. Yeah, you know, I'm really sorry about all this, Donald." Then he pulled a cigarette out. "Sometimes I get a little crazy with this one!" And pointed it at her. "It's not her, though, it's—"

"What are you doing?" Elizabeth didn't want either of them to hear the annoyance in her voice, nor did she want them to think her smoking rule was silly.

Brad looked down at the cigarette in his hand and laughed. "You see what I'm saying? You see?!"

Being around them both was too much, and she turned to the stairs. "Kids?! We have to go. It was nice meeting you, Donald."

Brad would always, always want a cigarette, and she would always, always be telling him not to. Elizabeth quickly did some computations in her head. "Maybe next time we'll talk more about yoga."

Her eyes stuck to Donald a moment longer than might've appeared normal to Brad, had he been watching. He was probably too nervous and focused on his own problems to ask Donald anything about yoga when she was gone. And even if he did, Elizabeth gambled that Donald would cover. "You know, I'm at my class every weekday at ten at The New Day Studios. They've got some great instructors over there."

That was all. She gathered up the kids and didn't even bother looking into the living room on the way back out. It was up to Donald now.

FRIDAY

She hadn't expected it to happen so soon, and she certainly hadn't expected him to figure out where she was, considering the blizzard had turned everything upside-down. At first, Elizabeth was actually a bit disappointed because she'd been looking forward to a week or two of anticipation, of possibility, before the actual reality of the situation changed it all into something else: disappointment in him if nothing happened, disappointment in herself if it did.

It was dark inside the café, and everyone's attention just naturally drifted to the huge plate-glass windows that presented such a blinding, new snowscape. She'd immediately recognized his odd way of moving in the morning glare, in the street, and she turned away to pull the gum out of her mouth.

Elizabeth had no idea how to greet Donald, so she pretended that all of it was a happy accident. After all, people knew her, and maybe it was. But his stare was manic now, rather than gentle, his eyes ringed with purple like something hunted. It wasn't a coincidence, and she began to panic that she'd mistaken the intensity of the previous morning as infatuation, when it might have just been creepiness.

But she knew she was more perceptive than that. "Donald! How are you?!"

Taking the opportunity to hug him, she was dismayed to find that underneath all his clothing, he was bonier than she'd imagined, and his wracking cough wasn't part of the picture, either. Was this the way it was with other people? "You sound sick."

But there was a deep appreciation of her comment somewhere in there, fighting its way to the surface. Maybe he'd just had a bad night.

"You're right. I probably shouldn't be out in public. But I wanted to see if I could catch you."

Elizabeth smiled, but there was a young couple behind her who had started a conversation with her earlier; they probably considered it their right now to eavesdrop. She looked around the crowded room.

"Sure, sure. I'm still waiting for my drink, but why don't we get out of people's way?" As she led him to a cappuccino-stained table, she considered the best course of action to determine exactly what was going on with him.

But once they were seated, Elizabeth found herself without words or direction—slightly uncomfortable, but actually a nice change. She was always in charge of words and direction. And anyway, this was his show now. She could plainly sense that he needed something from her; let him ask, and then she would decide what to do.

The silence lengthened. People nearby glanced at them, the energy at their table unmistakable. Donald had begun to sweat and squirm in his seat, agitation expressing itself in every way but words.

Did she always have to be the one in charge? "So Brad's coming down with something, too, I think. Either a cold or the flu, but you can tell because it always starts with a sore throat with him. He's always so predictable, even when he's sick. Was he like that at work, too?"

Donald relaxed at the choice of subject. "I always knew I could count on him." But even this seemed to drown in other, darker thoughts.

She didn't want to work all morning trying to figure out what was the deal with this man, so dropping her voice below the clatter of her environment, she laid her cards on the table. "Well, you know, I know Brad, too, so I knew that something, let's just say 'odd,' was going on when you were over the house. And I know when he's telling the truth and when he's not and how to eventually get to the truth, and he told me the truth about you two."

Donald sat back in his chair, nodding. "The truth?"

"Yeah."

"What's the truth?"

She leaned into him and lowered her voice. "What, you mean you don't know?"

"Well, he might have a different truth than I do."

That could actually be the case; Brad's story was an odd one. She lowered her voice even further. "I guess as he's gotten older, he needs, I don't know, affection more. Apparently, he wasn't getting the kind he needed from me, so he goes to you. You know, saying that, I realize that I should be jealous of what you seem to give him, and actually I said that to him, said that I should be jealous, but he says that it's a completely different thing."

"Because I'm a guy?"

"And because it's not *physical* physical, just holding him. But women are different. Do you want it to be *physical* physical?"

"Elizabeth, I want it to be what he wants it to be. He's married."

"Hmmm. I believe that. I believe that."

Donald withdrew, the gears almost visibly turning. There was cinnamon scattered across the table, and Elizabeth wanted to tell him to be careful and not get any on his cuff, but he wasn't her husband, her responsibility. Nonetheless, as he emerged from his thoughts, more and more hopeful, she was glad because she felt a little responsible for it. Even through his pallor, he was beautiful when unbound.

Elizabeth laughed slowly. "What a weird thing! A situation! Because I'm here, now, too. I don't know what to think. So were you hitting on me yesterday?"

A young woman approached the table with a paper cup and set it in front of Elizabeth. "You couldn't hear, so I thought I'd bring it over."

Elizabeth touched the woman's arm. "Oh, thank you!"

"No problem. It's crazy today!"

The woman, energized by the challenges of the day, returned to the wad of people at the counter.

Donald stared at the drink, his voice suddenly saturated with expectations. "She seemed nice."

"She seemed very nice. I love being around people who love their job, you know, because it's something we've all got to do, and it's so depressing to think that someone spends their whole life doing something they absolutely hate. And so many of us are like that, it's just sad. But, yeah, she seemed happy. I don't know."

Apparently, she'd said the right thing: "I totally agree! That was a really nice thing about her. I bet she would be great to get to know better."

"Sure." Why were they talking about the waitress? "Anyway, what were we talking about?"

Donald sat up in his seat, and Elizabeth could only describe it as a joyful rise. She could tell, now, what he looked like as an eight-year-old, winning a blue ribbon, getting to a punch line. "So you were saying that Brad told you. What are your thoughts?"

"I guess I'm all right with it, weirdly enough. It's nice to think that he's happier. I mean, who cares who he hugs, as long as it floats his boat, and I guess yours, too. Right?"

Another incredibly naked, intense look from Donald: his soul was like an X-ray she could feel on her face. Nothing seemed crazy anymore about any of it, although she wasn't sure why.

"Exactly! Elizabeth, you're amazing. I was really hoping that you'd say that. In fact, I was beginning to wonder if anyone could say something like that. I'm so glad I saw your van."

"What do you mean? Like what?"

"I don't know nice, thoughtful. Generous to people. Even to people you don't know."

No one had ever applied that phrase to Elizabeth Markowitz, least of all herself. But the strange thing was, she wanted to be that for Donald now. He seemed to see things in her that she wasn't even sure existed, but maybe he was right. Why not be generous for him?

He was grinning now like a crazy person. "You know, to be honest, I've been going a little crazy because I had to see you—but Brad. I just didn't know how to do this."

Now Elizabeth shrunk. "What do you mean?"

"Well, I knew I could never do anything to hurt him, but I could feel such a connection with you. And I was totally right: you and I really see—"

"Wait a minute. What, do you think I told him about this? What was there to tell? I mean, I didn't know if I'd ever even see you again!"

Watching Donald deflate, his eyes scarring over, Elizabeth instinctively drew in her extremities. Something died.

"You've got to be kidding me! I didn't even know what was going on with you! What would you want me to say? There was nothing to say!"

He got up and turned in an effort to hide his tears, but keeping his voice steady was impossible. "No, no. That's true. Listen, I've got someone waiting for me."

It had been an unbelievable two minutes. She had been exposed to a kind of energy the likes of which she couldn't comprehend, and it had been lavished then snatched away. She'd never felt denser in her life. "What would I say?"

"I know. It's me. I'm sorry."

"You *are* crazy."

He left without looking at her again, and she could only stare into her latte, feeling the people around her and wondering if they would have understood what had just happened.

She had no idea how to feel, so she drank her coffee, replaying their meeting over and over. She was determined not to flee the scene, and anyway, she wasn't sure that she wanted to get back home very soon. Home to Brad.

Outside, Donald was talking to a man with long hair sitting in a car. Watching the pain on their faces, the dismay, Elizabeth knew that what she should've been feeling was relief. She'd nearly stepped into a new world where everything wasn't stuffed down, but rather fished out and exposed to the light, every second a melodrama.

Who knows how she would've dealt with it. She wasn't like that. But looking at the other people in the room, quiet, busy, excited about the blizzard, she knew that she needed something else in her life. The petty emptiness was destroying her.

And she felt her marriage drape back over her, slowly, accumulating. Brad had proposed to her in a bus station of all places, and she remembered again the smell of urine and how she'd promised herself at the time that she'd only ever let it be ironic.

ANDIE

Andie's new rule was to live near a highway, so she wasn't surprised to see Donald's car pulling up to her place ten minutes early. She knew he would sit in his car until exactly four, at which point he would consult his cell phone—the only chronometer he trusted—and come up. She knew that he was going to be jumpy because he'd know that she knew that he was waiting downstairs, but he'd never bring it up. Nor would she.

Sitting back down at her vanity, Andie suddenly realized how much she missed knowing things about people, which brought her immediately back to the kitchen she'd shared with the others for those months, the electrical smell around the refrigerator and the different patch of vinyl flooring under the fern in the corner. It was kind of a dump, but it was kind of a home. The ordinary, intimate knowledge that comes from a shared life had been so intense for her, right even though it was mostly wrong. She'd had to concentrate to know whose hand it was under that table, the discussions instigated by Marjorie but usually centered on Donald. Of course, the whole group seemed to her to be ultimately centered on Donald, even though Donald's focus on the other three was at least the energy equivalent of their regard for him.

She'd called it a "family" when she was in it, but now it was a "group."

When Andie found herself idly wondering if Donald would like this particular eye shadow, she stopped. Eight minutes to go, and it felt as if it were starting all over again, so she walked out to his car.

He jumped out as soon as he saw her, and she was relieved to see the same thick appendages, the same style-less sweater. More than relieved, she was happy. But happy was usually a trap, and she dropped her eyes to her feet.

When she had to look back, when she was right in front of him, Andie saw that he'd been worn down further.

"Donald."

*　　　*　　　*

Donald squinted into the setting sun, his sun visor sparing only his hair now. He was just as intense as he'd ever been, their time apart apparently of no consequence whatsoever. But Andie had gone through a lot during their separation, had grown, and she found herself resenting the fact that he seemed to think that he still understood her absolutely.

"You look so great, Andie. I want to make love with you right now, and I say that because I can, with you."

"You can say that to Marjorie and Helmut."

"I don't have to say it to them."

The reality of Donald's double-sided honesty bloomed again inside of Andie, hot and warm, and her presence in the car became palpably more tenuous. They both tensed up.

Looking out the window, she finally acknowledged where they were. The old neighborhood was territory she'd avoided since she'd left the others, and the feelings it was igniting were stronger than she wanted them to be. Her breathing became shallower, but she refused to ask if they were going past the old place.

"You look tired, Donald."

Donald grinned. "Well."

"So you're going through a bad patch, then."

He turned his smile toward her, and it broke her heart. This was how it always started. This was the easy part.

"But I'm trying. In fact, I'm having a New Year's party. One of my friends is helping me organize it. For everyone I know."

She wanted to lift the handle on the door, which was so close to her finger. "Oh, Donald."

"What else am I supposed to do, you know? I'm trying new things. I know that if everyone just met each other, they'll get it. They'll really like each other. And that's why I thought, you know, you and Joseph. He doesn't know me too well yet, and you know me so well. You know everything about me. So I thought you two would be a great start."

"I don't want to have this conversation. The rest of us aren't—"

"I know, but—"

"No! No! No! Look, I love you. I love you. Drop me off at the nearest bus stop, and don't call me. This only ever gets worse."

Red flashed from a stop sign in the distance, and Andie started calculating the walk to a bus stop, the taxi fare.

"Andie, please! Okay, I'm going to prove it to you. Just spend some time with Joseph, and if I'm wrong, I promise never to call you again. Okay? He's fine with meeting you. Let me show you, please!"

"So what makes this different from what happened the other times you've tried this?"

"Because I'm going to tell him about me right away."

"So you haven't yet."

"But it's been the lying—"

"You weren't lying—"

"I was! That's always been the real problem. Now, after Sunday—"

"But you'll always be meeting new ones! You can't tell people that you love everybody *including them* five seconds after you meet them."

"I didn't tell Roberto for four years! And I don't blame him for what he did. I hated lying to him. I'd rather lose people."

"No, you wouldn't."

"And I won't. I know I won't."

Andie let the frosting lawns in the twilight sweep past. They'd passed the stop sign, and she was still in the car. She felt like she deserved a medal, compared to so many of the others. And although she couldn't blame him for continuing to flail around, she refused to have the same conversation so soon.

"How's your new job."

Donald didn't answer immediately, so Andie swung toward him, not surprised to see the familiar desolation.

"I'm going to be working on my own. At home. Make my own hours."

"You were working when I talked to you this afternoon, Donald." It was 4:15. "Was it because of this?"

"I haven't been giving people what they deserve lately because I've been so busy and everything, so I figured that right from the start, I'm going to do everything right with Joseph. Spend as much time with him as he wants. He's such a wonderful guy, Andie."

Donald slowed down, and before the car had come to a complete stop, she opened the door and stepped out into a crusting puddle. Rushing onto the nearby lawn, she turned away from the car and headed toward the next intersection, wondering what Donald's next step would be and how best to resist it. She was crying now.

Andie heard Donald pull up to the curb and turn the engine off. Was it going to be that easy to get away? But then an older, Asian man was standing before her.

"Hello." He looked very stiff in his bulky down jacket.

She stopped. "Hi. You're probably Joseph."

"That's right. And you must be Andie."

Donald was still in the car, watching as he leaned over his steering wheel, pleading. She could see his shoulders rapidly rise and fall, a possible prelude to another self-inflicted meltdown.

"Jesus Christ."

*   *   *

Joseph crossed his legs in the back seat. Andie had never seen anyone do that before, and in fact, this was the first time she'd ever equated a car seat with a sofa before. She wondered if people from the past imagined floating along the blacktop as if relaxing in their living rooms, refusing to acknowledge seatbelts or head-ons. Who knew what antiquated things people like Joseph believed?

His posture made him look quite at home back there, but she knew better. His eyes kept slipping off her and onto the oncoming cars' headlights.

"Joseph's wanted a sailboat his whole life. Wouldn't it be great if you fall in love with this one?"

Joseph cleared his throat. "Well, let's take a look at it, first."

Why was she driving to Connecticut? Andie turned to the old man pleasantly enough. "Where would you sail it, Joseph?"

"Well, I thought I'd start with a lake. When I get the hang of it, the ocean, maybe. It might be too much for me."

His hands were small but spoke of capabilities in many fields. Andie imagined them shaping a sculpture, writing checks, unfurling a sail. She squeezed her small, nail-bitten ones deeper into her lap.

Instantly, they passed 1814 Rhododendron Circle, where a fourteen-year-old girl, Patricia, spent every waking moment of her life gaily searching her house for Easter eggs.

The urge overtook Andie to determine exactly just how capable Joseph really was. She wasn't going to spend hours in the car talking about fucking sailboats. "So Donald told you that he and I used to live together, along with a couple of other people."

Joseph only leaned over pleasantly. "No, he hasn't told me too much about you." He looked past the two others through the windshield and then slowly sunk back, uncrossing his legs. And then he surprised her: "I don't want to sleep with Donald, but why not get to know someone who believes that they love you?"

Andie had to admit to herself, even though it might not have been particularly healthy, that she reveled in Joseph's confusion and discomfort as Donald proceeded to explain exactly what his situation, his affliction was. Joseph's mouth hung dumbly open as he gradually processed the disturbing information. But he had it coming—he'd assumed he could shock her by seeming worldlier, more sophisticated than she was just because he was old. She'd been in the trenches for the past year; she'd done more things than he'd ever dreamt of, things with four people in a bed, things that were radically opposed to the morals of ninety-nine percent of the country. She was totally worldly.

When Donald had told Andie, months after they'd become involved, she'd been so ashamed, enraged. She'd hated him for a long time but finally became flexible. She'd accepted and grown. She'd impressed herself just as much as she'd impressed Donald and then Helmut and Marjorie. At least for a while. And now, this little old guy in the back seat thought he was going to win this one? He was mistaken.

But then Joseph surprised her again. He sounded blandly interested as he asked Donald, "Is that so? And you've never met someone that you didn't feel that way about? Ever?"

Donald's joy blossomed at this, it overflowed. Joseph had been too easy. "If I don't look people in the eye, it doesn't happen. But I want to look everyone in the eye! That's the problem."

"Well, one of the problems." Andie knew this came out a little resentful, but if Joseph and Donald thought that everything was going to continue to be so touchy-feely, they were more self-deluded than they knew.

Joseph ignored her. "That's incredible. Although this means I really shouldn't be all that flattered. How can you possibly manage to live like this? It must be hellish." He was already doing the math.

"It's everything."

And the old man continued to reason everything through: "No wonder. Hmm. Forgive me for asking, Donald, but have you ever seen a professional about this?"

Andie watched the suburbs pass by; she had no idea where they were. The trip was getting worse and worse. It was as if the old guy had been instructed how best to work her nerves. Now he was opening the door to Donald's therapist, who had been so critical of Andie, who had blamed her for the weirdness in the group. As if a guy who loves and wants to sleep with every person he ever meets is the sane one.

"My parents tried, when I was smaller. And recently, but it didn't work out."

From the sound of Donald's voice, it had worked out just fine.

"Hattie?"

It was true.

"Oh, Donald. Fuck."

It was all beginning to make a lot more sense. Andie hadn't heard from Donald since she'd left—*she'd* had to call—because he was involved with this Hattie woman. After all, she was a "psychologist" and must have been telling him to stay clear of Andie. Of course he'd trust her. But how could you trust a therapist who only really wanted to sleep with you? Donald was such an idiot. Or a victim, at least.

Andie considered which organization she'd call to report this gross professional misconduct when Joseph turned his attention to her.

"How did it happen for you, Andie?"

She kept her response steady. "It happened for both of us. We passed each other in a parking garage and saw something in each other."

"But he sees something in everyone, doesn't he?"

He wanted to debate the validity of Donald's condition already? She noticed that the atmosphere in the back seat had cooled; the old man was no longer concerned by anything. He looked her in the eye.

Andie rolled out the standard responses to the questions everyone eventually asked her. "Everyone deserves love, on some level. It doesn't mean that it means less."

"But isn't that like saying that standards don't amount to anything?"

"We all have our own standards! Who's right?"

"Maybe the majority?"

"Is that why your wife married you? I mean, was she wrong about you?"

That shut him down. Maybe now Joseph would realize that he shouldn't ask questions before he really thought everything through. Maybe now, he'd understand the spider web that Donald spun; everyone tangled with him eventually got tangled with everyone else, on some level.

"So if your wife felt that way about you, why shouldn't Donald?"

"My wife loved *me*, not *everyone*."

"But was she wrong about you?"

"It's not right or wrong—"

"Exactly!"

"But wouldn't you rather have someone who loved only you because you were the only person they could love?"

Andie turned back around in her seat. Donald was forgetting to dust his dashboard. He never forgot to dust his dashboard. "I'm not about ownership. I know it's hard for most people to understand."

"But you don't live with Donald, anymore. Why not?"

"Maybe part of ownership is living together."

"Then I guess I want to own and be owned."

"Then what are you doing here?"

Joseph kept his cool; he chuckled. "Good question." And he laughed harder, apparently unaware or unconcerned that everything he was saying was wounding Donald. "I think I'm taking advantage of someone who wants to be owned."

"And it's you people who are destroying him."

Even this didn't seem to puncture his hide: "Donald, you've kept pretty quiet. Is it people like me who are destroying you?"

Of course, Donald would never stick up for himself, for Andie. "Nobody's destroying me. I'm not being destroyed, guys. I just wish you two would just see how much you have in common."

"No offense, but I don't see much at all, except for you. And what's wrong with that? There's no right or wrong with any of it."

Andie wished Donald understood that what he needed right now were people around him who really cared about him, who actually worried about him being torn apart.

"You look like shit, Donald."

"No, I don't."

He'd never, never understand.

Andie watched a Dairy Queen pass by, its post-holiday Christmas lights drooping badly. "Can you let me out here?"

Donald kneaded the steering wheel with both hands. "It would get better with you, Andie."

"Let me out. Please!"

Donald pulled into a mechanic's, and Andie immediately opened her door. "After we see the boat, I'll—"

The slamming door felt better than she'd expected, and Andie focused all of her attention on the distant Dairy Queen, imagining the hard curve of the plywood booth pushing into her spine. She'd sit under the bright lights and eat chili until Diane could pick her up. Diane would know what happened immediately because it had happened so many times before, and Andie began to craft her rebuttal, glad for something to keep her busy during the long wait.

THURSDAY

Andie's apartment had lots of plants, most of which had grown out of their attractive, retail appearance and now looked as if they were being kept alive almost against their will in the weak morning sun. Although she'd never cooked it in her life, the place smelled like pot roast under her wealth of potpourri, and it annoyed her, this lack of power.

Donald sat back on her black futon, stroking the orange cat that rubbed its incisors against his belt and purred unevenly. "Clyde remembers me."

"Why wouldn't he remember you?" Andie hated that her voice was nasal with impatience. She sat across from him, picking at the seam of her t-shirt. Donald was actually in her house.

"This seems like a great place."

"Next time, I'm going to spend more time looking. You know, when I moved in, I wasn't really moving in. I was moving out."

Donald frowned at her, pained, but remained still.

"Do you want something to drink?"

Donald shook his head, then: "You haven't started drinking coffee, have you?" He did look pretty tired.

"Do I seem like I've changed that much?"

"I don't know, Andie. I guess not."

She focused on pulling an errant thread. "I don't know, either." She got up and fished around in a kitchen drawer until she retrieved a pair of scissors. He'd done all of this to her, made her live like this, screwed up her life. If they were going to get back together, he was going to have to jump through a few hoops. "What would you say if I told you that I was sleeping with Joseph?"

The cat climbed higher on Donald, who continued to stroke his thin fur. "I don't know. I guess I'd ask you if it's really true."

She turned to face him, leaning on the doorway. "There was just something about him. I think that right now, I need that kind of intellectual, I don't know, fierceness. Everyone is so all about saying the right things, not rocking the boat. I just don't need that in my life right now."

"I saw your car at his house last night."

"Did you?"

She replaced the scissors in the drawer, having never cut the thread. They were the same pair that she had used with the group to wrap Christmas presents, before she'd moved in. While one of them turned their back, the others would wrap his or her presents all at once. She was the best at cutting the paper in a straight line, so this had somehow led to her ownership of the scissors. Of course, the model of fairness that they'd all lived by was galling to her now; life was utterly unfair, and trying to counteract that only made reality worse. She felt the hole now more than she felt the love then.

"Are you sleeping with him?"

"You, of all people, have no right to be jealous! That's a real laugh."

"I guess I can understand it. He's such a great guy—smart and careful."

"Careful?! He's not careful at all. I don't think you can even really see people through all that emotional haze you're surrounded by. I don't think you ever even saw me."

Donald put his head back on the futon and just looked into the corners of the ceiling.

"So, if you know me so well, why do you think I invited you over?"

"I don't know."

"I'm not sleeping with him. Do you even get jealous?"

"Every second of my life."

"I wonder if you really feel anything at all. I mean, you say you do, but do you really know what it's like to actually experience emotions? Because a weird, neurotic need isn't an emotion."

Donald took a deep, jagged breath. "Why else would I be here, Andie?"

"For a quick fuck. You know, that's still not off the table."

Chuckling, Donald faced Andie. "Whatever you want, Andie. Really."

Andie moved out of his line of sight so that she could start brewing tea and relinquish control of her face to her heart. It was always the same thing, in the end: she could never have what she wanted. That was her life's obstacle, but it was also the relentless kernel that she was determined to turn into a perfectly round, exquisite pearl.

"Would you do that? Mindless fucking? No words, no lies?"

"Yes."

Now she wasn't even sure what she wanted. "I don't want to sleep with Joseph, but, I don't know. I felt like I was closer to you with him than I do when I'm with you. We talked about you. He's one of the few of us who hasn't punched you in the face or keyed your car. We have that in common."

His answer was a little delayed: "That makes sense."

"But I can tell that he wants to sleep with me. Maybe if he did, it might be the same for you: I could tell you about it and it would be like you're sleeping with him through me. Because that's the closest you're going to get. Joseph likes you, but you're not getting into his pants no matter how hard you try."

Andie was glad that her voice sounded lighter now. It was the one thing she never could control well.

"So, anyway, I might come to your party. It wouldn't be about you, though. It would be for me. I'm looking at it like Donald AA. 'DA.' Maybe Joseph and I'll go together."

There were presently eleven types of tea in her cupboard. Normally, she would ask which kind the other person wanted, but today, she felt like strawberry green tea.

"If you couldn't tell, and I'm not embarrassed about this or anything, but you're still a problem for me. And ignoring it isn't making it go away. It's probably making it worse, if I know my luck. So I'm hitting it head-on, because you're not bigger than me, Donald. I'm not going to let you be that. You know? Good luck with all of your shit. Really. But, as if you don't already know, you're really fucked up, and I just can't give someone who's so fucked up that kind of control, anymore. I've got to take my life back to the sane side of town."

Andie laughed at her comment, pleased to hear her old self peeking out a little. She wanted Donald to see this, to know she was in charge now. They were going to share a cup of tea, and then she would tell him, politely, to leave. She needed to confront the issue, but part of that confrontation meant not wallowing. Wallowing was a motivation in the past, but it wasn't going to happen today.

When she'd finished with the tea, she saw Clyde first, stretched out completely across Donald's chest. He'd been hiding in the darkest parts of the apartment since she'd moved, and what had been frightening him was just as unclear as the inspiration for all of his other actions. But this was the first time he'd allowed himself this level of exposure, and once again, she felt the familiar, simultaneous awe and resentment of Donald's hold on others.

Then she saw that Donald was asleep.

The tea had cooled off enough that she probably wouldn't go to jail if she flung it in his face.

Hesitating at the edge of her kitchen, she turned back and put the mugs on the counter. She wrapped her hand around each cup and felt the sharp pain, which calmed her.

Returning to her guest, Andie contemplated kicking him in his crotch, as he'd slid down the slick, black material and his legs were splayed apart. He wouldn't blame her.

But he always sat like this, open to anything, trusting the universe even after its continual betrayal. Realizing that she couldn't possibly be the first person to kick him in the balls and wanting to preserve her special position among his acquaintances, she stood at the center of her living room and crossed her arms, her part of New Jersey suddenly passing out of favor of the sun.

As if in response, the radiator began to plink behind the sofa, and Andie found a warm buzz expanding in her stomach. She sat down in the chair farthest from Donald and closed her eyes, gradually accepting her desire to experience what little had been given her. She had him all to herself, at least for the moment, and judging by his pasty, hollow appearance, this pathetically involuntary moment they would be sharing—a mere nap—might even be more important to him than it was to her.

*   *   *

Although it had only been about fifteen minutes before Donald's cell phone alarm rang, Andie had the chance to dream: an A-frame house was situated at the center of a small, steep valley near a very busy ski resort. So many skiers passed by, chatting about their next run, their faces pink and chapped against the bright snow. None of them seemed at all concerned about the two rescue dogs desperately trying to get into the house, and on closer inspection, there was some kind of dread, a funereal pall to the place that contrasted so sharply with its carefree, mid-century vacation design. At every window, spider webs obscured the darkness inside.

At the base of Mt. Rainier, in their rented cabin, Rachel Benn finally told her mother, Annalee, that she would be changing her religion from Presbyterian to a radical branch of the Baptist faith. Something told Rachel not to confess that it was the real reason she had asked her mother to leave Tacoma for the week, so she kept this to herself.

Secretly, Annalee was glad, because it finally gave her a concrete reason to dislike her daughter. But then almost immediately, she wished that she could have rewound time and simply refused Rachel's indulgent, frivolous offer of the vacation. As she added this trip to the list of her life's grievances, Annalee calmly realized that a nagging undercurrent of resentment would have been better than a clear reason for loathing.

Rachel, on the other hand, delighted only in the thought of all the excellent skiing they'd both get in now that this weight was finally gone from her heart. She'd trusted in God, and he'd delivered.

Donald sighed as he hugged Andie, grinning into her neck. "Believe it or not, I'm really glad that you and Joseph are becoming friends. Being jealous has always been the least of my problems, but I don't ever want it to be a problem for you."

Donald hadn't shaved, and Andie was surprised to find that she was relieved by this, more than anything else. It was proof that his biological functions were continuing normally, even if she could feel sagging skin where a solid, packed torso used to hide under his clothing. Then the familiar ache returned: what she wanted was right here, yet it wasn't.

She broke the embrace. "I need you to leave now."

"Okay. Promise me you'll at least consider coming to my party. I really need you there."

"I don't know." She opened the door and looked out at the baseboard in the hall. A spider was arthritically trying to climb it. "And I don't care what you need! God. Goodbye."

She closed the door in his face, something she'd never actually done to anyone before. All she could feel was Donald on the other side, which made her wish that she'd slammed it.

*   *   *

Andie immediately noticed Donald after her eyes adjusted to the dim bar, then Joseph at the table. Donald actually looked mad about something, or at least preoccupied. Scanning the room, she sought out the best exit route because she'd never seen him angry before and wasn't sure how to deal with it. Whatever happened, she wasn't going to be bending over backwards to accommodate his odd requirements, anymore; now, it was his turn to do that for her, or she was gone.

When she got closer, Andie saw that there was a woman at the table, too, and when she reached the table, she didn't even bother trying to smile for her sake. She was middle-aged, frowning and had a caked layer of concealer on that, along with hair that was crackly from what must have been a deadly series of cheap home perms, made Andie want to laugh.

But Andie noticed the look that Donald gave the woman and finalized the plan for her hasty exit. She didn't owe him anything.

"Hey, Donald."

"Andie!" She hated that the bolt still rang through her; no one else would ever be this glad to see her ever again. "What are you doing here! Sit down!"

So Joseph hadn't told Donald she was coming. But there was something else, a hollowness to Donald's demeanor that was chilling to Andie. For the first time, he was trying.

Andie remained standing.

"This is Stacy. Stacy, Andie."

"Hey."

"Nice to meet you. Listen, I can't stay long." Andie signaled to Joseph that she was annoyed with him. "I don't mean to be rude, but I was hoping I could speak with you alone for a couple of minutes. Just for a couple of minutes."

Joseph crossed his arms and looked at the table. Something had happened, but no one was going to tell her about it.

And Donald didn't even seem all that interested in speaking with her. "Okay. Why don't we—"

"Just over there. Sorry."

She and Donald crossed the bar and sat at a booth at the dark end of the establishment. Someone's used napkin had been left on the Formica and still smelled of Thousand Island dressing.

"So, you and Joseph."

"What did he say?"

"Nothing. But you showing up like this…"

Something told her to stick to her original plan. "He wanted you to see that we get along. But everything's happening so fast. Even right now, I'm questioning my motive for being here. I don't know if you deserve it, both the good and the bad." Andie shook her head in short, quick jerks. "I'm not even making sense. I need so much time to work things out, but by the time I do, everything's changed again."

Donald sat back, studying her from a distance that hardened her, a little, and resurrected the tension, hope and dread, pulling at her insides.

"Maybe seeing me again after all this time, you're realizing that I'm not worth it."

"Andie, I feel exactly the same way I've always felt about you."

But she heard something else running under this remark—a shading that had never been a part of his vocabulary before. Things were changing again, and once again, she was going to be the loser.

"And that's why I'm here, Donald. I know this is going to sound calculated or something, but I swear it isn't. I wasn't totally honest before. I kind of like Joseph."

Donald frowned intensely as he considered her comment.

"And even though it's hard to believe, it's not about you. It might have been at first, but now that I've gotten a chance to get to know him, he's kind of liberating, in a way."

It was just a statement: "You've only known him for a couple of days."

"Look who's talking!"

Donald grimaced. "Okay."

"So I lied to you this morning: we did sleep together last night."

He merely continued to listen.

"And what I'm feeling for him has kind of made me reevaluate my relationship with you. The whole thing with you and Helmut and Marjorie—I needed a family. They kind of knew that, in a way—although I can't speak for their feelings for me—so it was easier separating from them. But you. That unconditional love. And now, I can see that it wasn't good for me. It *isn't* good for me."

She expected Donald to sob; he'd been doing a lot of it that week. Instead, clinically: "Why are you telling me this?"

"Fuck you."

But a vibration rang around inside of Andie, and she realized that her desire to exit had dissipated. Instead of rising, distributing sad smiles, and passing out of the pathetic dump and into the light of the rest of the world, as she'd planned, Andie found herself rooted to the booth.

She threw the old napkin onto the next table. "God, that thing stinks! You want to have a party here?!"

Andie glanced over at the others. Stacy was talking too loudly; Joseph was listening too intensely. But they seemed farther away than Andie remembered.

How did he do this to her every time? "Donald. That's a pretty nasty thing to say."

"But if I was just sort of a crutch for you, an emotional crutch. Or a tool, a thing—"

"I just didn't understand."

"But maybe that's the way everyone is to you—"

Now she did rise, her face flushing. "What the hell's wrong with you? Why are you treating me like this?"

A familiar cast of fear and pain returned to his eyes, and she was almost disappointed.

"I'm sorry. I don't want to upset you—"

"Look, I'm the same person I've always been, although definitely wiser. But you're looking at me like... I know this thing with Joseph is a lot to take in, but is *your* love real if it can disappear so quickly?"

"What do you mean?" He searched the space between them. "It hasn't disappeared, I'm just... It's just been kind of crazy today."

Andie realized that she suddenly found him incredibly attractive. Once, they'd had sex in the closet when Helmut and Marjorie had been in the kitchen, cooking as usual. Her brain had switched off, and for a moment when she'd been the one moving and had held him against the wall, she'd been grappling with nothing more than a warm side of beef. It excited her now, just as much as it annoyed her that it excited her. He'd been a thing then; he'd been a tool.

Andie took a deep breath. "I wanted to tell you about Joseph because I respect you and I didn't want you to worry about me, anymore. You know, if you're introducing everyone, other people might get involved with each other, too. Does knowing that I slept with one of your people make it easier or harder for you?"

Donald answered faster than he should have, his eyes on Joseph and the woman. "I don't know."

"But you're still jealous about Joseph and me."

He turned to face her, his eyes shining out clearly from an increasingly waxy face. "I always feel so many things. And you're right, it's what I want: all my friends to appreciate each other."

He sat up in his seat, making the preliminary movements to return to Joseph and the woman, tender under all his clothes. Andie had always found him attractive sexually, but this was something else. Suddenly, he wasn't nearly so earnest and clingy, and she knew that would make fucking him so much better. She wouldn't have to beat herself up for opening up and just treating him like some guy. Which he was, after all.

She counted the seconds in her head for as long as she could before speaking. "I mean, I don't know where it's going with him, but I guess I should thank you." She slid out of the booth before he did. "And we'll come to your party, even if it's here."

Looking down at her top, she smoothed it. "I guess it might even benefit us both if we kept in touch, Donald."

He received her signal, but instead of the grateful nod she was expecting, he looked over at Joseph and sighed. "I've got so much to do before Sunday."

Andie wanted to punch him, to make him acknowledge her fury, because once again, she'd prepared for the wrong scene. So all she could do was leave, a weak move now, an admission.

FRIDAY

The motel room even smelled like she imagined the '60s did: tangy, floral. Of course, Andie couldn't have possibly known what the decade really smelled like, but items from that time period always smelled so synthetic, so moist.

She was glad that she had the ugly room to focus on; otherwise, she would have been obsessing over the fact that she hadn't taken a shower beforehand, and she hated that. It had been more than fifteen minutes since she'd arrived, which meant that she could have taken a shower if she'd done it right away. But she'd waited, instead, and Andie would have been feeling more and more frustrated and negative, if not for the velvet, French provincial furniture to disgust her. The gold curtains gave her something to consider, too: at what other point in the country's existence had Americans felt so comfortable, so recklessly confident enough to decorate in actual, shiny gold?

There had probably been forty-thousand asses pressed on the satin bedspread over the years. Would that be a good thing to Donald? Did he love the people that he'd never met, too? Did he really love *everyone?* Sure enough, she checked it, and the bed sagged in the middle a good three inches.

Andie didn't love everyone. She wished her boss was more generous with her pay, so she wouldn't have to be in such a fleabag now. She wished the owner of the crap-hole had splashed out—at least during the '80s—so that she wasn't now dealing with the crust of fifty years of humanity. She wished she could've stayed away.

A knock. "Andie?"

A shock rose up her esophagus, but she got up slowly, resolute. Even though he'd called *her*, up until that second, she'd been unsure if the new Donald would come. The hard Donald.

"Andie? Don't open the door."

It hadn't even been ten seconds, and already it was starting.

"What are you talking about?"

His voice dropped. "Are you close to the door?"

Pressing her ear up, the cold immediately radiating down her neck, Andie wondered how many ears had touched that exact spot since 1965. Hopefully not too many.

"Donald—"

"Listen. One of your... of your fantasies."

She relaxed at the same time as she became charged. Andie knew what he was talking about.

"What do you mean?"

"Remember—?" The last bit of his sentence was pinched off by a series of violent coughs.

When he was finished: "Are you all right?"

"Open the door now." The edges of his words were roughened.

As the atmosphere of the place pushed in on her, it seemed to prevent her deep breath from working. Even so, the filthy room was in her now, a part of her, and she opened the door to find Donald with his eyes closed, his nose raw, his lips chapped. His head looked somehow narrower, elongated.

The scent of winter that surrounded him made her grasp one last time at walking out on it all: just passing him and heading out into the clean, normal day.

She was supposed to have her eyes closed, too, so she pretended. She probed around the air between them with her bag until Donald's hands closed on its other side. She didn't touch him—they weren't supposed to touch each other, either—but for reasons she didn't want to understand, she could feel Donald more than she ever had before.

Andie led him into the room this way, his feet tentative as they slid across the stained carpet. She knew he would never open his eyes because neither of them was supposed to, so he'd never know how hard she was looking at him. Donald's clothing was just as uninspired as always, but soon enough, they'd have his many layers dropped into discrete piles across the floor, and she'd recover more of her fantasy. Andie didn't want him flinging her clothes on any of the suspect surfaces in the room, except for maybe the bed linen, so she immediately started taking off her top. Hearing this cue, he did the same.

Donald used his belt as a blindfold, and it contrasted sharply with the pallor of his face. As he removed his t-shirt, Andie only just remembered to stifle the gasp that rose up in her: there were disgusting brown and green bruises across his chest. She made a mental note to seem surprised by them afterward, when the two of them were finally allowed to look at each other, but she wouldn't ask him where they came from. She could guess. In fact, Donald's body in general looked hopeless, and the old layer of fat, which had always seemed the only protective measure his body took against the world, had turned liquid beneath his skin.

Of more immediate concern to Andie, however, was the fact that Donald wasn't aroused—never, ever an issue previously. But her extremities were becoming weak and numb with her longing, and she faked feeling around the bed for a pillow a few seconds before bringing it up to Donald's body.

She had trailed through the order of things so many times in her mind, and now she really had a body before her, offered up to the hunger of her imagination. The first step was to gently stroke his right ear with the edge of the pillowcase, then slowly bring the pillow down, catching it on the whiskers across his neck. He looked relaxed by this, nothing more. Next, the edge of the pillowcase, light blue of all colors, was lowered to his chest, and she pretended to seek out his nipples with it, achieving her target more regularly than she would have if she hadn't seen what she was doing. But of course, Donald would never suspect a thing; he never did.

His breath shortening, Andie looked between them both, but he remained flaccid, a comment that couldn't be more frank. Hoping that a different tack might distract her from this, she held the pillow still at his belly, and he quickly took it up.

Andie's actions had always been predicated on the fact that in bed, Donald believed people did to him what they wanted to have done to themselves. Now, for the first time, there was an obstacle between them, and she became aware that what was lost in this equation was what Donald wanted done to him. But you had to be selfish in sex. It was the only way it really worked.

Unsurprisingly, he started with Andie's head, her ears and chin. It was quite a bit more awkward this time, and she got a mouthful of fragrant pillow. Inspecting the thing for stains couldn't possibly help the situation, so she closed her eyes for the first time. Soon enough, he had made his way down to her breasts, and that worked quite a bit better. Andie liked being the only one who was looking, at last the one with the secret power, so she watched him again. His face showed signs of strain, but the pillowcase was just the right softness and stiffness, so Andie began to forget about the room, the absent erection. Her heart beat faster as she felt herself sink into her fantasy: sergeant at arm's length, light gray horses stamping on the soft ground, the sun hitting places on her body it never should have reached.

But then she felt the moist comforter on her feet. The smell of raw sewerage infiltrated from the bathroom. Donald breathed through his mouth, a sloppy, overwrought sound. It wasn't just his uninterested penis—the grimace of concentration on Donald's face suggested he was trying too hard, but at the same time not enough. It was unsettling to recognize this in someone who'd always been so natural in his ways.

The local news theme blared out of the television next door, and Andie was reminded of the time. She grasped the pillow and pulled Donald onto the bed with it. He lay down on his back, his hand straying down to his groin. This was another unsettling first, but maybe unsettling was just what Andie needed. After all, Donald absolutely trusted that she had no idea what he was doing to himself. Andie was witnessing what few—if any—had ever seen before: something that Donald wanted for himself, by himself, with no others to dilute his desire with their own. Not even Andie.

Her eyesight dimmed, her head buzzed, his scent was plain to her now, and it went right down inside of her. Finally, she didn't have to be the only one out for herself. In fact, if she'd known that he was going to propose this, she would have brought along some of the items listed in this particular shadowy nook of her brain: feathers, a balloon, cold marbles.

Wanting to press the advantage she had over Donald, to make him feel it, she pushed the pillow down Donald's body, down to his crotch. There was no way her jaw-tightening excitement wouldn't infect him, there was just too much of it in her body.

It could have been that her rhythm was too fast or that she was too rough, but his hand came up and hovered over the pillow, tensed. She slowed down; she still had time, and now that he knew exactly what she expected of her turn, there wouldn't be any missed targets. She could afford to grant him a little mercy.

But Donald took off the belt and looked at her, bewildered. The air in the room stilled, cooled.

"This was what *you* wanted."

"So?"

"We were both supposed to have our eyes closed. That was the whole point, I thought. To be the same."

"So now you're going to tell me how to do my own fantasy?"

"But it was *your* fantasy!" He gagged on a series of coughs, his chest constricting, caving in. A cold wasn't supposed to be part of it, either.

"Yeah, and my fantasy was also supposed to have a soldier in a uniform! You didn't bother with that!"

She suddenly felt naked, the way he looked at her.

"It was supposed to be the same for both of us."

"Oh, my god. Nothing's ever the same for anybody! Don't you even know that?! Even if I'd kept my eyes closed! Nothing's the *same*."

Dropping his head against the pillow, he pushed his hair back.

"Why did you call me, Donald?"

His eyes slipped off her, disgusted—something else she thought she'd never see. But they returned soon enough, scanning her face for some answer she couldn't give.

"I wanted to see something, and I guess I have."

"This was a test."

"It seemed like the way I've been feeling, the way I've been acting, was having an effect on you."

What did she have to lose? "It *was* having an effect on me! For the first time, you weren't a total fucking pussy! I figured maybe this wouldn't be such a fucking train wreck, anymore. But I was wrong."

He nodded. "I thought that if I really tried, it would be better. There'd be something more."

"What the fuck is that supposed to mean?"

"But the more I try, the worse it gets."

She had to wait for him to stop coughing again, and it infuriated her. He was seriously ill, she could see that now, but that's what Marjorie and Helmut were for. Not her. "The worse what gets?"

"People."

"And what, now I represent all 'people?' God, I know you're crazy, but this is more fucked up than usual!"

She scooted off the bed, ready even to have her bare skin touch the carpet, if only for a moment. "You know, I don't love you. I never loved you. I guess I needed the attention to begin with, but I grew out of that. I grew up, Donald! Now, I just want to fuck you. No, not even that, anymore. If that makes me 'people,' then I guess I'm 'people.'"

Donald watched her as she rushed to dress, indifferent to his own nudity. He was thoughtful; he should have been crying. Over and over, Andie repeated the promise in her head not to look, not to speak, not to look, not to speak.

"I don't know what I'm going to do, Andie."

She got out of the room ten seconds too late. Just outside the door, a dream she'd had the night before joined with the present, forever, she knew, indelible. Her classmates in kindergarten all had to put a cherished item into a bonfire in order to graduate, and their faces glowed in the dusk, shiny with tears that blazed trails down their dirty faces. Obscure woods rose around them, owls hidden in pines.

Andie was the last, and she threw her Tonka Truck into the fire. The children cheered, and then there were cupcakes with translucent frosting and a cherry on top that tasted like wine.

HELMUT

MONDAY

Marjorie saw it first. Donald stood in the center of the kitchen, his shoulders slouching under the weight of something new and cruel.

"Uh-oh." Helmut added the latest wound to all of Donald's others as he embraced his friend, wishing he could absorb the pain through their shared heat, wishing he could shield him from a world filled with ignorance. But he only hugged tighter.

"Stacy? Or Brad?" Marjorie believed the pain was lighter than it was.

"Maybe I should work by myself? Some kind of job here?"

Helmut gently disengaged to look Donald in the face. He was simplifying the issue for Marjorie, trying to spare her, at least.

It worked: "Donald, that would kill you."

"Maybe. But *only* me."

Helmut's instinct was to hug Donald again, but then he imagined an embrace that never ended, always being necessary but never a solution. Donald didn't expect solutions, and yet Helmut still wished he could do more.

"Nobody's killing anybody. Now, Donald, do you want to tell us why you're so upset?"

He moved away from his partners, eager to avoid sharing his pain. "Smells great." But Donald knew it was hopeless, and that made Helmut feel even worse for him, frustrated that the only thing he was doing for Donald was twisting the knife, if only involuntarily.

And Helmut wanted to tell Marjorie to be quiet, but it was too late and unkind.

"You mean, why I'm upset this time? Same old thing. The lies. I'm so sorry, guys."

Marjorie, at least, seemed glad that things were out in the open. "I'm so sorry to hear that, Donald." Her education and experience had trained her to respond with passive empathy, but it seldom helped poor Donald.

153

Helmut knew that it was uncharitable to imagine her opening up Donald's chest with a cleaver and then putting a Band-aid on it; Marjorie loved him fiercely, too.

"I should have told Lourdes this morning, but I didn't."

Further uncharitable thoughts entered Helmut's head—thoughts that solved little themselves, thoughts of people who couldn't appreciate Donald for what he was, thoughts of Donald's inability to cut himself a break.

Instead, Helmut said simply: "Chickpea tagine?"

For the moment, Helmut's tension melted away: Donald was relieved.

"You always know just what to say."

*   *   *

That night, Helmut chose to be on the left side of Donald. Although he enjoyed being in any of the three spots, he felt a bit more comfortable as a satellite than at the supported center. His participation in their family was often delayed because of his careful diligence, so when at the prow of the triangle, he was often an anchor dragging in the mud. Instead, he preferred to trail the other two, taking time to prepare himself for their eventual requests, questions, demands. They depended on him for calm wisdom.

Unease radiated off the body next to him, prompting Helmut to wonder if it was ever right to want people to change, even if the change could only ever be for their own good.

He wanted to make love, too, his only outlet for expression that was immediate and unregulated, but it was clearly inappropriate, and soon, Helmut was dreaming.

He, Donald and Marjorie were in a mud-covered car somewhere in tropical South America, slowly following a wrecked, dirt path that was just coming into a haphazard village. Helmut suddenly remembered that he'd left Andie in the trunk and gave only a passing thought to all of the horrific potholes they'd just bounced in and out of, how many fast-moving, brown streams they'd just forded. What was done was done.

TUESDAY

"Andie called."

It wasn't a coincidence, really, because Helmut dreamt of her quite a bit. It certainly wasn't an omen.

But as Donald dug around in the cheerless refrigerator, Marjorie shot a look at Helmut: Andie wasn't going to help things at all.

"Oh?"

Could Marjorie's clients sense the stress in her voice as easily as Helmut could? It seemed so obvious to him, but just as obvious was her genuine desire to remain neutral for Donald, her practice of love much more endearing than Helmut's own polished, self-aware gestures.

And then Helmut replayed the high feelings Andie inspired in all of them, the solid minutes of laughter, the late nights of punched pillows and controlled responses, the fury. This was very bad timing.

"I'm going to look at a boat tomorrow evening with Joseph, and I invited her to join us. In Connecticut."

Donald both believed that he owed Marjorie and Helmut this information and longed to change the subject. Helmut could at least help there. "You look tired, Donald." The signs of Donald's tough periods were emerging: the puffy eyes, the dull hair, the tight neck. "And you must be starving." The loosening of skin on his arms and legs.

Donald squeezed Helmut's hand, glad of his partner's concern. "How are you guys doing? How was work?"

A quick inspection of Helmut and Marjorie seemed to make it clear to Donald that the conversation would remain squarely on him, and Helmut found himself marveling again at how a person could be so perceptive in some areas and so blind in others. But there were things we all had to learn alone, painfully, or not at all.

"I'm getting the parent vibe again."

Marjorie wasn't going to let it go. "We love Andie just as much as you do."

"What do you want me to do?"

A list immediately grew in Helmut's mind in response to the question, and he let it pass away, disassembling gently and naturally. Marjorie was right to push; something was going on with Andie, but there were larger issues lurking, too, that would explain Donald's downturn.

It was Helmut's turn to contribute, to show that he wasn't a cold, stone well. "Ahhh! We know! We know. But remember, buddy, this kind of involves us, too. Directly. How do we not get a little parental, or maybe the word would be 'interested?'"

"Well, you understand *why*, with her, at least. And Joseph's such a wonderful man. I think that when she gets to know him, in that kind of environment, focused on something else, and he doesn't—I'm not sure if he even likes me." Helmut wanted his pulse to slow; Donald was nearing the real issue. "It's harder for some people when they don't know, and they start imagining the rest of my life. This might be the perfect time for her to meet someone else. It would be very non-threatening, I think. Kind of a first step, maybe. And I think Joseph would actually prefer it."

Marjorie responded with, "How can anyone *not* like you," but the words "first step" echoed in Helmut's mind.

"I wonder how anyone *can*. But with him, it's not about me, it's about the effect I'm having, I think. You know."

Desperate, Donald had developed another plan to manage his life, rewritten rules to ease the discomfort he caused others. Helmut had witnessed similar initiatives during his time with Donald, and each one was disastrous, pitiable. For understandable reasons, Donald believed that people were good, that they had open hearts and minds. What was less clear was why he continually assumed others would react as he did, too.

Donald sat down, his exhaustion clear in every move he made. Helmut had to stop this before it went any further.

"In fact, I've been thinking about this. Because I think I'm coming into another hard patch, and I apologize in advance."

Arranging his face so that his churning reactions would remain hidden, Helmut nodded.

"I know it's short notice, but I've started inviting people over for a New Year's thing. My people."

To avoid Helmut's gaze, Donald asked Marjorie, "So, on a scale of one to ten?"

Helmut was exerting such control over his expression that Marjorie was on her own. He felt for her, but keeping his horror from Donald was more important to Helmut at this point—and perhaps just as important to keep it from her.

"Okay. But you have tried this before."

"I was thinking that maybe this time, I'd tell them all."

Helmut had to do something immediately. Donald had eventually told Roberto, and Roberto had tried to kill him. Of course, Helmut never believed that the man had been serious, but the truth had inspired a rage in Roberto that was harrowing. He'd been a quiet bookkeeper who'd slashed at Donald with a paring knife, slashed at a betrayal that couldn't possibly have scarred him as much as it had Donald. Now, the forgiven, physical scars crossed his palms, signifying nothing more than horizontal lines to Donald.

Helmut had to stop this.

*   *   *

He dreamt of Andie again, handing buckets down a long line of people trying to put out a fire near the harbor's edge of a sea town in Maine. The flames flew higher and higher in the distance, indistinct shouts rising with the black smoke. But Andie didn't hand the water-filled buckets to the woman next to her, she just placed them down before her, being careful to keep them geometrically neat.

Even surrounded by commotion and disturbed by the fire, Helmut marveled at the soaring clouds reflected in her sloshing water, each bucket enlarging the scuttling mosaic of blue and white.

WEDNESDAY

Helmut was still up when Donald finally returned home. He was drinking cocoa and drawing a cockleshell on a piece of thick, nubby paper at the kitchen table, considering contingencies and finalizing objectives.

"Oh, Donald. Another tough one?" Embracing him, Helmut could sense all the cold, exposed spots on Donald that he could never cover. The first time they'd met, Helmut had been surprised by the urge to swaddle him like a baby.

Donald pulled him even closer, trembling. "It was a lot colder in Connecticut, but it's getting pretty bad here, too."

He'd brought it up; Donald wanted to talk.

"So, I've got to ask: how's Andie?"

"She seemed good. She didn't go with us all the way."

Andie would destroy Donald just as surely as she would destroy herself, but Helmut was resolved to keep things light.

"God. Sounds like another story. You want some hot chocolate?" He gently disengaged and rubbed Donald's upper arms. He was still pink from the cold, his eyes smudged and unfocused by fatigue.

Smiling weakly at Helmut, Donald dropped onto a kitchen chair with all of his cold-weather clothing still piled on him. "I would love a hot chocolate. Thanks."

Helmut leaned against the old oven, its chrome handle squeaking under his weight. Overchallenged, harrowed, Donald was lost among his

Gortex and wool. Although Helmut had finally decided what he needed to do, there was a distinct possibility that it would only add to the wrenching of life that constantly threw Donald off true, leaving him battered in new ways. In order to lessen the chance of damaging his friend, Helmut had to be deliberate about initiating his plan, even if its inspiration was random, personal.

Helmut had seen huge skies years ago when he'd driven himself to college in Seattle. At the time, he'd wondered how anyone could live as the farmers did, who willfully separated from what he'd assumed was the natural state of mankind: the crowd. Of course, he'd grown up in Brooklyn.

Lost in Minnesota, he'd ended up on a dirt track that twisted around some pine trees in the sunlit distance. He stopped in the middle of the road. It was cool, nearing a late dusk. Some birds were calling to each other in the dark woods, and a pressing silence owned the land up to the horizon. Rows of crops spread off behind him and next to him, buzzing insects weaving through. His dust trail settled.

A fly landed on his dashboard, and he realized that he might be the only human being to ever look at the creature. There were no secret flies in Canarsie; everything had been possessed or changed or digested by someone else, probably hundreds. But this place and moment belonged completely to him.

Taking off all his clothing, he lay down, spread-eagled in the middle of the road, and watched the sky purple as his car ticked next to him. Only briefly did he consider the families closest to him but still miles away, eating their Fritos in their living rooms and watching Dynasty. He wished he still had that joint.

At least for that moment, Helmut was at the absolute apex of his environment's hierarchy; no one and nothing outranked him here. Without giving it much thought at all, he rolled onto his side and urinated onto the road, amazed at how quickly the dirt absorbed what he left there.

A fourteen-year-old girl named Annie was taking a break from reading about the gestation cycle of the hippopotamus to urinate. She was fantasizing again about getting away from her parents, who didn't seem to like her all that much, and moving to a spot that was more exotic than Tylerville, Manitoba. Presently, she was thinking about a plantation in Tanzania where she could play her violin on a rough-wood verandah for the workers after the harvest. Their respect for her would only make them toil even harder to bring in her crops. However, during a recital six months later, Annie forgot all her music and training and was never again exactly the same. Her world shrunk back to Tylerville, and she eventually married a man named Sam who lied to her about his drug use. Her last dream was of a Tanzanian hippopotamus, which filled her with a sharp, momentary pang of regret that gently passed into a horizon of forgetfulness.

It was time to make the first move. "I could make you some hot chocolate. Or we could do something crazy."

Donald's appreciation was always poised just beneath his surface, and seeing it break through the weariness allowed Helmut to tamp down his concern, a practice he'd had to master since meeting the man. Donald's whole body lifted up in appreciation, in bliss, and he gave more in that moment to Helmut than Helmut could ever, ever return.

It had to be true: Donald would always survive, even if soldiering on was a bit more work. His store of affection would counteract anything, including whatever Helmut threw his way.

He would always trust Helmut: "Let's do something crazy."

*   *   *

Helmut had misgivings immediately after choosing the spot. He'd driven out past Boonton and was lost in some woods, but the land never became expansive; the sky was always constricted by trees, and mailboxes seemed to pop up whenever he thought he might finally stop.

Eventually, he'd found what appeared to be a sort of meadow—an inappropriate description in late December—and pulled the car off the road so that its headlights illuminated the area. A tangle of stripped trees a few hundred feet away offered harsh relief from the darkness confronting the car.

Donald had fallen asleep almost as soon as they'd left home, and he now looked so owned by unconsciousness that Helmut hesitated. "Donald?" He gently rustled Donald's puffy arms.

"Is it the—? What, oh yeah." Donald grinned at Helmut and struggled to keep his eyes open. "I'll be—just give me a sec." He squinted through the windshield. "Where the heck have you taken me?"

"I don't know, but it doesn't matter."

Donald's eyes closed again, and he slurred a sentence out: "You're not going to kill me, are you?"

159

"Come on, you can go right back to sleep in a second. Then this will seem just like a dream we both shared. How does that sound?"

"Nice." Donald was losing his battle, so Helmut shut the car off. The cold air almost immediately began to invade the compartment. And then Helmut added concerns: the profound coldness of the night made him want to close in on himself, not unfold into his environment, like Minnesota. There was a glow off to the right indicating the proximity of the greater New York City metropolitan area and several million people. A hoary track originated nearby and disappeared off into the outer reaches of the open space, attesting to recent, frequent tractor or pick-up activity. The place was saturated by humankind.

Putting all of his trust in serendipity, Helmut opened his door. "Come on." It took no time for his face to sting. "Just for a second, Donald."

The reality of the night's temperature did the trick, and Donald was soon conscious and walking next to Helmut over the crunchy, hardened ground. The headlights provided grasping shadows that joined the blackness to the men, and Helmut began to wonder that, even if he had taken Donald to his abandoned, summered Midwest acre, whether his companion could have ever completely shared the experience. But he couldn't allow Donald to suspect his doubts, so he briefly and cheerfully recounted what had become his Minnesota fable.

"They have loons there, don't they?"

"You know, sometimes I wish I just had you to myself, like this. I don't think so much for me, but imagine how simple it would be for you."

But none of it was right; Helmut could feel the nearby residents on top of him here. Hundreds of people probably drove by this spot every day, maybe some of them even picnicking in the summer, playing Frisbee with their retrievers. It would never be just theirs. It would never fulfill Helmut's vision.

"Imagine only one person to love."

Donald shivered as he grinned, the steam that rose off of him catching the offensive light. He looked up, squinting at the spread of stars. "It's too late for that."

Helmut noticed a section of brown grass that appeared relatively smooth, and he lay down, leaving a space for Donald. But Donald remained upright, looking around him.

"Too late, too late, too late." Helmut found himself echoing now; it was so easy to become sad around Donald. But it was also a part of the package, and Helmut reminded himself that he respected that. "Maybe it's too late the day we're born."

Now Donald sat down on the hard patch of land that Helmut had chosen, and only afterwards did Helmut realize what a chill the frozen earth must have sent into him.

But he had to continue with his strategy. "This would be so much better if we were looking up at a far-off, summer sky."

Donald's gloved hand sought out Helmut's. "It's wonderful to be outside and not worry about seeing anyone. I don't do it enough. Thanks."

Helmut recognized the flutter in Donald's voice, a sign that he was on the verge of weeping. Knowing this would change the chemistry of their few moments in the dead of winter, in the dead of the New Jersey night, Helmut decided it was the right time: "Let's move away to the country. You know I can do my job anywhere, and even rural areas need social workers, so Marjorie would adjust. Let's just go. Tomorrow. I'm serious. We can celebrate New Year's in our new home in the middle of nowhere." Helmut shifted on his side, glad to see through the slashes of light and shadow that Donald wasn't crying.

"Or maybe the desert. Alaska. I don't care. Someplace that could finally give you some peace. Because all this is grinding you down, Donald. Look at you. I don't know how much more of people you can take."

A rumble of a vehicle approached from the northwest, and the two men sprung up, a reflex of their particular love. It was a dark green truck, and when the driver saw the two men walking quickly back to their car, he slowed down.

Squinting at the two of them for a moment, he came to the conclusion that they looked harmless enough and rolled his window down a bit. "You guys having car problems?"

"We lost a dog. Thought he was here." Helmut positioned himself between Donald and the man.

"Geez. In this weather?"

He pulled his truck up next to Helmut's car and turned off the engine. "Why don't you let me help you guys look."

They'd almost reached their car, Helmut feeling Donald's hesitation dragging at his back. "Oh, that's great of you to offer, really, but we think he's somewhere else. Maybe closer to home."

"What does he look like? I just live down the road."

The dynamics were shifting, Helmut's plan quickly dissolving into bad luck. Realizing that it was pointless to avoid it, he looked over at Donald and found him staring openly at the man. The man was still looking at Helmut, though, or he would have rolled up his window and quickly pulled away.

He had bushy black eyebrows and moustache, but his hair was full and white, which somehow made him look like a puppet, each element of his head deliberately chosen and placed. His eyes were small and hard. The Nutcracker soldier.

It was a ludicrous reaction to have at this point in their relationship, but Helmut found himself wondering what Donald could possibly see in the guy. Why was he still plagued with these thoughts, thoughts that only served to distract Helmut from more important matters, like avoiding confrontations?

He opened his car door. "A Rottweiler Pit-bull mix. He's actually pretty mean. We're just going to check closer to home, but thanks."

Strangely, the man's gaze slid off of him in disappointment. "Sure."

Donald would have recognized this change in the man's demeanor, too, so Helmut immediately began to compose tactics to counteract the situation Donald was about to create. His mind momentarily jumped to the young woman at Sea World and the ensuing physical altercation that resulted in Donald's two caps and a bridge. Helmut hadn't seen it coming and hadn't acted quickly enough. Since then, he'd studiously avoided spending time with Donald in public; it might have been cowardly, but he genuinely felt that he only made things worse. And being in love with Donald meant letting him interact with the human race in the only manner he could and praying for the best.

But it was happening in front of Helmut now.

"That's really nice of you to offer." Donald's voice was saturated with an intensity wholly inappropriate for the situation, and the man noticed.

"Well."

A still silence ensued while Helmut's mind raced for the quickest, least dramatic exit. Every second, he was aware of the shifting forces inside of Donald, and this only served to slow down his problem-solving abilities. In addition, the man had a shotgun on a rack behind his head.

Helmut aimed his next comment at Donald: "So, anyway, I—"

"Actually, you know it's kind of funny because I'm just going home from the vet's, well, emergency vet, as a matter of fact. Well, not just going home. I've been driving around a while. My dog had a wrecked heart, apparently." The man now talked only to Donald. "I guess it's kind of my fault because I kind of stopped her heart-worm pills a while back." He looked down to rub his steering wheel, his fingernails ringed in black. "I never even liked her that much. She was always so scared of everything."

Helmut's next words were strangled when he saw Donald's face: his weak caution had been chased away by a genuine horror at the man's situation.

"I'm so sorry."

As Donald approached the truck, Helmut felt himself melting back into the shadows, his body temperature dipping to meet that of his environment. Now, Helmut and Donald's private spot in the middle of the New Jersey woods had become a scene for something entirely different. Once again, Helmut was physically sharing what was in reality always shared, anyway. Why did he attempt to deny it, to prevent it?

The man continued to talk, and Donald continued to listen, rapturously, as he fell head-over-heels. It was gratifying to see that Donald's pain was in remission, and Helmut actually felt ashamed that he hadn't had the capacity to lessen it himself. But these were simply the rules of the game in which he'd chosen to participate. The stranger clearly needed to share his pain with someone else, and no one else on earth was better.

Helmut turned to the stark relief of the barren meadow, committing it to memory as best he could. The still, arctic atmosphere was so invasive that he couldn't even imagine August here: the bright, insect-covered weeds, the birds passing in and out of waving leaves.

Nonetheless, Helmut reassured himself that at least this would always be a special time and place for Donald. The reason why it would be special—and the fact that almost every time and place was special for Donald—mattered less to Helmut at that moment, and he was glad of it. Things were fine: Donald was happy, and Helmut had broached his subject. This meant that he was free, now, to continue on to his next step.

Helmut waited, and the meadow seemed to contract itself into a postcard as the two men continued in lowered tones, somehow cozy now, and contained.

THURSDAY

"Let's take a shower."

Once he'd dragged himself out of bed that morning, Donald had looked like a pained zombie. It was Helmut's fault. He should have known that Donald would want to be up with the rest of the family, that he'd never catch up on all the sleep he'd missed the night before.

But just as he was increasingly concerned with Donald's health, Helmut also recognized that he was pleased on some level; he needed the severity of Donald's condition laid bare—*temporarily*—because it would, in all probability, help his case with Marjorie.

She'd sent Donald right back to bed, but Helmut knew it was a futile gesture. Donald had already pledged the day to Joseph.

"Come on." He led Marjorie to the bathroom and pulled off his sweats. "Christ, how does the tile get so cold? They've got the heat on downstairs."

"Shh!"

Helmut noticed that the water was taking longer to warm than normal and that Marjorie's flesh was covered with goose bumps. He drew her to him and rubbed her behind, which he knew would be her coldest spot, except for her feet. It was as generous as the rest of her, pliant and relaxed, and Helmut's gut began to heat. They hadn't made love at all that week; Donald's sadness had negated it.

"So listen. I've got an idea, and it's a crazier one than usual. But I'm completely serious."

"Do I want to know?" Marjorie could read Helmut better than she could most people; she'd become familiar with his patterns. He found himself hesitating.

"You first. I want to watch you."

"Get into the tub? I've stopped trying to figure you people out."

"What people?"

"Men. I never even bothered trying to figure women out."

Once in the shower, Helmut began to seriously doubt himself. He'd continue, but she wasn't responding to his touch, she was waiting, detached.

"So he can't hear us in here."

"What?"

It wasn't the right time. Marjorie was always cranky in the morning, unfocused.

"I've never kept anything from him. Or you. You know that, and it's completely true. Never."

Marjorie pressed his hands off of her. "You're scaring me now."

"This life is destroying him. Look at him. And it isn't something he's doing to himself. Not really. He doesn't control his life. It just doesn't work that way."

"Okay." She was putting her impartiality into gear, the fence-riding of social work.

Helmut wanted to shock her back to the personal and was annoyed that he needed to. "Jesus Christ! You know what it's been like, Marjorie! On the sidelines. Don't tell me you're not just as frustrated as I am."

"We agreed when we got together that we'd never, ever do anything like this, Helmut. Gang up. We're having a secret conversation, for Christ's sake."

He noted that he was even more irritated because she was right and redoubled his efforts. "Did you see him this morning?! He couldn't even walk straight."

"We're always there for him if he needs us. He knows that."

"Passively!" She wasn't getting it. Like everyone else, she didn't see Donald's condition, she saw what Donald wanted her to see, what she wanted to see. "Look, the guy last night scared me. How many people is he involved with now who could be on the edge like that guy? I don't know if he was really on the edge or not, but wouldn't someone who was disturbed be more likely to get involved with Donald? I mean, it is kind of a crazy situation. And Donald is losing his strength to deal with things."

"Nobody who's ever gotten involved with Donald has really hurt him. Really hurt him."

Over the last few months, Donald would routinely come home with rope burns on his ankles or odd patches on his skin, burned somehow or affected by chemicals. No one ever talked about it, and Helmut wasn't about to start now.

"We don't know that. And anyway, that's not what I'm most worried about. I'm most worried about what's happening to him now."

"I don't want to do this, anymore—discuss him as if he isn't here." She flung the shower curtain open, admitting the frigid breeze.

"Marjorie, he wouldn't mind. When has he ever minded anything that we've done for him? Being passive means giving everyone else permission to call the shots. Who *should* be controlling his life? Because *he's* not."

"Giving up control *is* control!"

"That's nonsense."

"But we're supposed to be supporting him, not manipulating him."

"But we do! Everyone does! What, do you think you're not on some level controlling his life? What about Hattie? You were the one encouraging him to drop her—"

"He was going to, anyway! I was supporting his decision, not making it for him!"

"You're getting the floor wet."

Helmut only realized that he'd been watching how the side of Marjorie's breast moved with her words after she closed the curtain and it was thrown back into the obscurity of gray steam. They'd never made exasperated love before. He found himself just as exasperated with her blindness to Donald's decline as he was drawn to her wet curves and soft places.

"He's entitled to his own life, Helmut."

And his own death.

Helmut would try again later, maybe let some of what he'd said sink in. But it had to be soon; Donald's party was only a few days away, and Helmut was sure that it would be devastating for Donald. He couldn't let it happen. "There's no more room inside of him for all of this, Marjorie."

"I know!" Marjorie was finished. "I know that."

"All right, all right. But why don't you just think about what I'm saying. Maybe it'll make a little more sense when he ends up in the hospital or something. Sick."

"He's not that bad, for god's sake."

But Marjorie trusted Helmut. When she looked at Donald now, she'd see what he meant, she'd understand the significance. She'd be open to Helmut's plan.

*　　*　　*

Marjorie was embarrassing herself, eager to make sense of something that could never, ever make sense to her. She'd been grilling Joseph in the kitchen for five minutes, and now she wanted to escort the man home—a situation he clearly didn't want to live through. Helmut pulled off some toilet paper, wishing his bowels would move a little more quickly.

It was strange. Marjorie and Helmut had been together before Donald, and she'd joined Helmut in the search for new family members. But when he found a candidate, she was always indifferent; she'd never been particularly enthusiastic about any of his choices until Donald. So why did she suddenly want to fall for every person that Donald did? Helmut's nominees had been carefully chosen for both his and her tastes, needs, and desires. He'd really put some thought into the dynamics of their relationship and those of the potential new one. Helmut had been positively methodical, but his efforts had been utterly dismissed by Marjorie. And now, even though the people Donald became involved with were simply the ones who didn't ignore him, laugh at him or try to kill him, she was chomping at the bit to be captivated by each one.

Helmut knew her primary motivation was a desire to make Donald's life a bit easier and perhaps even learn a little more about him in the process. Her heart was always in the right place, and that was why Helmut loved her. But Marjorie really did have to calm down.

Helmut flushed the toilet as she said, "No, hold on, I'll just get my coat."

She retreated into the bedroom, and Helmut made his entrance. At first glance, Joseph appeared insightful, well-mannered, and pleasant, and Helmut began to wonder if perhaps Marjorie hadn't been right to try and get to know him.

"You must be Joseph."

Helmut's plate-like hand enveloped Joseph's, and he was glad to see that the old man wasn't guarded with him. He smiled up at Helmut fearlessly.

Donald wouldn't look at him, and immediately, Helmut felt the absence of the bottomless well of Donald's eyes. It had never been denied him before.

But Helmut wasn't going to worry yet and instead turned his attention to the matter at hand as Marjorie joined them. "Hey, Marjorie, haven't you been coughing an awful lot today? Are you sure you want to go out in this?"

There might not even be anything to worry about with Donald.

"It's just a couple of blocks." Marjorie wasn't looking at Donald, either.

Something must have happened between the two of them, maybe something to do with Joseph. Something Helmut must have missed while in the bathroom. "Oh, okay. Well, it was nice to meet you, Joseph. I hope to see you again. Maybe at Donald's party?"

Joseph's face fell; he'd been hoping that Helmut would save him. "I think so."

"Fantastic. Oh, you know what, Marjorie?" Helmut quickly walked into the bedroom. What had he missed? The atmosphere in the kitchen was leaden, caused by something more than just Marjorie's awkwardness.

"What? Helmut? What's up?"

Joseph might be able to tell him.

"He's such a mystery, sometimes. Are you married, Joseph?"

"I was."

"Oh, is that right? Divorced or—"

Helmut thundered back down the hall and straight to the back door. "Colleen called earlier, Marjorie, and I couldn't speak with her. She really needs to talk to someone, and you're so much better at it than I am."

As he gestured for Joseph to exit, Helmut knew that Marjorie would be hurt by this, but not yet. And once she did realize what Helmut had done, she'd want to believe otherwise, she'd want to give him the benefit of the doubt.

"She really sounds bad, Marjorie." But he still had some time before she figured it out.

Marjorie's eyes swung back and forth, bovine and confused, and Helmut's stomach buzzed in empathy. She knew she was the one without a clue again, her girlish vulnerability still there, still alive after all the wounds of her long life.

Joseph was merely relieved. "Pleasure meeting you, Marjorie. I'll talk to you later, Donald?"

Hacking, Donald dragged himself up from the table and embraced Joseph. He must have come down with a cold that made his limbs appear dead, the light in his eyes appear smothered.

A dizziness generated by dread made Helmut's next words difficult, but he'd learned enough to know that fear was seldom worth giving in to. He forced down his panic. "I'll be right back guys." And he was out of the stifling room.

"It's awfully nice of you to walk me home, Helmut, but it's really not necessary."

Helmut needed a second to plan. "To be honest, I was going to use this opportunity to grab a smoke. No one likes me smoking at home."

"Oh. I see."

Helmut could see Marjorie and Donald speaking on the other side of the lace curtains. Donald would be asleep by the time he got back. "They can't see me here, right? I'm a real outlaw, eh!" Cupping a cigarette, his lighter immediately melting a few unfortunate snowflakes, Helmut forced himself back into his conversation with Joseph. "I'll stay right here. Or I could come with you. I mean, would you mind that?"

"Yes, I would."

In spite of himself and of the scene unfolding a few feet away from him, Helmut laughed. He still could be caught off guard by the divide that separated his outside from his inside, and he was glad to find himself on autopilot with Joseph. Joseph was a smart man; Joseph could help him.

"That being said, I would appreciate it if you did."

Helmut moved some of the snow on the porch with his foot to create a miniature snow angel and sucked the smoke deep into his lungs. If he could just continue to appear relaxed, he might be able to determine what had happened to Donald since the morning that had changed him. And later, if he decided it was prudent, he might even share his plan with Joseph for Donald's future. The man seemed kind; he might join in the effort to help Donald to accept it.

"Oh, good, because I'd freeze to death just standing here. Which way are we going?"

*   *   *

Helmut would dream that night about the spot near the apartment building where the two of them had stood. Gophers were underneath them working the dry, frozen earth, cooperating to make sure that the ground where they'd be walking would hold the men up. The gophers understood so much more than Helmut could ever hope to, and they knew how important it was that he and Joseph not be swallowed up by the earth, which was very close to happening. Somewhere nearby was a busy gopher metropolis, and the workers ran back and forth, bringing news.

Helmut suspected that the gophers' city was beneath the playground of a nearby elementary school, and in his dream, this seemed to make absolutely perfect sense.

A teen-aged girl named Park Min dreamt of a new use for the powder recently developed to produce fireworks. Gophers had told her exactly what to do with it, and they chattered on and on about how important their information was. But when she awoke, she had forgotten.

For the rest of her life, Min would half-wonder if directly under her feet, gophers were gathering gunpowder in a concerted effort to stun the world. These thoughts made her uncomfortable.

FRIDAY

Helmut was looking out the kitchen window at a slow-moving snow plow when Donald came up behind him. Part of navigating life with a larger, loving group was respecting privacy in whatever ways possible, so he chose not to turn. Helmut had been staring too much at Donald that morning, anyway.

"Oh, good. They're clearing it." Donald's voice was drained of Donald, and Helmut vowed that he wouldn't convince himself later that it was just his imagination, his panic.

"It's at least a foot."

Coughing so long that he gasped for air, Donald beat his own chest, the sound disturbingly hollow. Helmut decided to face him. Donald had been keeping things from the family, too; that was clear at this point. Helmut wasn't the only one. Something had changed.

After Donald finally caught his breath, Helmut rubbed his shoulder, concerned. "Hey, why don't you stick around here, today? I need some help with installing that program from Eunice. You know I'll just crash the thing without you."

Donald's voice was hoarse now. "I'd love to help. How about tonight? After dinner?"

"You're having dinner with us?"

Marjorie would be sure that Donald ate.

"Yeah, I thought so. Maybe invite Joseph, if that's all right with you."

This was a new situation. "Absolutely." Helmut wished that he wasn't in such turmoil, so that he'd be better equipped to digest unexpected information and formulate his best responses. Did Donald want to add Joseph to the family? Did Joseph?

"So what did you think of him? Joseph."

At least Helmut knew how to deal with this question. Joseph had warned him.

But he wanted it to appear as if he were really considering the question, so Helmut gazed over Donald's shoulder and up into a corner of the kitchen's ceiling. He'd lived in the apartment for years but had never really noticed this particular spot before. It was eerie to realize that it had always been there, unseen, waiting.

Everything that was going to happen to Helmut, to Donald, was waiting, unseen.

"Let's see. He was very intelligent, very personable. He was charming, I thought. Clear and open."

"But how did you *feel*? When you first saw him."

Somehow, Helmut had misunderstood the information Joseph had explained to him; he'd given the wrong answer.

He retreated: "To be honest, I try not to form opinions until I get to know people. First impressions aren't fair."

"Hmm." This seemed to catch Donald off guard, and he nodded vigorously for a moment, reminding Helmut of the recent past, of his clearer times. "But you do form first impressions, even if they aren't fair."

"Well, I don't know as if I even do, anymore. I think it's been beaten out of me." Helmut chuckled, hoping his unease with Donald's red, dilated eyes, which were crossing slightly now, wasn't as apparent as it felt.

"Really?"

"People change, Donald. You know that. I've evolved, or maybe devolved. I don't know."

Helmut ached to talk with Joseph again, to clarify what Donald had confessed at Burger King. A flailing helplessness rose up in him now, scratching at the base of his throat, and it rose up because Donald appeared momentarily cut adrift by Helmut's comment, weighing interpretations, struggling at some private balance with a defeated glaze.

Against Helmut's better judgment, an anguished reflex: "Donald, how can I help you?"

Affection flooded back into Donald's face, and he blushed, looking down at Helmut's chest.

"How can you help." But Donald's mind was elsewhere. "What do you have planned this morning?"

*   *   *

Virtually no one was on the road, which had been transformed into a kind of pioneer trail through an only somewhat familiar landscape. Despite the salt and plowing, Helmut drove slowly, spooked by the lack of normal activity in the neighborhood. But there were a few children who hadn't yet learned to curse blizzards, and the sun conspired with them to remind Helmut of a time when exhaustion inside a snow suit was the best thing there ever was.

For a moment, his heart didn't ache.

"You said The New Day Studios?" Helmut knew enough not to ask about Donald's sudden interest in yoga, but he was hoping he'd be told about the person, sooner or later.

"Yeah."

The sunglasses felt odd on Helmut's face, but the reflected light was agonizing, otherwise. It had been so long since he'd thought to wear them; months of gray, freezing rain had forced him to always look down, to dismiss the importance of his surroundings and their right to be observed. But now that it was so bright and clear, he still couldn't look head-on at Montclair.

Helmut's sunglasses also hid his eyes from Donald. "Do you think they'll be open, today?"

"I don't know."

"Gosh, I haven't done yoga in years."

The place was closed. There wasn't even any way to tell where the parking lot was, so Helmut just slowed down, his eyes trained on Donald more than was probably safe.

"Sorry about that."

"Wait a minute. Could we stop at the coffee place over there?" Donald was focused on a maroon minivan.

"Sure."

It appeared to be the only open place in town, and quite a few people with the day off were celebrating their morning there.

Helmut found a parking space that faced directly inside, but he left the car running, unsure of the next step. Donald's attention would normally hit the ground when he was confronted with large groups of people, but this time, Helmut bore the full force of his gaze.

So he turned to Donald and smiled openly. Something was going on.

"Pretty packed in there." Donald wanted him to return his attention to the bodies in the restaurant. The crystalline light obscured the people on the other side of the glass, weaving or stationary in the murky environment, their bright winter wear dulled into steamy shadows.

Helmut watched the people, glad for his sunglasses. "You know, I got a one-sided Q-Tip this morning." In the bag, they'd all looked alike, but Helmut had been wrong about that. "Organisms. Isn't that what you said to Joseph yesterday?"

Helmut braced himself for Donald's surprise at this admission, but he surprised Helmut, instead. Donald looked up into the crowd, his eyes picking out and studying every person, his face crumpling into a different grief for each.

"Donald! Donald, please. We're just not as gifted as you are. We're ignorant, disabled. You know that."

"Do those people look disabled to you?"

Helmut's stomach dropped: he'd come to depend on Donald's exquisite single-mindedness, his beautiful, humane incomprehension. But now he was realizing that it was more than dependence; Donald's condition had gradually taken over Helmut's spirituality, proving it and being proven by it, acting as its central gear now and at the heart of his perceived world. Somewhere, Donald's faith had become Helmut's.

But it was gone. Helmut was cut loose.

His mind scrambled at responses, even as he willed himself to breathe. "How do they look to you?"

"I don't know. There's a question mark over everything. It's never happened before."

"But isn't part of real love accepting and forgiving faults?"

Immediately, Helmut was aware that it was possibly the worst thing he could've said. *Real* love?!

But Donald's shoulders merely relaxed, and he placed his hand over Helmut's.

"Exactly."

The play of writhing pain and boundless gratitude on Donald's face was hypnotic to Helmut. It took him a moment to realize his mouth actually hung open. "I don't understand."

Someone in the coffee house caught Donald's attention, a self-possessed woman with long dark hair, and he underwent yet another shift.

His eyes softened and he leaned forward, his hand instinctively rising up to the door handle.

Helmut underwent a shift, too. Now, he found himself actually getting angry, an emotion he'd gradually managed to comb out of his heart over the years. But here it was again. Exactly when had he accepted responsibility to be just as victimized as Donald was by the torture of his emotions? And more than victimized—this time he felt as if he were in the police line-up, too.

He wouldn't give voice to this frustration, but the impatience that rose up in Helmut was compelling him to broach the solution he'd recently developed for Donald. He even got as far as opening his mouth before recognizing that Donald seemed different with this infatuation, so he sat back, instead. The usual ecstasy inspired by a new relationship, or whatever this woman was, seemed diminished, mitigated in Donald. Even this sacred phenomenon had been crippled by his sudden doubt.

It saddened Helmut, and he desperately struggled to feel the empathy he knew Donald deserved. After all, he was having a much tougher time than Helmut was, and as Donald tore himself up peering at the woman, Helmut struggled against his lower self and its annoyance, its impatience—probably its jealousy.

He'd also learned that Donald would be aware of at least some of what he was battling with, and sure enough, he squeezed Helmut's hand. "I'm sorry."

Helmut swallowed. It was impossible to be angry with Donald for long before his grace emerged. There had been that day in Atlantic City, the woman that Donald had immediately befriended. She was rough, homeless, a little crazy; she'd memorized the March 1977 McCall's that she carried around with her and called herself Iowa. Helmut had been appalled, but by the end of their time there, Donald had almost taught his partners what there was to love about her. Almost, and that was all Helmut needed. "Go ahead. We'll talk later."

As he watched Donald hurry inside the cafe, nearly slipping on the first, wet step, Helmut instinctively knew that Donald's latest agony was caused by one of his other people, possibly this one, and rage at his own impotence gripped him again.

But there would only ever be one real casualty in all of this; he had to remember that. Clarity would allow Helmut to center himself, and then he'd know how to take the next step.

*   *   *

Helmut had witnessed glimpses of the short scene in the café: one minute, the two of them were delighted with each other, and the next, the woman was confused and Donald crushed. As he made his way through the crowd, it was clear that Donald was even worse now, his mouth pulled back like a betrayed animal. Again, Helmut found himself resenting Donald a little, slightly disgusted, and he knew this was an irrational and wholly unwarranted reaction. In fact, his lack of empathy lately seemed to be in direct proportion to how much Donald needed it.

Ultimately, it was disappointing, which gave Helmut something to do other than facing Donald's plummet.

But in a few seconds, he would have to, and honest compassion was just as necessary at this moment as it was deserved. Unfortunately, managing his resentment took Helmut time, it was a process, and Donald was six steps away from the door. It was one thing to hide thoughts from Donald, but it was a serious challenge to keep him from sensing animosity.

Squinting, Donald emerged into the bright street, his illness plain. Helmut weighed his options, panic rising as he rejected every one, so he was relieved when Donald only came up to his window. Helmut couldn't tell if the scowl he wore—a first for Donald—was because of the sun or what had happened a minute before with the woman.

"I'm going to walk home." The temperature was dropping, and it was at least ten, long blocks.

Donald wouldn't look Helmut in the eye.

"Okay."

Unevenly cleared, the sidewalk stretched away into hardening yards and trees, the sunlight's progress on them halting, stilled by the whipping wind.

Reflexively, Helmut rolled up his window, and he watched Donald make his tentative way into the steady blowing, adding shame to his list of negative emotions. Closing his eyes, he squeezed, squeezed at the foulness in his heart. Only after Donald was two blocks away was Helmut able to push things aside a bit, reorganize priorities, and get out of the car in pursuit.

It wasn't hard catching up to Donald, but Helmut hung back when he did, realizing how seldom his friend ever sought out privacy of any kind. His back seemed shallower now, powerless.

Until that week, Donald had kept his life compartmentalized, but he'd always basked in the company at home, sometimes even following Helmut around a bit more than he might have liked. And although Donald occasionally withdrew to hide emotions that belonged to his other compartments, it was always out of respect for his partners' feelings, rather than a desire to keep them in the dark.

Things were never going to be the same.

"Donald?"

He turned around, a distracted, haunted, almost angry staring.

"I'm so sorry. But do you think you're up to walking home?"

Donald's body supported Helmut's assertion by shivering.

The question was too strong: "What did that woman do to you?"

Donald's posture snapped to attention. "Are you mad at me?"

A reflex to breathe in deeply at this point gripped Helmut, but he knew that the bitter air would just make him tenser. So he looked at the green house closest to them instead, imagining himself inside, disassembling the browning Christmas tree at the picture window.

"I don't know how to answer that."

"You just did."

"Let's just get back in the car. You shouldn't be out in this. You're really sick, Donald." Helmut noticed that the next section of sidewalk hadn't been shoveled at all. "Look, I don't want to—why should I respect emotions when I know they're wrong? I know they're wrong, Donald. I just can't get them under control at the minute, and it's not fair to you."

Donald hugged himself. "Fair feelings." He looked in the direction of the reminder, the artifact of the Christmas tree. "They're just about the worst thing in the world."

Things were spiraling. "Let's just go back to the car. Please."

"So why are you angry, then? Because I'm having a hard time, right now?"

"Please, Donald."

Donald started walking in the direction of the car. "But is that it?"

"Let's have this discussion later—"

"But I don't want only *some* of your feelings, the ones you choose to let out. I don't want what I *deserve*. I want to know the *truth*."

Helmut was immediately aware that Donald was walking slower than usual, more deliberately. He was ready to catch him if necessary, and this occupation helped refocus Helmut, bring him out of his head. "All right.

All right. It's just that you go through so much with other people. Things have been kind of steady for you and me and Marjorie, but it's always seemed to us that things weren't so healthy with your other friends. You've kind of kept them separate, kept your difficulties to yourself. Possibly more. We've done our best to respect that. And maybe that instinct was right. Maybe mixing us all up just creates more tension among us and possibly more resentment toward you. That's all. But you see? It's not fair."

Donald kept his head down, his lungs rumbling in an extended cough. But at least the wind was at his back, now. Finally: "The party."

"The party. Maybe, I don't know. Look, it's frustrating for me to see you go through all this. And because I feel I can't do anything about it, I get frustrated with you. Allowing all of this to happen to yourself. I mean, for Christ's sake, Donald, once a week you come home covered in bruises! I want to respect that, but it's so fucking hard!"

"And you're worried about the party."

"Just like I'm worried about what happened in there just now that's made you so upset. I worry which one of them beats you up, tortures you, whatever. Which ones make you unhappy. Which one said something to you yesterday that's suddenly made you question everything you've ever felt. I've known things go on, but I've never had to be in the same room with them. And you've never been this bad."

Donald swiveled sharply toward Helmut, and of all things a grin slowly bloomed on his face. "You don't miss a thing, do you." He batted Helmut with his elbow. "You know, you're my scarecrow. Your fairness is one of the things that I most love about you. Maybe I need to be more like you."

The car was only a few hundred feet away now. Donald bent over, coughs wracking his body, and Helmut put his arm over Donald's shoulder, looking up at the café and straining to ascertain who was and wasn't still in the place. Nothing was ever simple.

"I'm taking you to Dr. Francelli right now. Or the emergency room."

Donald didn't reply; he'd righted himself and was lost in the obscurity of the café again. The day had become even brighter, and the dark forms there were probably too indistinct to make much of an impact on him. But he showed no signs of turning away from them all, packed together, corralled, a moment's glimpse of a hand tugging a bracelet, a moustache receiving the steam from a paper cup. Helmut found himself staring, too, wondering what his memories of this place and time would be in ten years, wondering if his own selective shifts in memory were anything like Donald's instant perceptions—keeping the good stuff, ignoring the bad—and if this was dead, now. He wondered if Donald had ever confronted a mass of humanity like this before, even one as lost in murky anonymity. Helmut had never seen him do it, and he wished more than ever that he could understand what was happening.

But he understood enough to know that he had to get Donald away from all of this. Immediately.

Only when a middle-aged couple burst out into the street did Donald drop his face and open the car door. "Okay. But let me make a call first."

Stavi had found the joey at the bottom of the hill at the back of the house, in the shade, but just about to be exposed to the sun. It was clearly not long for this world: it looked like an organ more than anything else, something that was never meant to be seen alive by human eyes. It breathed and moved a little, but the gravity and the dirty ground worked against it, sharp pebbles sticking to its gummy skin. Stavi knew how it felt to be so helpless. In fact, he felt the exact same way.

He'd never been all that interested in the valley's wildlife; at the moment, he spent most of his time with his Rubik's Cube, but before that, there had been Dr. Who, a Mechano set, drawings of space ships. He knew enough from school to recognize that this joey belonged next to its mother, so he folded up his shirt, and grimacing wildly as he picked up the thing, held it next to his belly in an ersatz pouch, and raced back up to the house.

No one was home. His mother didn't like him calling her at work, and Stavi wouldn't call his stepfather, so he warmed up some milk with one hand as he held up the pouch with the other. The shirt was too large for him—his mother always bought clothes he could grow into, but he wore them out before he got there—so he only noticed that the joey had climbed up and out of the pouch after seeing it on the floor. It was dead.

This was his stepfather's fault: he'd put in the hard, beige tiles. It was his mother's fault: why couldn't she buy him clothes that touched his body somewhere other than his shoulders? It was his fault: maybe the joey's mother would have come back for it. But it was her fault, too: how could she not notice that her baby was gone?

Picking the thing up with a piece of kitchen roll, Stavi was suddenly struck by the fact that it was really all the joey's fault, and he cried for the last time in his life.

*   *   *

That was it: Martin Luther King's assassination. The balcony seemed like it was waiting for a sniper, itching for a scene. Helmut knocked on the door to 243 again, the wind blowing further into him up here.

Seeing Andie, if only from a distance and the safety of his car, had scared Helmut. She was still material, still reacting, still flashing her eyes. He'd been something like in love with her once, something that, when its components were separated and analyzed, consisted mostly of lust, flattery, intrigue, and a literal last grasp at youth. He'd certainly analyzed it since she'd left, and the overwhelming result was thankfulness that he could still be fooled, that his johnson could still do the thinking for the two of them. He was glad there was still a little youth in him yet and that the transformation into gentle master wasn't yet complete. Of course, this seemed only selfish and callous at the time. But it had yielded a particular impression, a hybrid of mistake and experience that would take years to mature into either wisdom or festering regret. What sagacity he did possess had at least provided this much knowledge: he'd just have to wait and see which.

Helmut had come to the conclusion that after things ended with Andie, there was nothing else to be done; it was history. Now, though, it was clear that there was something he'd failed to consider, and that was Donald. Helmut had respected Donald's usual distance after Andie left. There'd been a group therapy session with Marjorie, and he and Donald had scratched the surface of the breakup a few times, but it had all been so tactful, respectful.

Early on, Helmut and Marjorie had agreed that this was the best course of action with someone so fundamentally impossible to fathom. But now, standing on the icy walkway that overlooked a depressing row of cars covered in dried slush, Helmut recognized that he wasn't nearly the sage he thought he was. If he had been, he would've known that Donald might've welcomed a broach of the subject of their mutual misery; after all, Andie hadn't been a private affair like the others. They'd all shared the break-up, and obviously, Donald would never get over it.

Then again, this probably wouldn't have worked for Donald, anyway. He must have realized that Andie's departure hadn't been much of a blow to either Helmut or Marjorie, and so must have strenuously avoided burdening them with his own agony. No one really ever put Donald first, even himself.

Helmut knocked, this time harder. He was getting frustrated. He'd waited too long for this, but he couldn't inform Donald of his solution with a motel door between them. "Donald? Do you want me hanging around right now?"

There was a chip in the door's paint that went down, down: white, tan, pink. Inside, there was the start of a sentence, then a wheezed-out cough that Helmut could actually feel through the brass door knob.

Finally: "I think I'm going to stay in here for a while."

"Oh."

Yelling this into the harsh wind made it sound even feebler to Helmut's ears, so he simply sunk down on the cracking concrete in front of the door, balling up against the winter. Helmut could feel the eyes of the gunman upon him, and he actually chuckled. How else would he ever find himself in such bizarre situations? Who else. A life without Donald momentarily spread out before him full of peanut butter sandwiches, endless, regular rhythms, bowling.

"I'm just going to stick around here at the door, if that's all right."

"Why?"

A foreign word for Donald. Helmut stumbled. "You still know me, Donald."

Helmut was in the shade here, and he felt it. The wind numbed the right side of his face, and he was beginning to get a headache that radiated from his cheekbone. Even James Earl Ray got blown away by a gust.

But then the door opened behind him, and he felt heat on his neck drenched in mold and disinfectant. The cold had only encouraged his stiffness, so it took Helmut an awkward while to get up and enter the room, an old, humid place.

Donald lay on the bed, nude, and stared at the ceiling. The oversaturated colors assaulting him made him look paler, agreeing only with the yellowish tones of his bruises. Then he pulled a sheet across himself, refusing for the first time since Helmut had known him to be inspected, consumed.

"'I still know you.'" It was a rumination for Donald. "I wish I was smarter."

"Donald, what the hell is going on? Please."

He smiled at Helmut, but it was like a wound. "I just wish I could figure a way out of this before my party."

Helmut sat at the end of the bed, afraid to touch his friend. "You're still planning on that?"

"I just never realized how different I am. I mean, now... I just don't know how I made it this far! I must be so stupid."

Donald watched Helmut carefully at this point, any kindness there retreating, making way for unfamiliar workings.

"So what's smart, then? Are the rest of us smart?"

Donald's eyes returned to the ceiling. "I thought so."

"Look, what I'm about to say is incredibly selfish. But look at it from my perspective for just a second—"

"But don't you see, I *can't* look at it from your perspective! I thought I could, but I've been guessing all this time, about other people. And I've been wrong."

"What's right, then? Do I know myself better than you do?"

"I don't *know* anything."

"And maybe our brains just get in the way of real knowledge."

"No. I don't think so. Not now."

What had felt wonderful a moment before now strangled Helmut: the room was stifling. He unraveled his scarf and opened his coat. Sitting down in a chair, he faced Donald and waited.

"Do you still love me, Donald? Or is that gone, too?"

"I still love you."

"And everybody else?"

"And everybody else. But it's different now. I don't *like* some of them, anymore. I don't think I can do both at the same time."

"So what do you see in me now?"

Helmut still expected a turn of the head, a reassuring smile. It had always, always been there before.

Donald only studied the ceiling carefully, while Helmut watched an artery in his neck swell and contract, just like any other human's.

"Okay, Donald. We're leaving New Jersey today. No New Year's party. No other people. Just you and me and Marjorie, if she wants to. If she doesn't, just you and me. Consider it kidnapping if you don't want to go, because I will force you, and that way, it won't be your fault. You can blame me. But I'm not letting this go on any longer. You're going to kill yourself with these other people, and I'm just not going to let it happen.

I've rented a cabin in the Poconos for a week until we can find a more secluded place for you. Someplace where you won't have to see anyone else ever again, except for the people who really love you and care about your health and your future. It's time somebody put your wellbeing first, before anything else."

Helmut threw the pamphlet and keys for the cabin on the bed next to Donald, who continued to stare above him, and he rubbed the arm of the chair to remind himself that the earth at least hadn't abandoned its laws.

"Okay."

The word produced another coughing jag, which gave Helmut a chance to feel his heart beat, to finally recognize the sweat that covered his body.

Donald wiped his lips. "I don't know what else to do. I guess I am getting pretty sick, and it's a problem if I don't care about it."

"It'll be tough at first, Donald, but you've made it this far with all your break-ups. I know they're bad, but this way, you won't have any more. No more guilt; no more running around all day trying to satisfy everyone's demands. I think what's happening to you is that you're finally realizing we're not worth it. Because we're not."

This comment wounded Donald, and he writhed in the bed, stretching the sheets, gritting his teeth. "All right. But if I decide that I want to come back for the party, you have to let me. I might want to tie things up with everyone. I can't just drop them like that! I can't do that!"

"Okay. Okay, Donald. You know I'm not enjoying telling you what to do with your life. That's not why I'm doing this at all. You know that, right? You know this is for you?"

"Yes!" Donald's voice screeched out, attesting to the torment of regret that must have been spreading in him already. But finally, he looked at Helmut, and there was some love there. It was true. "I know you're doing this for me, Helmut. I know you're just trying to save me. I love you."

Helmut felt that he could touch Donald now, so he hugged Donald's lumpy body to himself and kissed his ear and neck. "Thank you."

And then he pulled away. He had what he wanted, what he'd been praying for: Donald's trust. He could do anything now.

"I'm going to call Marjorie. I haven't really discussed any of this with her yet, but now that you're on board, I think she'll see that it's the right thing to do. I want to get to that cabin right away; I don't even want to go back home. Either Marjorie or I can drive back to the apartment and pick up some stuff, and we'll just deal with the rest later. Nothing matters but you."

Finally acknowledging that he had to urinate urgently, Helmut rose, grabbing Donald's ankle under the covers. "You're going to be all right! I promise."

The same countless, contradictory emotions that had always pulled at Donald's face were pulling at it now, but he reached up and rubbed Helmut's elbow. "Thank you."

The bathroom would probably be a horror.

"But we were thinking about going to the doctor, weren't we?" Donald's voice echoed around the bathroom, which was a horror: cracked, aqua tiles, grout blackened by generations of splash back. In his rural life, Helmut would only have to worry about his own mess. "That's true."

A basin made of molded resin designed to look like marble dominated one wall. On its surface were multiple burns, their dark bubbles immortalized, and a guest at some point had carved into it: "Evergreen Motel sucks balls."

Helmut grinned; he could now. The correct capitalization meant that it had probably been left by someone twenty or thirty years earlier—the disadvantaged period before email and texting. Helmut felt even more encouraged, for some reason: the Evergreen hadn't decayed, it had been designed as a shithole all along for the shithole people of shithole New Jersey.

Pissing felt as if he was ridding himself of more than water, it was a physical expression of his relief. He yelled toward the other room: "To be honest, I'd be surprised if Dr. Francelli would be around on a Friday afternoon before a holiday. We'll see how you do on the drive. I have a feeling she'd say that all you need is rest, anyway. You can get some shut-eye in the car, and then we'll get you into bed. It's probably the best thing to do with a cold, which I'm sure is all it is."

The flush was deafening, the water ice cold on his hands. After the sickening torpor just on the other side of the door, the draught in the john was glorious. Helmut began to map out a route to the cabin in his head, to consider the alternatives. "You know, I could use a break from the world, myself, to be honest. And we could even decide to stay a little longer at the cabin, if we want to."

Only then did he face the smile in the mirror and recoil. It displayed such a terrible well of immaturity, pushed down but not out. In so many things he was a man, but there was no denying this adolescent disregard, a betrayal, and Helmut sobered immediately. It was much worse than a cold; they both knew that. And anything Helmut said now, to himself or to Donald, could never entirely fill up the depth of selfishness he'd just exposed them both to.

Still, Helmut tried. "But listen to me! Your health is more important than my escape plan. First we should try the doctor. Donald?"

The empty room was still a shock, and it seemed so much filthier now, obscene. He'd left only his cell phone on the bed stand; the pamphlet and keys to the cabin were gone.

Helmut's first and lasting reaction was fury, which swung back toward himself and hardened later, gradually and permanently.

All through those months, it had ground Enoch down, such a simple, stupid thing. And then his sister and her kids moved in right after, which seemed to cement it, this terrible rawness that fed itself. He told them he was angry about the dust because they asked, and it was just about the only good use for the storms. But the dust wasn't the cause at all. Marion knew that much. And Alberta knew more than to ask.

One day, Enoch realized that Alberta's kids were afraid of him, and without his family, absolutely none of it made sense: the fight, the farm, hanging on. And the next week, Marion got sick in her lungs.

When it was cold, not much of the dust could get under the blankets, and it only turned the inside of his nose brown and produced mud in his eyes and ears. But when it was hot, it forced the dust everywhere—down his navel, way up into his privates. Not that they ever discussed any of that, but this was how it must have happened to Marion. This was how it had all started.

Who knew exactly where the dust came from? Mexico, maybe. Of course, being Marion, she'd told him right away, and showed him, too --a white, sappy excretion from between her legs. They had always been fellow warriors, sufferers, and they kept back little from each other.

Enoch felt so terrible for her when he saw it, but for some reason, a word infiltrated his mind, an awful word that mocked his wife: marionnaise. He had to leave the room to keep her from seeing his horrible laughter, and this was the simple moment that began the crushing down of his wife.

She thought he was disgusted, and it was true: he was disgusted with himself. At first, she was devastated by confusion and embarrassment, those questioning eyes set in a flushed, round face. Then it was disbelief and betrayal, and he never saw her eyes again. Enoch never could tell her the truth, so he began to resent her for it even though to do so was worse than ridiculous.

They never had relations again, and by the time Alberta showed, they were hardly acknowledging each other. In just about the worst kind of horror, Enoch watched his wife die without the means to an apology. Then, as punishment, he spent the rest of his long life on the farm, one foul word ever scraping in his ears.

During his last few hours, he asked the woman with him to fill his mouth and nose and ears with dust and choke him out of the world. But she didn't understand or didn't listen.

STACY

MONDAY

Brad came in twenty minutes after Donald had arrived—twenty minutes late—and he kind of smiled at the top of Donald's head in a weird way. Brad was starting to sweat.

"You really have to start showing up on time, Donald."

Stacy took the pencil out of her mouth. "An old guy slipped and fell."

"Of course, he did. Can I—?" Brad pointed at the door, and as usual, Donald was thrilled to go because it was less time he had to spend at his desk, working.

*   *   *

The sun was doing that annoying thing where it would get brighter and then darker and then brighter and then darker, over and over. A lot of people at the office didn't have a window, but all it was really good for was constantly reminding Stacy that there was something else going on, something more interesting.

Stacy watched him closely when he returned. Donald grinned back, a lock of his hair falling over his forehead like a kid in a commercial.

"Brad's always whisking you away to meetings."

"I know."

"What did he want?"

"He just needed to go over a few things."

"Uh-huh." Stacy said it as icily as she could. She knew that's all it would take.

Sure enough: "What's wrong, Stacy?" And he looked at her with his puppy-dog eyes, way more worked up than he should've been.

"Well, it's just that I know you're lying. I know you're lying to Brad. And I know you're lying to me. Not that you owe me the truth or anything. But Brad really likes you. He trusts you."

187

He was constantly making her feel bad about things; now, it was his turn to see what it was like.

But his face broke into a thousand shards, and once again, Stacy was made to feel bad about some little thing she said to him.

"What do you want to know, Stacy? I'll tell you anything. You know that."

"Hey, I don't want to know anything. It's none of my business."

He still looked as if Stacy had clubbed him, and she felt her pulse behind her ears banging away. "Did you finish that spreadsheet for waste management?"

"What am I lying to you about?"

Translation: he didn't finish the spreadsheet, although Stacy knew that already because she checked on his computer when he was with Brad.

"I don't know because if I did know, you wouldn't be lying to me. But I don't care! I need that spreadsheet, so if you could just print it out."

She had to stop having conversations with Donald because half the time, he'd get thrown into a funk, and she was stuck doing all the work for their department. When would she learn to keep her mouth shut with him? It was as if any little thing sent him off in some stupid direction—a direction that never pointed toward work.

But there was a simple solution: "Look, I know I owe you a little, but I was kind of wondering if I could borrow another twenty or so. Until payday."

Donald whipped out his wallet, and she had the money before she could think what to do with it.

He was relieved, as usual. Glad. "Are you sure that's all you need?"

"It should be. Thanks."

He handed Stacy another twenty. "Just in case."

Why did she smile at him then? She was still mad at him.

*   *   *

Stacy started to type furiously when she sensed him approaching.

"Hey."

"Hi, Stacy." He was staring at her again.

She flicked her eyes in his direction for a millisecond. "What? Brad's looking for that spreadsheet—"

Then Brad's kids ran into the room, and the girl ran to a corner of the room.

Why was Stacy always getting in trouble for her work? It was a wonder she got anything done, with Donald constantly in her face and her boss's kids treating her workspace like a playground.

The girl screamed, "Freeze!" And the boy froze, both children panting in place. Stacy had to be nice to the kids, so she smiled a little at them. When she looked over at Donald, though, he'd buried his face in his monitor.

Then Brad ran into the room, more panicked than he needed to be. She had never worked in a place where everyone was so much more worked up about little things than they needed to be. Brad looked as if his kids were playing near a shark tank.

"Hey, guys. Come on now. Come back to my office, okay?"

"It's no biggie, Brad!"

Brad practically yanked the kids out the door. "Come on. Let's let them work. Sorry guys."

As usual, Donald was acting weird. Ever since the kids had walked into the room, he'd been stiff, furiously interested in his work.

"What was his deal?"

He was working up to another one of his lies.

"Donald?"

Then he raised his eyes to her, and his terror was a shockwave across their desks. She wanted to kill him for doing that to her, but all she did was shiver and turn away.

"God! Whatever."

Stacy's mother had turned away, too, after seeing a ghost or an angel when she was twelve in her grandpa's barn one rainy, spring morning. She'd told her horse in the paddock that she was looking for an apple, but in reality, she just wanted to get out of the damp cold, and the barn was a few degrees warmer. For ever after, she was uncomfortable with the lie she'd told her horse because she associated the guilt with the appearance of the lady, even after she ceased believing any of it really happened.

An old woman was standing half hidden behind a wall, turned to a stack of hay bales. Stacy's mother stopped as soon as she saw her, trying but failing to get her completely into focus. This was the only reason why she hadn't immediately addressed the woman, because in all other ways, she seemed perfectly real—probably a wanderer just turned around in the woods next to the farm.

Also, ghosts were supposed to scare you, not be scared of you. And angels were made only of light and love. But when the woman turned toward Stacy's mother, the absolute terror in her eyes was ice water thrown at the girl. Her first thought was that there was something horrible behind her, something that little girls from Hardwicke Township were never supposed to see. But the woman was looking directly at her; only her eyes were in sharp focus, and they were just as sharply focused.

Stacy's mother ran and ran. But she could never completely outdistance the terror of never knowing what there was about her that was so horrifying. Never again could anyone or anything keep her from occasionally gagging on the fear she had of herself.

She never told anyone about the encounter, first because her horse died a week later, and later because she gradually realized it must have been just a child's mistake.

Stacy struggled alone with Donald's helpless stare now, which she'd never asked for and certainly didn't deserve.

"What is your deal? They're just little kids."

"I know."

It was drama as usual, so Stacy quickly left the room. The stifling heat in the hall was a different kind of stifling heat.

TUESDAY

"You couldn't call?" Stacy was surprised that her voice sounded more concerned than she felt. Because she just felt annoyed. How did he always get away with being so late?!

Donald dropped down at his desk, his eyes rimmed in pink.

"Donald, you have got to get yourself together. Seriously. Brad is on the warpath."

"How are you doing?"

"Me?!" Stacy's eye contact with Donald was done for the day. "Worried about your job is how I'm doing."

"I'm sorry, Stacy." Donald begged her and thanked her at the same time, somehow.

"I mean, how am I supposed to get your work done, too? I can barely keep up with my own!"

Inspecting his lap, he nodded slowly. "I'll stay late tonight."

"That would be nice of you. You know, I feel like I'm always covering for you, and all you ever do is apologize. To me, to Brad. I don't know about Brad, but I kind of feel like I deserve to be treated better than that."

Stacy refused to look up at him because he'd gone really silent and she didn't want to see why.

"Why don't you go in to Brad now. Before he comes in here."

Donald rose. His voice sounded funny, of course. "That's a great idea. Thank you, Stacy."

He was thanking her for yelling at him again. He must have known that it made her feel worse, as if it were her fault.

"He's not going to buy your lame excuse of the day for being late, Donald. Not today."

*　　*　　*

When Donald returned to his desk, Stacy kept her back to him at the small file cabinet. She stared at one word of the application in her hand: "refuse." For a second, she felt both of its meanings at once, and it depressed her.

"What happened? You were in there forever."

"I had to sign something."

"All that time? Just for a signature?"

Donald's voice was unsteady. "He had to talk to me about it, too."

"I told you!"

"I'm always late. It makes his life so much harder." Stacy felt the warmth of his gaze envelop her, even though her back was to him. "And yours, too. I'm really sorry about that."

He was doing it again: making her feel bad about being justifiably resentful of his behavior. "Whatever. Oh, and I don't have that money for you. Sorry."

"No problem."

Stacy imagined stuffing dollar bills down Donald's throat, but even in her fantasy, he didn't resist.

When she went to the other file cabinet, she could look at the back of his head, at the monk's bare patch growing there. It had noticeably increased since Donald had started working at Environmental Services, and the thought made Stacy annoyed with his body, too, in a weird way, for taking advantage of him. He probably didn't even know how much balder he was getting, which was happening because of all the stress he generated for no reason.

She wasn't about to tell him. That wasn't part of her job description.

*　　*　　*

He was late coming back from lunch, but only by ten minutes.

"It's been nice working with you."

Donald looked up at the clock. "For ten minutes?"

"Maybe." She shrugged without slowing her eighty words per minute. "Probably not, but god!"

"I'm having a New Year's party on Sunday. I'm really hoping you can come, Stacy."

"What?" They weren't friends! She didn't even slow down. "I can't, but thanks."

Stacy hadn't been invited to a party on New Year's Eve for five years. All of her friends had kids now and stopped wanting to have any fun. In fact, the thought of having that kind of fun was so alien to her that it almost seemed obscene.

But she was only twenty-nine. Wasn't obscene still supposed to be a good thing?

She briefly inspected his boring sweater. Any party he threw definitely would be the opposite of obscene, but there were the other, shadowy reasons that warned.

Donald had been hanging over her, but now he dropped into his seat. "There really isn't any point if you can't come."

She was so surprised by this that she had to look up at him for a second, although she was immediately sorry. "Me?!" Her glass paperclip holder had a chip in the corner. She'd never noticed that before.

"Listen, I kind of live far away from you. Let me—" He dug into his pockets and retrieved a couple of crumpled twenties, which he carefully smoothed out on his desk. "—for a cab. Please."

He really meant it: for a cab. He made it so much easier for her, always really meaning everything. He made it easier, but at the same time, he made it harder.

There was no way Stacy was going to go.

"Okay. Thanks."

WEDNESDAY

"Oh my god! Somebody alert the media!" Stacy waved her hands in the air above her new, silver-plated hair clip. "It's party boy, and he's on time!"

Donald had arrived distracted, a frown pointed a few feet ahead of him, but his expression transformed when he saw Stacy. Almost immediately, she felt annoyed that it had taken him a bit longer than usual to change after looking at her. "What is it, this time?"

"Nothing, now! Did I really make it?" Donald glanced up at the clock as he slid into his seat. "Yes!" He turned full-force to his office mate, beaming. "How are you doing, Stacy?"

She'd been asked this question a million times after her motorcycle accident four years earlier. In fact, during their first week together in the office, she'd told Donald all about it, and he'd been interested in all the details—something that nobody else was, not even her own mother. And one of the details was that she hated being asked, 'How are you doing, Stacy?' as if it were more than just a social nicety. Which was exactly what he was doing now, and she rolled her eyes.

Donald immediately recoiled. "I take that back! I'm sorry, Stacy, I don't know what I was thinking."

He was annoying her already—even the way he looked. He was so tired that his face actually drooped.

"Whatever."

"But to say that. To you. It's so stupid because I know better!"

"That's true."

"I'm so sorry."

Why did everything have to be such a big deal? But Stacy felt a little thrill go through her, for some reason.

Now downcast, he flipped on his computer, pulled some papers out of a file. He stared through the screen, the computer performing its routine of flashing numbers and words. "What good am I if I can't even keep things like that straight."

"Can I say: drama queen? God, get over yourself, already. I'm fine, thank you for asking."

Donald managed to grin at her, but it was one of those grins that he meant, rather than felt. Something else was bugging him, something from his murky outer life, and she definitely didn't want to know what it was.

Working with him was like being in a soap opera on fast forward, and she knew he'd just keep apologizing to her for hours if she didn't change the subject. "So about the party. Is it going to be at your house?"

He kept smiling at her, but he didn't even mean it, anymore. "I think so."

"You think so? Isn't it kind of late to just now be inviting people and planning it? Duh. How many people are coming?"

Donald shrugged. "Five to maybe seventy-five."

"*Five to seventy-five?!* You are in serious trouble."

"I've never thrown one before. Like this."

"You didn't say anything about my new hair clip."

"It's beautiful, Stacy. It makes you look like royalty. Did you ever see Grace Kelly in a movie?"

"No." She checked with both hands to make sure that the clip was still perfectly placed.

"You've always reminded me of Grace Kelly when she was really young. She was a real princess."

"God! Whatever. Just get that thing for the mayor's office done. I can't keep covering for you."

Finally, he got to work. The pores on his nose were ginormous. Stacy hated how he was such a big, goofy idiot.

"You know, Brenda had her birthday party at Rascal's."

*   *   *

She knew what had happened as soon as she saw his face.

"God. What's wrong?"

Donald came toward her like he was sleepwalking, and she got serious hug vibes off of him, so she immediately turned her back to get a file out of her desk. Thank god he usually seemed to understand what she was thinking, because when she glanced back, he was at his desk.

"If I gave you my home phone number, would you call me?"

"You got fired. Donald, what did you do?"

"I'm giving you my home number." He started to write on one of his little squares of scrap paper, his eyes crinkling up with tears.

"Donald, what happened."

"I have to leave early." He handed her his scrap. "I just can't work here. I wish I could." Why did he think he could look at her like that? "I really want us to stay in touch, Stacy. I can take you out to eat, or we can do whatever you want. And we're going to see each other on Sunday, right?"

Stacy gritted her teeth, realizing that she'd have to wait now to get out of that party. It would be harder now.

She deserved compensation for her trouble. "They said they needed fifty bucks to reserve the room."

Donald wiped his eyes with his sleeve. "Okay. Can I give it to you now?"

She should have said a hundred, or even more. "Yeah."

Now his nose started running, and he grabbed a tissue five seconds too late. It was disgusting.

"Plus another fifty." If Donald wasn't going to be around, anymore, he couldn't keep asking her about the money. And even if he did figure it out, he wouldn't care. He wouldn't do anything. And she'd never give him her home number, anyway.

Stacy's pen ran out of ink five seconds after she'd taken it out of the box, and she threw the stupid thing hard into her waste basket.

Donald wasn't going to be around anymore.

She took the next pen out and jammed it onto her pad, making loops. It felt good to push down so hard that she ripped the paper. Donald was almost retarded, in a way.

Flipping down to ground zero, Stacy ripped the pages out of her pad, crumpled them up in a satisfying ball, and chucked it into the trash so hard that it bounced. Her pad would have the swirly indentations for a long time, and since she didn't want to be reminded of what a piece of garbage the pen was, she threw out the whole pad. It was a waste, but that wasn't her problem.

Maybe she would really call Rascal's and set something up. Or maybe not.

"Thank you so much for your help, Stacy. You're a lifesaver."

His money was brand new, never even folded before, and as usual, she got the feeling that it was a burden to Donald. He didn't even want to touch it, which made the bills just seem like disappointing paper with squiggles on them.

But she took the cash and never looked at him in the face again until he was gone.

When Simone was twenty, she and her best friend Kylie had gone to a frat party in Glassboro where she convinced Kylie to enter a drinking contest with some guy named Clark, and Kylie drank so much that she had a little brain damage and had to drop out of college. Simone didn't really like Kylie all that much after that night because she was different in a way, and so she avoided her until the phone calls stopped.

Eleven years later, when she was moving back to New Jersey, Simone found a book that she'd borrowed from Kylie in one of her old boxes. It was called Finding Your Passion. *Simone briefly thought about finally reading it but threw it out, the book just a morsel in the line of eight, big trash bags that were lined up near the curb and announced to all her neighbors that she'd finally given up on their fucking town and was headed back where people weren't all assholes. Simone knew that being Californians, they wouldn't even notice her absence, much less care, and she hated them even more for it. But she did briefly wonder on the car trip back home if she shouldn't have saved that book, because it was high time she started focusing on herself.*

Right after Donald walked out the door, Stacy wished for a second that she worked in a store full of tropical fish. The bright colors there could glide through her mind and settle like a sheet over a bed, slowly and completely.

THURSDAY

There were a few people in late middle-age on the far side of the bar, looking left and right without enthusiasm. The scent of burnt tobacco still persisted in the dirty carpet and the grease trapped in hundreds of corners around the place. Donald squinted in the murkiness until Stacy was practically a foot in front of his face.

"It's not that dark! So what took so long."

But she immediately wished she wasn't so close to him, because he looked as if his grandmother had just died.

"A friend is going to meet us here for lunch."

"Guy or girl."

"Guy." Donald wasn't a one-word-sentence kind of guy. Had he talked to Bob? Did he know that Rascal's didn't need all that money? Stacy had known that meeting him at the bar would be a huge mistake, but she wanted to make sure that things went smoothly so that he wouldn't get mad at her later.

Then he tried to look happy, or maybe he was, a little. "What's going on with you? You look great! I've never seen you in your civvies before."

Stacy was muffin-topping over her skinny jeans, and it pissed her off. "Yeah. I guess you dress the same all the time."

"Pretty much."

"You're such a wild man. So? Are you going to buy me a drink or what?"

"Sure."

They approached the bar and Gabbi, who was so slight that her fingers only made it halfway around a cocktail shaker. Stacy wondered how she could even hold down her job with such little fingers.

"Hey, guys! I was wondering when you were going to visit me, Stacy."

196

"I was waiting until the guy with the cash showed up. Vodka rocks. Wait, he's paying, so make it a double."

Stacy turned to Donald, who was staring at the bartender with one of his weird expressions. This time, though, he also looked mad, or maybe confused, too.

From her long-suffering experience, Stacy knew that it was time to change the subject. "Brad didn't come in today, and I didn't have anything to do, so I'm taking the rest of the day off." Had Donald called Rascal's about the deposit? "Hello?!"

Donald swiveled toward Stacy, now concerned. "Brad didn't come in?"

"What do you care, anymore. Uhhmmm, I think Gabbi's waiting?"

"Oh, sorry. A Coke, please." He said this to the brass bar at his stomach.

Gabbi punched Stacy in the arm. "He's cute. Where have you been hiding him?"

"God, Gabbi! You're such a nympho. He's a good tipper. You don't have to fake flirt with him."

"Who's faking?"

Donald's pupils had dilated to such a degree that Stacy was reminded of her grandmother right before she died, her eyes seeing more things than just what was in front of her. But Donald's eyes also looked like that guy's who she'd slept with a few years ago. He'd been much too eager, and she'd hardly felt him on top of her. He'd been really hot to trot and had that same look, as if he were about to eat something good.

"Donald? Remember me? You know, I think you'd love Gabbi's husband; he's great at pool."

Gabbi placed the cocktail down before her. "I've never seen you so jealous before, Stacy!"

"And we're ending this conversation right now."

Donald forced a smile when Gabbi handed him his drink. Stacy shouldn't have been surprised that he was even weirder outside of the office. She was starting to have serious doubts about this whole thing again, but at least the alcohol gave her something else to focus on: her throat and then the warming.

After Gabbi returned to the barflies at the other end: "You don't really like her, do you? She's like ten pounds, and she totally flirts with everybody that walks in here, guys and girls. She's a total fake."

The hungry look had retreated a little, and there was a new kind of hardness in the tired lines around Donald's eyes that Stacy had never seen before. If he did know about the deposit, would he even say anything?

"Anyway, I don't think I can come on New Year's. I've got something else going on."

She was glad of the more familiar reaction she received with this statement.

"You have to come, Stacy!"

"I don't have to do anything. Look, I got this whole thing set up for you, didn't I? So now we're even."

"Even." He said it like the answer to a game show. Weird.

"Yeah. Even. I'm just going to go to the restroom."

In the bathroom, there was a lot of paint on the edges of the mirror. The person who'd done it hadn't even tried. Stacy hated people like that, but sometimes, it didn't really matter. What if there weren't any sloppy drips on the crappy mirror of some stupid bar? Would Rascal's suddenly become the Ritz?

After she went, she didn't even bother to wash her hands. Why bother in this dump?

Donald was talking with some little, old Asian man in a way that quickly made it clear that this was the guy he'd invited along.

"Great." Stacy almost wanted Donald to hear her; he'd even screwed up the possibility for her to meet some cute guy. And this was what his friends were like? Some Oriental senior? She was definitely not coming to the party. Talk about a freak show.

"Stacy, this is Joseph. Joseph, Stacy."

"Oh, pleasure to meet you, Stacy." But the old guy was looking at Donald as if he were worried about something, or surprised. Or maybe scared. Apparently, Donald's buddies were just as weird as he was, not that it would ever matter to her again.

"Hi. So, anyway, I'm going to have to get out of here—"

"You don't want another drink? Or lunch?" Donald had become a little more balanced now that his friend had showed up.

"You're buying?"

"Of course."

The calculation was easy: she didn't have anything else to do. "Okay."

Stacy led them to the table closest to the stained-glass window; it felt the most like a restaurant and the least like a bar there.

"You know, I haven't been in a bar in years, and now two in as many days." Joseph said this for Donald's benefit, not hers. "So how are you doing, Donald?"

"Oh, you know. I think I may be coming down with something."

Stacy had seen Donald sick before; he'd never been so grumpy then. She deserved that money for all the work she did setting up the party at Rascal's, and that's exactly what she'd tell him if he brought it up.

Of course, Gabbi had to deliver the menus herself, even though there was a waitress around somewhere.

"Have you spoken with Andie since last night?" The little old guy was still ignoring her.

At first, Stacy was relieved, because it seemed that the two of them were going to talk about stuff she didn't know or care about, but then she resented being excluded. "So how do you guys know each other?"

Joseph answered: "We're neighbors."

"Oh." There was tons more to it than that, but Stacy wracked her brain to come up with something entirely different to talk about. "So I'm thinking about dyeing my hair. I always liked red. I'm getting real sick of brown." She frowned it out again: "Brown."

Then the men looked up at someone standing behind her, and Stacy twisted in her seat to find a young woman with shiny, straight brown hair holding some expensive purse in front of her. She looked like one of those girls who had just graduated college and was waiting for the next chapter in her life to start. By paying careful attention to every aspect of her appearance, she'd made sure she looked better than everyone else in the room.

"Hey, Donald." Of course, these two words meant about a hundred things, and Stacy rolled her eyes. This one was going to be even weirder than the Chinese guy. Were all of Donald's friends like this? Every little thing so significant, so fraught?

"Andie! What are you doing here? Sit down!"

Andie's eyes bounced all over the place: she didn't want to stay, even though Donald had become a little more animated since she'd arrived.

"This is Stacy. Stacy, Andie."

"Hey."

"Nice to meet you. Listen, I can't stay long."

Stacy began to review the many excuses she could give for getting up and leaving that minute.

The girl hovered over Donald. "I don't mean to be rude, but I was hoping I could speak with you alone for a couple of minutes. Just for a couple of minutes."

Joseph crossed his arms meaningfully, and Stacy realized that if she just got up and left, no one would even notice.

"Okay. Why don't we—"

Andie pointed to the other end of the dining area. "Just over there. Sorry."

So this left Stacy with the old guy. But maybe it was for the best. She could say that she had a headache and leave, and she wouldn't have to worry about Donald's X-ray vision burning a hole through her brain in search of the truth.

But then she realized that she had an opportunity to find out what the deal was with Donald, even though she wasn't all that interested.

"So you guys are neighbors. What's it like living in the same neighborhood? Because working with him was insane."

Joseph's attention was on Donald and the girl. "Oh, you two worked together?"

"Yeah, up until yesterday, when he just decided to get up and leave in the middle of the day. Our boss can put up with a lot of stuff, but Donald's just too much."

For whatever reason, this got the old guy's attention, and he was suddenly annoyed with her. "Tell me, is it that Donald's too much or that the rest of us are just not enough?"

"What?! I don't know about you, but there's nothing wrong with me. And there's definitely something wrong with him."

This was insane. She had to get out. The old guy was looking at her like she was lying or something, and she wasn't, although what she said might have sounded a little nastier than she'd wanted it to.

"Anyway, I promised him that I'd set his little party up here. I owe him a few favors, I guess, and he's not that bad. Are you coming to that thing?"

"I think so."

He was fixated with the others again, so Stacy made her move to leave. She was done with Donald.

"I'm not."

FRIDAY

"And now, they're going to be delivered late." Stacy was still regretting that she hadn't stayed online long enough to finish the transaction for her sister's shoes. After all, Debbie's birthday was in three days, and she lived on Guam. But there had definitely been something about Donald's voice on the phone that had made her log off. He'd sounded tired, but there had also been the vague echo of a threat of danger that, in other people, she always respected.

"Of course, I guess I can afford to get them shipped priority now." She wouldn't; she'd tell Debbie that they'd been out of stock. "Although they'll still probably be late."

And this was the point at which Donald would apologize.

Instead: "There's a drive-through ATM in back."

Stacy dropped her eyes to her instrument panel. "And I'm almost out of gas, too."

"Don't worry about that. I'll cover it."

"I'm not worried, I'm just still wondering why I've agreed to this. It's going to screw up my whole weekend."

Instead of an apology, this time she only got silence.

"So maybe I won't."

The area around the bank hadn't been plowed, and Stacy had to carefully follow the tracks left by a few other, hardier customers. "And what are the roads going to be like? I think we should forget about this."

"What about seven fifty then?"

His new voice was scaring her, now, and it mixed with the excitement the money was generating in her stomach.

"What? Are you serious? Okay, but you're not going to murder me and dump my body out in the middle of nowhere, are you? Because that's what you're acting like."

He looked at her with his old eyes, but the voice was still the same. "I'm not going to murder you."

"So why are you pissed at me?"

Donald got out of the car and walked up to the ATM machine. While she watched him, Stacy pretended to weigh her options, but gave up on that pretty soon because $750 would buy that black, leather sofa. She'd finally have a piece of furniture that would make her apartment smell new for a while and wasn't covered in weird stains.

Donald came back, still looking pissed. She deserved the money for doing this, but she didn't have to take his attitude, too. That wasn't part of the deal.

"It would only give me five hundred."

"What, now you're not even going to put on your seatbelt? So?"

"So we can go to the Bank of America down the street."

"So why are you pissed at me?"

"I'm not." He rubbed his forehead too hard. "Well, not for any good reason."

"Oh. Thanks for clearing that up. You better give me that money right now, because I might decide to kick you out of my car if you're going to be like this the whole time."

When he handed it over, Stacy tried to put the wad of money in her pocket smoothly, as if she were really expecting it.

The parking lot at the next bank had been neatly salted, and she pulled up to the door. She'd have enough left over for those curtains.

"Okay. So when you get back this time, I want you to be nice. I'm not spending the next couple of days stuck with you like this."

Donald pulled a nasty tissue out of his coat and dabbed at his nose. "Okay."

Stacy was probably going to get the flu off of him, on top of everything else. She'd already told him that it was dumb to be driving around when he looked so bad, so she'd done her duty and had nothing to feel guilty about. He was a grown-up, kind of. But he looked like death warmed over.

And he was moving more slowly today, like he was unsure of the ground. It was probably some kind of cold medicine that was doing it. Maybe she could blame his especially weird behavior on that, too, because she certainly hadn't done anything to him. He'd apparently never figured out the thing with the deposit at Rascal's.

Stacy's heartbeat got out of whack for a second when she saw the rest of her money glide out of the bank, and she smoothed her jacket down to remind herself to be cool. She wasn't doing anything wrong.

Walking back, as he looked up at the empty sky, Donald's hair blew up in the wind. He had no idea, but he looked especially goofy, and Stacy tittered until he returned to his seat.

"It's two-sixty."

She took the money. "That's fine. So? What's your deal?"

"I just need to get away from everyone for a while."

"What, I'm not someone?"

"Of course, you're someone." But it wasn't like he would've said it before. It almost sounded like a put-down.

So she just started driving while she considered the best arrangement to cover that wine-cooler stain on the carpet with her new couch. Donald didn't want to talk, anyway, and it wasn't long before he fell asleep, his mouth gaping at the roof of the car because there was no way he was breathing through that nose.

*   *   *

The map Donald had given Stacy stopped making sense after she left Mount Pocono. It was the last purple of dusk and the snow was so much higher here and the snowplows didn't seem as concerned about getting everything off the road as they had been in Orange and the street signs were impossible to read because there were no streetlights.

Stacy stopped. "Donald? Donald?"

It took him a long time to really wake up, and he looked around confused. It was a bit of a relief to find that he was glad to see her, but then his expression darkened. "Oh."

She didn't need to know what that meant, either. $760. "Some help here? I can't find this last road." She thrust the sheet at him and pointed at it. "I've been up and down this one for a half an hour now, and there is no Oak Creek Trail."

"She said it would be hard to spot."

"Oh, that's great. Did she say how we would see it?"

"No."

"So call her."

"I don't have my cell phone."

"What! Mine broke last week! So we're in the middle of nowhere here, and we don't have a phone?"

"I'm sure there's one in the cabin."

"Donald! I'm here, too, you know. I could freeze to death, too. It would be nice if you, like, started thinking about someone else besides yourself for once. And your weird urges."

Donald shook his head while he looked at her glove box. "We'll just go down the road again. I'll help you look."

"Or we could just go home. I'll just keep half the money."

Donald always used to smile a lot. Stacy was okay with that. But now he laughed, and she'd never noticed that he had much of a sense of humor before. Plus, the laugh was nasty, or maybe not nasty, but not nice.

She turned away from him and looked out her window. Even if she did have that coming, she had her money. If he was going to be nasty, she'd just leave, and it would be his fault. There was no way she'd give it back. There was no way she was going to give up that black leather sofa now. See how much he laughed when she just left him there.

But she'd have to endure more than this before she could leave and not feel weird. The laughing wouldn't be enough when she told people who knew him what had happened. It was a good start, but not enough—especially if Donald talked to them, too. Seven-hundred and sixty dollars was a lot of money. She'd have to put up with $760 worth of crap, and right now, she was probably only at $250 or maybe $300, since he snoozed all through her trying to find the street on this stupid road in the middle of nowhere for the last half an hour, and he wasn't even bothering to thank her now for all her help.

From where she'd stopped, there was a view through the naked trees, over the glowing snow, out onto a small valley that seemed completely empty of people—no lights, no roads, no telephone lines. The day was almost completely gone, the light here clearer than any she'd ever seen, and the dark much, much darker. It was so still, and Stacy was sure that if she turned off the car, it would be quiet, too, the incredible cold absorbing all of life's sounds.

Humanity and its signs could've been down there, under and through the murky pines, but Stacy didn't want them to be. Her family had always vacationed in cities, the couple of times they vacationed at all. And the only place she'd been to on her own was Cozumel a couple of times, which she'd experienced with millions of other people who drank from sweating plastic and smelled like suntan lotion and sex.

But now, even though Donald was being a nightmare and trying to make her feel bad, she also felt more important, more special, being somewhere that no one else could share. So Stacy decided that if nobody else was around in her mind, then they weren't there at all. Plus, it was too late to drive home now, anyway.

She was pleased that Donald hadn't understood her silence: "Stacy, I'm sorry I've been so—"

"Wait a minute. Up there. There's a house."

She got out before he could finish his apology and walked up to a diseased trunk with a little, home-made sign on it. *Oak Creek Trail.* Looking up the hill, she noticed that there was a ribbon of land extending toward the summit that had no trees on it, just virgin, crusting snow that was getting squeakier, and farther and farther from its liquid state, as the temperature continued its plunge.

Stacy had only been out of the car for less than a minute, but the hot air that hit her cheeks when she returned made the situation more real: "We're going to have to walk up there."

"The cabin's up there?"

"And I bet it's going to be ice cold inside, too. It's, like, below zero up here. It's bad."

"We can't drive?"

Stacy merely expelled some air and rolled her eyes. "I'm just going to have to leave my car here. Didn't that lady know her driveway wouldn't be cleared?"

"She lives in Florida."

"Whatever." It was completely dark now, the headlights only blaring out a couple of nearby saplings before petering out in the denseness all around them. As he feebly got out of the car, Donald stared around himself like an idiot before Stacy turned off the engine.

"Or we could just hang around here all night." But she actually wanted to feel her boots break through the snow's shell above her, she wanted the muscles in her legs to strain at the incline. They didn't even have a flashlight, and there was no nearby, brooding Manhattan to help out the half moon, but she didn't even care. It was all completely crazy. Stacy wanted to climb a mountain in Pennsylvania in the middle of the night, and the revelation thrilled her, although she wasn't about to tell Donald about it because he'd only overreact.

She grabbed her bag from the trunk, and they started up. It was steeper than it looked, and Donald kept stopping and closing his eyes, sometimes breathing rapidly, sometimes coughing unproductively. This and the cold didn't bother Stacy too much, though. She stopped with him, and looked around, her eyes adjusting to the shadows surrounding her that were too frigid even to keep fear alive in them. Everything was still, turned in on itself. And the silence was made even deeper by the snow, which absorbed it and then pushed it right into Stacy's head, right into her eardrums. She could even smell it, a dry refusal. It was like the end of nature.

"Where the hell have you taken me?"

Donald took a deep breath and plunged a leg into the next stretch of accumulation. "I don't know."

She laughed, even though all of his responses that day had been dumb. "So why do you want to get away from everybody?"

The house was just above them now. The expansive windows covering its façade indicated a beautiful view over the same valley Stacy had inspected earlier. It looked really nice.

Donald hadn't answered her, just continued his slow plod up the hill behind her.

"Okay, if you don't want to talk." She was glad her back was to him, because she was grinning at the cabin.

"Well. I'm not really here to talk." Translation: she wasn't getting paid to talk, but she didn't care. By now, she had reached the porch, where some Adirondack chairs were caught in drifts.

"Give me the key." The snow was lighter in places, and some of it had sifted through the gaps between the floorboards, but it had built up against the house. Stacy started to kick at the section in front of the door until she'd finally reached her destination.

"The lock looks frozen." But her breath caught as she grabbed the handle, fumbling in her gloves, and it immediately gave way. "The door isn't even locked!"

She imagined what it must be like to live in a place where people could leave their doors unlocked for even a minute, and she found it actually frightening, for some reason. "We'll be lucky if there's any furniture in there."

The living room was cold, but really pretty, too. It smelled like frozen potpourri, and Stacy imagined the lady, in her fifties, hair dyed red, sweater with reindeer on it, a perfume trail that made her feel a little like she did in high-school.

"God, where's the thermostat?" But Stacy stopped to take off her boots before she walked farther in. It all looked so hotel clean. "Yikes, the floor is like walking on ice!" Jumping from one foot to another, she tittered her way around the room, eventually locating the thermostat in the hallway and setting it to eighty-five degrees. There was an immediate roar somewhere, and she loved the cabin even more for not letting her down.

Donald was already sitting on the couch, his boots heavy on the rug, hugging himself for warmth.

"It'll warm up pretty quickly. So do you care which bedroom you get? There are two bedrooms, right?"

"Three." There was a shiver in the word, and Stacy turned her attention to the expansive stone fireplace.

"Do you want me to try and light a fire? I've never done it before, but how hard could it be?"

There were already some logs ready to go, so she applied her lighter to one for a few seconds before moving away. "It's probably too cold to light now. So there are three bedrooms? Maybe I can use one to sleep in, and then one for, like, my own private living room! *You* don't want two of them, do you?"

"No." Now he was chattering so strongly that it was getting hard to understand him.

"It'll warm up soon." The rankness of burning dust blew from the registers. "See?" She took a closer look at the living room. "Why does she have the sofa turned away from the window? That's so stupid! I'm going to have to move all this furniture around. And that chair should be on this side, too, so—"

"Stacy."

"What?"

"We're not moving the furniture."

"Why not? We paid for the place."

"Just leave it where it is."

"God. I thought you wanted me here, Mr. Buzzkill."

He closed his eyes as he tried to lean back.

"What, you don't want me to enjoy myself? Why did you invite me, then?"

A noticeable shiver was his only response.

"Donald, why did you invite me!"

"Stacy! Because I needed someone to drive me here. That's all."

"But why me?"

"Because. Because I like you."

"You've got a really weird way of showing it."

"I'm just tired."

"No. No, I don't want to be here for the next two days, wondering why I'm here. I'm not that stupid."

"Because you're the only one who doesn't act like you like me."

That brought it up to $400. Maybe even $450. "Whatever."

"I'm sorry. That's not what I mean. I mean that you don't try to turn me into something that you want. Or that you need. You're honest about everything, I guess. With me, with yourself. And I have to try and figure some things out, because right now, I feel like everyone's just out for themselves, you know? Like nobody really gets anyone else." He was losing his battle to control the shaking, so he took a deep breath before continuing. "I'm going to be seeing a lot of friends at my party, and I just want to have everything back to normal. So I just can't have people needing anything from me right now. I need time to think."

"Okay." Stacy grabbed her suitcase and hurried into the hallway, opening a couple of doors. The bedrooms looked pretty much the same, so she picked one with a king-sized bed that was right next to another bedroom that had a couple of twins. That one could be her private living room.

Closing the door on Donald, who looked small, flimsy on the couch by himself, Stacy was confronted with the blackness of a big window with only an arresting reflection of herself. She didn't look like she felt, because she knew she felt pretty excited to be there.

Quickly turning her attention to her suitcase, she wished she could see what her view was like. Maybe if it was better out of her private living room, she could switch, although she didn't like the idea of sleeping on a narrow bed. But the big bed before her was way too heavy for her to move alone, and she knew that Donald would never help her. Not if he was going to continue to be in such a stupid mood.

SATURDAY

There were only some stale Apple Jacks and some even staler tea. It was exciting, though, eating something different than her normal oatmeal and coffee, even if the Apple Jacks were dry and the tea tasted like browned water. They were different.

The interior was brilliant, a million reflections of white light swapping back and forth from inside to outside and back. There seemed to be no source to it, it came from everywhere and was everything. At home, she always kept her two windows tightly blinded because all she could see was her neighbor's bathroom five feet away out of one and a run-down White Castle out of the other. Here, there were snow-draped firs and wavy hills surrounding her, and definitely, definitely no people in the little valley. There was no reason to deny the light here.

So Stacy became a part of it. She let her robe drop back over the chair as she leaned back and stretched, her slippers gliding sensuously over the clean, warm, vinyl floor. At home, she would've been annoyed that it was nearly noon and Donald hadn't even bothered to get up, but here, now, this just meant that she had the run of the place, almost like she owned it. She didn't even want to watch television, she just wanted to sit in each one of the chairs in the house to see what the individual experiences were like. There were so many chairs!

Still, she could check if he wanted some Apple Jacks. They'd never thought to bring any food, and Donald hadn't even bothered to pack a bag, so it really wasn't her problem. But the pleasant cabin was wearing off on her. She sort of felt like earning her $310. Plus, she wanted to prove to him that she really didn't want anything else from him, not like those people she'd met at the bar. She'd get him some breakfast and then just leave him alone.

In fact, Stacy kind of felt like a different person here, in a way. It was wearing off on her, and she wanted to match the white spotlessness, the expanse of rooms, the unashamed windows. She could be more like the person Donald thought she was here; it was possible, and it was something she felt like trying, at least for a while. Just for the Poconos.

The whole place was trimmed in light-colored, knotty pine. When she was a kid, she always felt bad in rooms trimmed in knotty pine because she imagined all the Christmas trees that never had a chance to wear tinsel or a star. Now it hardly bothered her as she inspected an especially large knot on Donald's door. For some reason, she thought of him when sometimes he came out of Brad's office and looked kind of hurt and alone. Just for that, she knocked directly on the knot, hard.

"Donald? It's noon."

Her own voice was ten times louder here, and she could feel it reach the farthest corners of the cabin—places she hadn't even visited yet. She liked the feeling of filling up the house, so she did it again: "Donald? Do you want some Apple Jacks? There's no milk and they taste funny, but it's better than nothing. Or tea. There are some old tea bags. Donald?"

Stillness again. If she held perfectly still here, in the hall in the middle of the house, she could hear her own body making noises. New Jersey was so loud.

"Donald?" Of course, he was probably sick. He'd been shaking and sweating the night before. How much did nurses make an hour? "I'm coming in."

Stacy was expecting a dark room, but when she opened the door, she was greeted by sunshine even more raw than in the living room.

"You got skylights!" She stared right up at the kind of winter sky that revealed itself as infinite outer space.

His bed was huge, too, and for the first time since Stacy knew him, he looked insignificant. At least she thought it was him; there was a narrow bump in the middle of the bed.

"You know, this room is really worth two of the other rooms. You totally lucked out. Donald?"

There was no way he could sleep through her voice; it was bouncing all over the place. Stacy approached the bed and shook the bump. Even the comforter was nicer on this bed—real down inside beige, crinkly cotton. She'd only gotten some kind of home-style quilt thing.

"Donald?"

Finally, he stirred, his face slowly emerging from the crash of pillows. He looked really bad, and Stacy could distinctly smell nursing home coming from the heat trapped under the comforter.

"What?" He only whispered it.

"Are you okay? You look worse."

"No."

"Well, I guess you picked the right room to be sick in!"

Then Stacy noticed the private, white bathroom that Donald had—with even more skylights. Then she noticed the French doors and a private balcony. Then she noticed something on the balcony.

Rising slowly, almost afraid to approach it, Stacy squealed as soon as she was sure.

"Oh my god! There's a hot tub out there! You got a hot tub! I am totally going to do that! And you can see right out over everything from here! You so got the best room!"

Why had she thought that she'd gotten the best room last night? She hadn't even bothered to check them all. "But you know, with all these skylights, it's so bright in here. Maybe you'd be better off somewhere else. You know, darker, so you can rest."

There was an odd, filled silence, and then Donald did something like laugh, but it was too choked, too shallow to be a laugh.

She decided that it wasn't a laugh. "Anyway, do you want anything? Apple Jacks?"

His shiny face pressed itself up and out of the covers, and he struggled to breathe for a moment. He was still sort of whispering. "You know, Stacy, it's so funny that I never totally appreciated you before."

The old Donald would've meant this, and he did sound like the old Donald. But she wasn't taking any chances. "Maybe you'd feel better with some tea?"

"People actually do some pretty funny things. Like me, for instance. And funny's not bad, exactly. Not *always*." But he didn't sound particularly amused.

"What do you mean—funny ha-ha, or funny strange?"

"I think they're the same thing."

"Whatever, I'm getting you some tea. You look like hell, and you sound like hell."

His head dropped back. "Water. Please. Just water."

Stacy wasn't sure if she was the butt of a joke. If she was, then it was worth $50 at least, because she hadn't done anything to deserve it. She'd been careful to be a perfect housemate since they'd arrived. She was even nice enough to get Donald's water out of the little, filtered water spout and not just the regular faucet, which would've taken much less time.

He'd fallen back asleep when she returned, so she put the glass on the bedside table and quietly approached the French doors. Everything they would ever dream of needing or wanting for the weekend was here, except for food.

Gino Bartolo had spread out breadfruit and mangoes and coconuts and guavas and bananas and other, even more exotic fruit on the table in his galley. After Papeete, he was looking forward to gentle beaches with transparent, bath waves and graceful, gray clouds always gesturing heavenward. Instead of thinking about the war, he mashed up one of the mangoes in his hand and let its juice run down his arm, spread across his face. Another reason to jump in the water, which didn't have it out for you here. This water didn't want you dead.

As he looked up from his bobbing body, into the sun and over the stern toward his cabin, Gino attempted to determine what his children were doing now. Either asleep or in school. A building wave came up behind him, and he and the boat rolled and dipped, briefly reminding him of the rougher seas of his past, but only briefly. Then he distinctly heard all his beautiful fruit hit the floor, and he knew it wouldn't be the same, now, but that eventually, in time, everyone would understand why he was bobbing alone in the Pacific thousands and thousands of miles away, worried about fatal bruising to his wondrous collection.

He had to take back the sea.

*   *   *

Donald had been watching her for a while, and Stacy knew it. She was careful to keep her back to him, but it was also the best position to see the valley from, anyway. She was also very, very conscious of her bra strap. She'd never dreamt of bringing a bathing suit—or, needless to say, underwear for public consumption—so it was a very awkward situation for her. No one was supposed to see her beige bra—especially Donald.

She was more exposed at this point because she'd had to rise up a bit from the frothing water. It was scorching. But she'd sink back down in a minute or two, after the water evaporated on her skin in the polar wind and her upper body was frozen. Suddenly, she looked down, even more horrified: her nipples were totally obvious in the wet bra! She rechecked the proximity of her towel and turned to reassure herself of her escape route when she saw white legs approaching. It was complete nudity: Donald, with some terrible criss-cross bruises on his chest so her gaze was a millisecond longer than she wanted it to be, and his groin, which was like a dark bruise lower down.

It was Donald's room, but the hot tub belonged to the whole cabin, so when he opened the door, she was furious: "Donald! What are you doing!"

He came around her right, so she turned her head to the left and closed her eyes. Assuming a very awkward position, she sunk below the foam to her chin. "What's wrong with you? You are not coming in here like that!"

Stacy felt the water shift, rise; she heard the little splashes. "I'm getting out, then."

"Wow. It's hot."

"I'm getting out."

"You can't see anything now. Open your eyes."

"I'm getting out."

"Okay, but wait a minute."

Her head still straining away from him, Stacy opened her eyes. The hills were even more inspired, the air even clearer of everything.

"I wanted to ask you something." He was still whispering, taking little breaths between words, which seemed painful to him in lots of ways.

"What happened to your chest?"

The hum of the water pump, the fizzling bubbles—they suddenly roared in the absence of his response.

Finally: "I fell."

"You fell?! Sounds like you should be asking *yourself* some questions."

He was quiet again, except for a long, drawn-out, failed cough. The towel was within reach, but if her bra was transparent, what would her panties be like?

"What are you most proud of?"

"What? Donald, give me a break."

"Really, though."

"What about you?"

"Nothing. I haven't done anything I'm proud of. Everything I've done has been for myself."

That didn't sound right at all to Stacy, but who was she to argue? "So you can't be proud of things you do for yourself."

"I don't think so. No."

She was getting annoyed by his self-pity. "You've done a few things for me."

"But for myself. You were right. I'm just as selfish as everyone else."

This was definitely a path Stacy didn't want to continue down. She wanted to stay as clean as the mountainside. "Whatever. Close your eyes, because I'm getting out."

Again, only the humming, the frothing.

"Are your eyes closed?"

"What's it been like for you being in love?"

"Are you trying to wreck this whole trip for me?"

"Of course not, I just need to know. Please!"

"You don't *need* to know anything. Why do you *need* to know that?"

More wheezing. "Because I'm in love with you, and I need to remember why."

Stacy rose and turned toward the towel; he wouldn't see much. "And that's it. That's your $760." The cold just shocked her into saying more. "You're going to have to get someone else to pick you up, because I'm leaving now, and I'm not taking you with me. I'm sorry, I've really tried to help, but you're not going to do this to me."

"You must've known, though—"

"Is there a phone here? I didn't see a phone."

"I don't want anything from you. I do this to everybody."

Something made sense, and she paused after wrapping the towel around herself, but only for a second. "Give me the number of someone who can pick you up, and I'll call them from that town. But I'm not waiting. Do *what* to everybody?"

"Fall for them when I see them."

"What do you mean: everybody?"

"Everybody. But it doesn't make sense to me, anymore."

"Everybody?! Of course, it doesn't make sense! That's crazy! Who do you want me to call?"

"Please stay. You don't have to do anything. I really need you here."

"Who do you want me to call?" Did that 'everyone' include Brad?

"Please. I'm going crazy with this—"

"Donald—"

"You can have this room. You could have the hot tub all to yourself."

"No way."

"Then you can have this room and the other room. And I'll give you another $500." But Donald sounded like he already knew what her response was going to be, and his voice collapsed into oblivion.

Stacy's hand was on the frozen door handle. She could see the squares of light on the floor of the master bedroom cast by the skylights inside.

Skylights.

But then a sudden wave of nausea grasped her, and she swung around at him. "Shut up! You know, you try and make me look like some kind of money-grubbing bitch, but you're the one who's screwed up! You're a freak, and now I know why! You've totally wrecked this whole thing for me!" Something inside of her wanted to stop. "I don't care if you do think you love me, because it doesn't count when the person who loves you is crazy! I had to work with you in the same room, and I've been nice to you a couple of times, but all this ends right now. And you can figure out your own way back home."

Instead of looking upset, Donald just stared at her, lost, which just proved her point: he was crazy. "Please, Stacy. Tomorrow night, I just can't—"

"It isn't my fault! So stop blaming me!"

Satisfied, she passed into the master bedroom with its thick, cream carpeting, and then through the toasty hall back to her bedroom, which had a really nice view, too. It would only take a second to pack up her few things, and even though he didn't deserve it, she'd call Donald's cell phone when she got home. Someone might pick it up.

It was even prettier in the living room now, and she hadn't even gotten the chance to sit in all the chairs. He wrecked it all for her! But it was too late now; she wanted to leave on this crest of emotion.

Pulling on her boots, Stacy found herself next to those snowed-in Adirondack chairs again. The place wasn't going anywhere. She could come back, maybe in the summer—by herself!—and actually enjoy the experience. The place could still be special to her, no matter what happened before.

The walk back down the hill through the snow was harder. Her boots were slipping in the footprints from the night before, so she had to blaze a new trail, and this hid its own treacheries of rocks and holes under the surface. Although the temperature seemed to be dropping even further—or maybe it was because of her wet hair—her back still felt hot, exposed; it was expecting Donald.

She stopped halfway down when the graceful, slender trunks around her were too much to ignore. It was the purity that did it: no dirt, no animals, nothing bad was there. To her, in Jersey, winter woods were sinister hiding places, tramp-filled vacant lots, secret-activity areas, filthy slush-edged private property with vague menacings of owners' shotguns. Plus, they were sullied further by their summer states, when they were muddy, bug-infested patches littered with rotting frog corpses and fungi and rain-swollen porn. Here, she just had to pause in the simple, untouched stillness.

She'd enjoyed being like the light in the cabin. But it hadn't even lasted an hour, thanks to Donald.

And he hadn't bothered to follow her. He wasn't even watching her from one of the cabin's soaring windows. He loved everybody?! How was she supposed to feel about that! Real love was picking out the special one, your perfect person. How could *everyone* be perfect?! She'd always kind of known that there was something mentally wrong with Donald, but this explained everything. Was the New Year's party supposed to become an orgy?! Did that make her a pimp, somehow, for helping him out at Rascal's?!

Then she thought of Donald and knew that she was getting silly. She still despised him for taking her here and then driving her away, for not even remembering *why* he loved her, but he wasn't *mean*. Mean wasn't really the same as wanting to have sex with her, even though it felt that way.

Still, in her very limited, far-off experience, being in love meant having a long list of reasons why you loved someone, even if that list was a joke to you a few years later. She'd certainly never tried to get Donald to love her, and in fact, he forced her to be kind of nasty to him, but when she was in love with Jimmy, the first thing she did was *forget* all the bad stuff about him. And then she *built up* the good stuff. It sounded as if Donald had it the other way around.

Stacy knew she had lots of good stuff; if Donald didn't know what it was, then it was not her problem, and he was even stupider and crazier than she thought.

She continued her slow trek down the hill until she saw it.

*   *   *

"Donald! Donald!" The white light and enveloping heat of the living room was wonderful, but Stacy's mind was too blanched by her shock to enjoy it. "Donald."

His door was still partially open; she stood at its edge and looked away. "Donald?" Cautiously, she peered in: the bed and bathroom were empty. "Donald."

She certainly didn't want to talk to him when he was naked, but he had to still be in the hot tub. She pushed the door slowly open, ready to rip her eyes off of his figure when she saw him.

His head was slumped over and bright red.

"Jesus Christ." As she ran to the deck, she was glad that the French doors were closed because there had been too much annoyance and not enough worry in her voice.

"Donald! Donald!" He didn't want to wake up, so she ran to the bathroom, snatched a pristine, white towel that was as thick as a stack of her own at home, and grasped him under the shoulders, pulling him out to his navel. Unwilling to be alone with him nude again, she carefully placed the towel over his midsection as she continued to pull, but he slipped away from her right hand and landed with his face in the snow.

"God!" His torso was turned halfway away from her, so she was able to drape the towel the way she wanted. Unfortunately, she wasn't sure how to get him into the bedroom besides dragging him, and if she did, the towel would slide off.

Her solution was to wad the towel over his crotch and pull him by both hands. His skin was really loose, so it dragged under him, but she finally got him next to the bed. Here, she decided to take the bedclothes and a pillow off and make him as comfortable as possible on the floor. There was no way she was going to try and lift him back into bed. She was not getting paid enough for that.

"Donald?" Besides drunks at parties, she'd never seen someone out like this before. Stacy looked around the room for some ideas. The glass of water she'd brought was still on the table above her head, but how would throwing water on him wake him up if he'd just come out of a bunch of water? He'd probably just been in for too long.

And his breathing was fast, too, which didn't seem good.

"Donald?" Stacy slapped him across the face a few times. It wasn't as difficult as she thought it would be. "Donald!"

He didn't recognize her when he opened his eyes; she was just an object to focus on. It was too weird, so she took the opportunity to turn off the hot tub and close the door to the deck. Stacy felt relieved that she'd come back, but scared, then, at the thought of what would've happened if she hadn't. Very quickly, this all turned sour in her stomach when she considered everything she'd been put through since she'd agreed to all of it. And now this.

"You came back." He made it sound like proof, even though it was so faint.

"Yeah." When she turned toward him, he looked stupid there on the floor.

"I guess I passed out?"

"I guess so."

"You came back."

"Yeah. Somebody hit my car."

Donald didn't even apologize, now, for the car or for the way he looked away from her as if she was the one who was naked.

"Because I drove you up here. Because I had to park in the road because the lady didn't bother to plow her driveway." Almost immediately, Stacy was glad that Donald wasn't looking at her, anymore.

"I'll pay for it."

"Yeah, well don't worry about it. The woman who hit it left a note on the windshield, and she says she's going to pay for it. She lives up the road."

"So you're going to stay?"

"Only until I can get a rental car and get back home. She can pay for that, too. Or you can. This whole thing has been a total nightmare." Stacy noticed that he was still red. "I wish I'd never come."

"Me, too." This was so soft that it was almost like the silence mumbling.

What did he want from her? None of this was her fault! It was the same as that time she had borrowed his stapler and broke it. It was an office; she had to staple things. It wasn't her fault that he had a crappy stapler, it wasn't her fault that he wasn't there to ask. She needed a stapler! It wasn't her fault! Donald never said a thing about it, but she could tell he was disappointed in her then, too—probably because she didn't replace it. Although then, he didn't know he was disappointed. He'd just said he was glad that she felt comfortable borrowing his things and that he'd only gotten it at a dollar store, anyway.

But now they were someplace entirely different and he knew he was disappointed and she hated it, hated him.

"*And* I'm going to have to get you to the emergency room, somehow, because you're all red and you're passing out now."

"I'll be okay."

"God! Please. You knew you were sick, yesterday! You shouldn't have done any of this."

Stacy hadn't realized how much she depended on Donald's apologies until they dried up. He just stared off into a corner of the room.

"*That's* a reason: I'm taking you to the ER. And I'm mad at you for not taking care of yourself. Two reasons." She swung her legs on the edge of the bed, back and forth.

Stacy could tell he knew what she was talking about because he didn't move. "But you *know* I'm looking for reasons now."

"So? What do you think, people don't know that the other person is looking for reasons right from the first date? That's why guys give flowers and girls dress up and flirt and stuff."

"But that's because they already *like* somebody, and they want the other person to feel the same way."

He'd obviously already tried to come up with every argument against her proof that she wasn't a monster. Why was she bothering?

"So driving you to the emergency room when I'd rather be home means I don't care about you?"

He coughed up a laugh at this, but it was weak. "I think so."

"Why do you want to make me feel like such a bitch?"

Once again, no note of conciliation: "I don't."

"Whatever. Whatever! I'm going to find that lady." Stacy stepped over Donald. "I mean, what do you want from me?"

"I don't know!" He suddenly sounded more frustrated than she was. Even his hacking sounded furious.

For some reason, this calmed Stacy. "You know, there are a ton of reasons to love me, or you wouldn't. You're not *that* crazy."

She thought he shrugged down there, under the covers.

"Whatever! I'm going." And she passed through the sunny cabin again, noticing for the first time a set of Russian dolls in the hallway laid out like anthropomorphic stairs, their eyes considering her one moment, sightless the next.

*   *   *

Connie was a take-charge kind of lady, so she was the first person through the door. She'd been sure to mention a few times that she knew the people who owned the cabin, and this, plus her locality, seemed somehow to trump Donald and Stacy's rent. In fact, Stacy was surprised to find that Connie's presumptions about her beautiful cabin didn't bother her, as she was drawn along in the wake of the lady's urgent bustle.

"Where, in the master bedroom?"

"Yeah." Stacy followed behind the woman, who was built like a cartoon hen, all broad upper body, inconsequential neck and legs.

Connie knocked, but it was cursory, and she soon swooped down on Donald.

"Donald? Donald?"

He turned his head away from Connie, and Stacy's stomach dropped. It was worse than anything else she'd seen all weekend.

"Do you understand what I'm saying?" Connie delivered this with a hospital briskness. "Donald?"

"Yes."

She hadn't expected Connie to arise so quickly, so when she was face-to-face with the lady, Stacy winced. "You see what I mean?"

"We'll take my car to the medical center."

"Now?"

Connie turned her back on Stacy. "Donald, we're going to go to the hospital now. Can you get up?"

After one of his shallow, gut-squeezing coughs: "It's just a cold."

"I actually work in a doctor's office. My daughter hit Stacy's car, and when Stacy came over and told me that you'd fainted, I thought I should take a look for myself. Donald, it's more than a cold, and you need to see a doctor right away."

"I'll be okay."

Connie returned her attention to Stacy and frowned. "What are we going to do, here?"

"What's wrong with him?"

"That's for a doctor to say, but we really need to get him over there."

"But if he doesn't want to go—"

"Stacy."

"All right. All right. Can you just leave us alone for a second?"

"You know, he may be a bit confused right now because of the fever, but—"

For a second, Stacy embraced this thought, but it was a lot harder to convince herself of stuff now, for some reason. Stuff that wasn't really true. So this was a novel experience for her and *another* reason for Donald, if he ever noticed it. "I'll talk to him."

When Connie had gone, Stacy approximated the woman's tone: "Donald, you have to go with us now. Connie works in a doctor's office."

His face was still turned away. "At the front desk."

"It doesn't matter where—" But she'd already heard the dry giggle under the luxurious expanse of cotton on the floor. "It's because of the new people you'll meet, isn't it. Feeling things for them."

Donald was silenced, and Stacy sat back down on the bed. "See? I might be a little smarter than you thought. And another thing: did you ever think that maybe you're so depressed about your life because you're sick?"

"It isn't that."

"Then what is it?"

He rolled over. "Don't worry. There's nothing you can say now, and there's nothing you can do. The pressure's off."

"Fine." Stacy felt tears burning the corners of her eyes; it reminded her of her childhood and its impotency's overwhelming frustrations. She worked to keep her voice somewhat even and her mind in the present. "So, you want to wait until you're passed out again and we have to call an ambulance?"

"Just go home. I'll be fine."

"I'm not going to let you do this."

"Why not?"

"Because I'm not a bad person, Donald! I'm not going to let you be right about me."

Her outburst seemed to have no effect on him.

Stacy turned toward his suitcase in the corner, now glad that she was crying and that he'd seen it. She retrieved some clothes and threw them at him.

"We'll be back in two minutes for you. You're going to the hospital whether you're dressed or not."

Connie was seated in the middle of the living room, her coat now open, her gaze stretching out over the valley, her wide eyebrows arching when she saw Stacy. "Is everything okay?"

"He's dressing. He's kind of depressed." Connie seemed to understand what she meant. "He won't look at you, probably. He's not trying to be rude."

"How are you doing?"

"Oh. You know." Stacy didn't want this woman to see her so upset, so she walked over to the kitchen and acted as if she was looking for something. When she could: "How far away is the hospital?"

"About a half an hour. But they're really good over there. You've got nothing to worry about. My younger daughter broke her arm last year, and they were just great about it."

"I was supposed to be going home, now, but with Donald like this…"

"Of course."

"I mean, I just can't leave him like this. It wouldn't be right."

"Sure."

"I'm just going to check on him."

Stacy returned, knocking like Connie had. "Donald? Are you ready?"

He hadn't moved. "Donald." Her eyes began to sting again. "This isn't my fault." But words were just sounds coming out of her mouth now. She ripped the comforter off of Donald, perfectly happy to allow her eyes to graze his backside, and began to tug his underwear up his limp legs. "And what about that time I let you have my lunch? You know, I was lying when I said I hated turkey. Why would I bring a turkey sandwich if I hated it? I just wasn't hungry, but I could've left it in the refrigerator for the next day."

But old sandwiches got hard on the outside and soggy on the inside. Stacy's face was dripping onto Donald. "I'm here *now*, Donald! I'm still here! I *want* to help! What difference does it make *why*? It's not for me! It's for you."

"It's for you." Donald's odd, feeble voice was quickly lost under the bed. "Turns out we're all pretty much the same, so don't worry. Everything I've done has been for myself, too. It's okay."

The corduroy pants were more work; even though he'd gotten skinnier, Donald was still a big man. And he wasn't helping Stacy at all.

"Okay. I don't know about you, but sure, I guess I'm kind of selfish or whatever. Maybe everybody is. But I'm not going to stop getting you dressed. And nothing you say will get me to give up on getting you to the hospital. I don't care what you say, that's a good thing, no matter why I'm doing it."

"Well, as long as it helps you feel better about yourself."

Stacy was now above his right cheek; she suddenly recognized an urge to spit on him for that, mostly because he was right. But she kept her voice light and hard. "There's nothing you can say."

Her mind was exploding in so many directions that she had no idea how to prove him wrong. Donald had picked her out of everybody he loved as the worst one—and maybe he was right—so how was she, of all people, supposed to prove that she was more than just selfish? She hated him for it, but maybe she deserved it, a little.

So Stacy simply focused on his shirt. She got one arm on and roughly rolled him over. His eyes were closed now. "Can you walk to the car, or are we going to have to carry you?"

Donald remained silent, so she finished buttoning him up and returned to Connie.

"We're going to have to carry him down the hill."

Connie stared at Stacy's tear-ravaged face before responding. "Maybe I should get my husband over here—"

"I'll carry him down, then. Or we can drag him."

"Wait. The Gallardo's have a sled in the garage, I think."

Connie disappeared through a door in the kitchen, and Stacy sat in one of the chairs that she'd never tried before. It was just like every other chair she'd ever sat in. Her breath kept catching, and now, when she looked out onto the valley, all she saw was empty space, miles and distance and wasted time.

Connie poked her chicken head through the door. "I guess it's a good thing that we got so much snow."

*   *   *

Donald was all dead weight. He was conscious, but he kept his eyes closed, a reaction that Stacy had never had to outsmart before, so her thoughts raged even more desperately, ineffectually. Looking down at his clenched eyelids as she and Connie slowly eased him down the hill, Stacy just couldn't come up with an answer that would make them open back up and see her.

The naked trunks still leaned into the cabin's driveway; their virginal depths still caught on Stacy's imagination. But now, the sun had changed its position, and the flaws in their bark were spotlit. Now the random, messy twigs and crusty dead patches were the same as the messiness and death of her New Jersey. And every time Stacy came up with a selfless, amazing deed performed by someone, it could always be turned around. The saints were saints because they wanted to be thought of as saints; they wanted to go to heaven; they wanted people to worship them, which people then promptly did. To make matters worse, she'd experienced relatively little charity in her own life: others rarely did her any good deeds, and she responded to the world by seldom bothering with kindness, either. The few selfless acts she'd performed had felt like implicit admissions to weakness or secret feelings, or unearned rewards, or just plain too much work. And when Stacy did recall the scattered examples of her nice behavior, without exception, she'd just been looking for a thank-you, a return favor, or a more advantageous position. If these were the motivations for everyone else, she'd been right all along not to do anyone any favors.

As they eased the sled down next to Connie's car, Stacy watched Donald's thin hair sticking up from his forehead and waving in the breeze. It was still the same. She realized that her motivations for kindness had never been his. He'd never really wanted anything in return from her except what she wanted to give him back—which hadn't been much. Although he might have befriended her to make himself feel good, that certainly wasn't the crime he was making it out to be. Plus, there *had* to be some collateral, positive effects from Donald's relationships with others that didn't originate in selfishness. She just couldn't think of any.

And Stacy had time to, during the ride to the hospital. Connie would occasionally mention points of local interest as they approached them, but otherwise, she was mostly silent, allowing Stacy the chance to sweep her eyes across the swelling landscape while silencing increasingly desperate sobs in the back seat with Donald. Donald, who was sleeping again, his breathing short and shallow, had collapsed against his door, and Stacy allowed herself to really study him for the first time. Those were the same hands that had typed on the computer across from her desk, and those were the same feet that had tapped against the corner of the desk that would still be across from hers on Tuesday. Stacy realized, finally, that she'd never even truly looked at him before, mostly because she'd been disturbed by his weird behavior and then guilty about the way their friendship developed. She added this fact to all the others she'd have to regret: she'd never really seen him.

In fact, Donald's left hand was very pale, almost lavender now. She covered it with her own because she just couldn't look at it like that, and anyway, she could bring it back from its icy state this way. If he'd been awake, he'd have said that she held his hand just for her own good, and maybe it was true.

There were clouds gathering in the west now, and they were the flat, battleship clouds that reminded her of Orange in the winter, the kind that threatened January and inflicted February. The clouds were exactly the same in the Poconos, and long after all of this was over, she'd see clouds like them and think of this horrible drive and how nothing she saw, nothing she heard, had helped her find a way to redeem herself.

Stacy realized that Connie was staring at her in the rearview mirror, and she wiped her nose.

"He'll be fine, now. Don't worry."

Instead of Stacy's hand warming Donald's, she found that his had become the source of cold creeping up her veins.

*   *   *

When they reached the emergency room entrance, Connie turned around to the back seat, straining to keep her eyes off of Donald. Stacy knew why: the redness in Donald's face had become patchy now, and it alternated with the purplish-white color of his hands. Stacy didn't know if she was crying for him or herself, anymore.

"Okay, I'm going to stay in here. You go in, because you know more about him and what's going on. Okay?"

Stacy nodded and quickly entered the hospital. There was only one baby crying in a corner and not even any blood, so her hiccupping hysteria looked much more out of place than it would have in the ERs at home. She didn't care.

"How can I help you." The man behind the counter didn't look bored, exactly, but his eyes rested firmly on Stacy's and dismissed her red, wet, tortured face.

"My friend Donald is sick."

"Okay. How is he sick, exactly."

"He's not awake, and he's not breathing much, and his face is blotchy and he's cold."

The man considered what Stacy said for a moment, his eyes passing over the waiting room and out the doors. "Okay. He's outside?" She nodded. "I'll just get someone to help him in, all right?" She nodded again.

He left through a door behind him for a second, and Stacy took a deep breath of the hospital air and grabbed the polished Formica before her. Donald was right: there wasn't anything she could say. People go to emergency rooms, and they're driven to emergency rooms by people, and sometimes people cause other people to be in emergency rooms. People just wandered around, breathing for themselves and struggling for themselves and taking for themselves. An old man was snoring in a chair near her, and she didn't even care if he lived or died. Because soon, he'd be dead and she'd be dead and the screaming baby would be dead and that was that. It was kind of the way she'd always felt, deep down inside, but now it was so much worse because she knew it was there, and she didn't want it to be, anymore. Blaming Donald didn't even work because she couldn't blame Donald for the world.

At least the Formica was warming under her hand. That was something.

A couple of other people hurried past her and out the sliding doors with a gurney, and their speed made Stacy feel worse. Then the man at the counter returned with a clipboard.

"Okay. We'll just need a little more information. How do you know the man?"

"He's a friend. We used to work together."

"Do you happen to know anything about his medical history?"

"No."

"Do you know if he has health insurance?"

"No. But I've got $760 on me, right now."

"Well, you may not have to worry about that. If you could just fill this out to the best of your knowledge, we'll get him to a doctor right away."

Stacy took the clipboard and stared at it. Something was different; the edges bit into the flesh of her palms. She looked up and saw Donald being strapped in and her heart jumped. Between them was the same clinical expanse that contained the same misery and uncertainty of the other people, but it wasn't just that, anymore.

She dropped the clipboard on the edge of the counter and it fell and hit the tile, but she ran back out toward the winter, through the doors to Donald.

Connie's face was pinched by worry now, and she stopped talking to the men when she saw Stacy approaching.

"They're going to take good care of him, Stacy. They're bringing him in right now."

Stacy came up to Donald, and now she hoped he was just closing his eyes. She didn't even need him to open them.

"Donald? Donald, I just told them I'd pay for this with the money you gave me, and I swear I didn't even think of myself. Not once! You can ask the man in there. It really was just for you!"

Connie grasped Stacy's arms to remove her from the orderlies' way. "You can tell him all about it, later, sweetheart. Just let the gentlemen do their job right now."

"Donald! Don't you see! I'm different, now!"

The men kept their eyes off of Stacy and started to wheel their patient into the hospital.

Connie held Stacy back. "You can tell him later, Stacy. When he can understand you better."

Donald was enveloped by the electric doors, and then Stacy was left staring at her own reflection: her smile was the first odd thing she noticed, but so much of her looked strange.

Stacy didn't fight Connie; she knew she was right. She'd tell him later, tell him how she'd changed and that it was all because of him, and that this was the reason he was looking for.

She'd just wait.

SUNDAY

When Stacy walked into Rascal's:

Helmut turned quickly away from her and back to slouching over the last stool at the bar. Every face that wasn't Donald's made the pain more acute, but also eased it, the conflicting emotions joining with the whisky and amplified by it. Helmut knew that each stranger's arrival added to the probability that Donald was suffering so terribly that he was unable to attend the party that had meant so much to him—or worse, that its importance had died away during the weekend along with a part of himself. But every swing of the front door also meant that it was a little less likely Helmut would have to endure saying goodbye to Donald—saying goodbye and apologizing because even though Helmut loved him more than ever, he finally understood that the trek into the wilderness was his alone. And his purpose would be to grow into a man if he could, and that man, instead of participating in the destruction of Donald Hanak, would somehow be wise enough to prevent it.

Andie was standing next to the warm engine of her car in Rascal's parking lot, watching Joseph carefully get out of her car. This was one of those times when she wanted to crush him in her arms so hard that she'd feel his weak bones snap and he'd look up at her, confusion and contrition in his black eyes. She knew it wasn't his fault he was born so long ago; she just wanted him to respect her for hating that their ages distanced them from each other in so many ways. It didn't seem to bother him much at all. Then again, she liked the distance because it allowed her to be herself more with Joseph, and that was a good thing. He never encouraged her negative behavior at the same time as encouraging her positive behavior because he didn't encourage behavior at all. Donald had made her selfish like that: he loved her indiscriminately, no matter what she did. And for this and so many other reasons, he'd probably gotten what he'd deserved at the Evergreen. But she'd still decided to come to his party because it was important to Joseph and because she wanted to explain her relationship with him to Donald and also check to be sure that he was all right. He'd been so strange in the motel room, the light in his eyes like a kite lost and receding into the horizon.

Elizabeth was staring at the dust on a plastic plant near her head, wondering why Donald would ever consider having a party in such a shithole. Then she wondered why

229

on earth she presumed to know the first thing about what Donald would consider. But she wanted to understand more about him, now that she'd told Brad about what she'd done in the cafe, and Brad had gushed on and on about how great Donald was. She'd been surprised at first that he hadn't understood what she'd just confessed; then gradually, it became clear that her husband's definitions had changed, definitions of morality, definitions of love. So she'd been honest with herself and him and had expressed her interest in a three-way, and then the conversation had swung back to Donald's perfection. Elizabeth was glad that Brad was finally allowing himself to feel again instead of trying to be a thinker, and the possibilities for her future had multiplied before her in a very pleasant fashion.

Joseph was struggling to right himself on the ice as he got out of Andie's car. He'd not looked forward to a party—not really looked forward to anything—for so long that his heart was actually beating harder. He could feel it. It wasn't because of his near fall; he was really, really looking forward to Donald's party, and his plan was to do whatever he could to help Donald with his goal for the evening and make up for the disappointment his friend was suffering. So Joseph would introduce people to each other, try to find their special gifts, facilitate new friendships and appreciation among Donald's tribe, and soothe the frayed nerves that were bound to arise when Donald explained that he loved each one individually, equally, completely. Of course, he also wanted to reassure Donald that he was enjoying his fling with Andie and that he'd keep an eye on her; but tonight, Joseph was most excited that he'd finally be able to begin paying back Donald for everything he'd done for him. Tonight, no one would be an organism.

Hattie was staring at herself in the ladies' room mirror in Rascal's, a drop of white paint on its surface covering the reflection of one of her eyes. She wished both of her eyes could be covered, they were so bloodshot, so needy. She'd been crying for the past three days and desperately wanted to look levelheaded when Donald's friends discovered that it was she who had injured him so, who had opened his eyes to things he should never have seen. She abhorred the idea of causing so much conflict at Donald's party because she knew it would just hurt him more, and this made her cry, too. But she still believed he wanted her there, needed her there. Of course, she'd also been crying a little for Reggie, for her gentle dismissal of him and the shock of discovering that their part-time relationship meant so much more to him than she'd ever imagined. And even though this was only an opening gesture, Hattie wanted Donald to know that she had gladly given up Reggie's twenty percent for one percent of him. She prayed that Donald would be a little comforted by this and also by her acceptance that their one percent together would inevitably harm Donald just as Hattie would be harmed by it, render love to him just as she hoped she was still loved. She understood now: all of it was one, indivisible gift that she was ready to share with him, and so here she was at Rascal's, staring at her mending self in the mirror and wondering if lipstick would make matters any better.

Marjorie was in her kitchen, staring at dried, brown drips on the front of the oven but unable to do anything about them. Only a week ago, the three of them had been so happy. It had just been a week. She still wasn't exactly sure what had happened, why Donald had left, why Helmut was leaving. She'd been in the same spot for an hour now; Donald hadn't returned home and Helmut hadn't called from the bar to report their lover's appearance. The situation felt so expected to her, almost familiar, although this was certainly the first time something like this had happened. But she trusted that feeling because Donald would've trusted it—she really was sometimes the odd man out, and it had always hurt her. Always. As usual, she was feeling so much—anger, fear, foreboding—but she felt discomfort in her butt, too. Marjorie had always hated these kitchen chairs but had never bothered to ask if Donald and Helmut did, too. How many years was she prepared to live with a sore ass? So she got up, cleaned the stains off the front of her oven and decided to finally act—track down Donald, beg Helmut to stay. Donald would've. And after all, if she ended up alone, there really wouldn't be any reason to do anything, anymore, and she'd just sit in her kitchen all night, staring at appliances and waiting, waiting for something to happen.

Brad was squeezing Elizabeth's hand under the table and looking around the bar, wondering if all the patrons were Donald's friends or if the two of them had come too early. Since he'd told Elizabeth about Donald—and especially since she'd told him about her meeting with Donald in the café—Brad had felt as if his life were one single thing again. It was fantastic. He was deathly ill with the flu, but it was still fantastic, and there was no way he was going to miss Donald's party. Plus, since they'd both been honest about Donald and themselves, Elizabeth had been holding him in her arms again, and that was maybe the best thing of all. So now Brad had Elizabeth, and Brad had Donald, and Brad might even have Donald and Elizabeth, although the details of that were still fuzzy to him and something that he planned to leave for later. Right now, he was just looking forward to embracing his friend the second he came in the door, right in front of everyone and right in front of Elizabeth, and for a long, long, sweet time. The reasons why he couldn't were all gone now, and it was fantastic.

Eric was at Provencal with his on-again/off-again lover, Rachelle, staring at people willing themselves to idiotic behavior just because it was the last day of the year and passionately regretting that he hadn't accepted the invitation to Carlos' loft party in the Bowery, instead. Having just paid $30 for a plate of hard-boiled eggs and anchovies, Eric watched Rachelle's eyes as they settled on the most expensive section of the wine list. He'd arranged this date weeks ago, when he'd assumed that his opening would *have generated a few sales, but that had all gone south once he'd decided to scrap his original theme, and now he was all about credit cards. It wouldn't be for long, though. A few days earlier, he'd inspected the first portrait he'd done in the collection, an acrylic, and realized that instead of focusing each and every piece on the total, abject passivity of one subject, he would instead investigate the concept of free will through a series of acrylic portraits of different people. He'd simply work with each one, exercising them into opening up and exposing themselves as the first model had done. But these exercises would have to go in a different direction because he'd been a little too manipulative recently, too involved, and the work felt false and forced. Eric wanted to return to the spirit of that first portrait, before all of his antagonistic machinations, and back to the original, dazzling willingness that radiated from it. Besides, 'victim' had recently been done to absolute death.*

Lourdes was checking her handbag for the fourth time that night to be sure that the hand lotion was really there. She'd been in Rascal's for several hours already, and it gave her something to do because she didn't want to approach any others there. She'd wait until Donald arrived. Maybe she wouldn't be too shy with his friends, she wouldn't embarrass him, and then at some point during the night, she could speak with him alone for a few minutes. She'd tell him what a wonderful time she was having and that she was no longer concerned with what anyone or Joselito thought of her friendship with him because it was beautiful. Then maybe she would open up her purse just a little and show him the hand lotion there; he would understand, he always understood her. Her hand lotion would tell him instantly that she was never going to call him her angel again because angels were one-way, and she wanted to be both ways for him, give back everything he gave her in the car. Maybe then he would know, too, that the brownies had been a terrible mistake; he'd been sick, and she should have had him come up to rest. She knew that now; she knew that he wasn't an angel because only angels never needed rest. So Lourdes just sat back, smiling, and waited for her first glimpse of Donald.

Just before, the patient somehow passed into consciousness and looked up at Zaïda. She'd heard of such miracles, impossible clarity rising up out of the failing for a few seconds, but she'd never been able to believe in them, herself. In fact, only an hour earlier, an old man with a burst blood vessel in his eye had punched her in the face as she'd tried to take his temperature.

Everything and everyone had made her forget it, her need to be recognized, to be truly seen. She'd buried it so long ago with her sand sculpture, under the waves in her old country. But when this strange man looked up at Zaïda, she felt as if someone had finally, finally, finally dived deep down, right into her soul. And it must have been a good soul, because he smiled as only someone who truly knew her could ever have smiled at her. His smile was so much and it was enough, and she felt calm and blessed and ready now for her next patient, her next shift, her next decade.

For a moment, just before, the man had really seen Zaïda.

www.ingramcontent.com/pod-product-compliance
Lightning Source LLC
Chambersburg PA
CBHW050422260626
47156CB00003B/1112